THE NAMELESS TRILOGY BOOK 2

JENNIFER JENKINS

Cover Design by Melissa Williams Design

Cover Photo by Arielle Levy

Published by Oliver-Heber Books

0 9 8 7 6 5 4 3 2 1

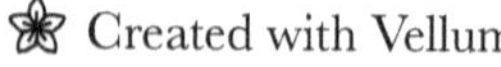 Created with Vellum

PRAISE FOR CLANLESS

"Jenkins weaves an unforgettable story that will forever be ingrained in your heart! With believable characters, epic romance and nonstop action this is a must-read series!"
—Bridget, Dark Faerie Tales

"Absolutely breathtaking! Jenkins brings this world to life with vivid imagery, beautiful writing, swoon-worthy romance, and compelling characters! You will root for Zo and Gryphon to find
one another and for love to prevail in this world of darkness and death"
—Jaime, Two Chicks on Books

"Jenkins yet again transports us into this wilderness where we want to decide if we are a Wolf, or a Ram. Where we hope we're not Clanless, but now being Nameless has a sense of pride and hope accompanied with it. The action adventure that goes on within this book is enough to make you wish you were fighting alongside Gryphon, Gabe, and Zo. The relationships that get bonded make you wish you were on the receiving end of the love that gets shared.
Yet, Jenkins makes you feel as though you are. She lets you in, and secretly makes the characters love you as you love them."
—Bri, Once Upon A Twilight

"Last year, Jennifer Jenkins' Nameless utterly enchanted me with its solid characters, swoony romance and riveting world building. With the way the book ended, I was more than excited to get to Clanless. There's always a little part of me that's worried that a sequel won't live up to its predecessor, but this was a second book that was superior to the exceptional Nameless in so many ways. Jennifer Jenkins has a real gem with this series and with Clanless in particular, she proves just how clever, romantic and addictive her writing and stories are."
—Nick, Nick & Nereyda's Infinite Booklist

"Clanless by Jennifer Jenkins is everything I expected and more! It's filled with so much action, I could hardly catch my breath! I was completely lost in the pages. The romance will leave you with tons of butterflies in your stomach. Loved it!"
—Damaris, Good Choice Reading

"What an awesome sequel! NAMELESS was a book I couldn't devour fast enough, and CLANLESS left me wanting more! This is an action packed fantasy ripe with betrayal, romance, danger and action. Nothing is as it seems. Jenkins had me on the edge of my seat with her twist and turns, and surprising ending! I need more."
—Katie, Mundie Moms

For Casey, Liberty, and Boston.
No matter where life takes you, you'll always be my clan.

CHAPTER ONE

G ryphon never thought he'd die at the hands of the Ram. Of course, he never thought he'd become a traitor to his clan, either.

He awaited a likely public execution, sitting in a patch of mud outside the walls of Ram's Gate, his clan's stronghold, as rain filtered through the trees overhead. Bristled ropes rubbed raw his bound ankles. Iron manacles secured his wrists behind his back. Gryphon clutched the hidden key to his restraints inside a bloody fist and glared at a man he never thought he'd call an enemy.

Zander, Gryphon's captain, stood at attention as the rain rolled off his brown hair and banked along the harsh angles of his cheekbones and jaw. He held a seven-foot spear like a walking stick, the blunt end buried in the mud at his feet. His short sword was sheathed at his hip, his round shield slung across his back. The perfect Ram warrior, and one of the best swordsmen Gryphon had ever known.

The fifteen members of his mess sat like stones in a field, unmoving but hard and very present. Most of Gryphon's former mess, including his best friend, Ajax, kept their backs to him, as if his treason were contagious. Some slept under thick wool blankets that repelled the rain while others stewed with the restlessness that plagued so many warriors.

No one bothered to light a fire. Whether they were too impatient to find something dry enough to burn or felt they deserved the cold, Gryphon didn't know. Ram were experts at self-*discipline*—not to be confused with self-control.

Inside Ram's Gate, Gryphon grew up training every day until his body ached. On days he struggled to do everything his leaders asked of him, he would sentence himself to mountain sprints until he literally passed out from exhaustion. Like every other Ram boy, he willingly walked into scheduled yearly beatings that were meant to train his body to block pain, making him nearly invincible on the battlefield.

A little rain was nothing.

Sitting cross-legged in the mud with his hands chained behind his back, Gryphon let the rain muffle the sound of his struggle to insert the small key into the unseen lock of his manacles. Each metallic scrape wound his nerves that much tighter. His wrists burned from bending at an awkward angle and his shoulders strained as he struggled to keep his face a mask of indifference.

Zander watched him, barely blinking. Gryphon needed to distract him—to break his intent focus.

"Why do you think they haven't let down the rope ladder?" Gryphon asked, speaking as though his impending execution meant little to him.

Zander's lip raised in a snarl. "Barnabas has the Raven invasion to prepare for, the gate to repair. He will deal with you in his own time."

Gryphon adjusted his grip on the key to approach the lock from a different angle.

"It seems Barnabas is content to let you sit out in the cold for the night. Do you think you'll lose your command over this?" Gryphon raised his chin and smiled.

Zander drew a knife so fast Gryphon fumbled with the key. "Barnabas ordered you brought back alive, but I don't think he'd mind if I took out your tongue."

Gryphon had been trained to use the emotions of his enemies against them. People made mistakes when they weren't stable. Plus, the conversation muffled the sound of the key scraping futilely against the metal lock behind his back.

A few of the heads in the wet camp turned to watch the exchange.

Zander leaned back, battling with his composure. "I might lose my command, but I'll return to my bunk with our brothers of the mess and rest well after seeing your body hang from a noose." He shook his head. "I knew you had a strange fascination with that slave—that *Wolf*. I just didn't realize your treason extended to all the Nameless inside the Gate."

Just yesterday, Gryphon had inadvertently helped

hundreds of Nameless slaves flee the massive walls of Ram's Gate. To slow the Ram pursuit, he disabled the only exit—a gate so large it required forty Nameless to open it. Even though only a fraction of the Nameless slaves escaped, it would be days before the chain connecting the gate to the counterweight could be repaired.

The key finally slipped into the lock. Gryphon let his head fall back, just a fraction, and closed his eyes in relief. Zander's hate-filled gaze greeted him as he opened his eyes, but that didn't stop him from turning the key. The lock clicked open, the sound lost in the rain.

With one hand free, Gryphon still kept both hands behind his back, though he relaxed his shoulders some to alleviate the ache from being bound. The metal key in Gryphon's hand was warm. The grooves pressed uncomfortably into his palm, but Gryphon didn't loosen his hold, refusing to let go of the hope Ajax had given him.

Not only was the key his only chance of escaping the certain death that awaited him inside the giant walls of his clan, but it also represented a dim hope that Zo was still alive. That Ajax—Gryphon's best friend—hadn't followed through with Zander's order to find and kill her and the others after Gryphon's capture.

The vivid scenes of the morning replayed in Gryphon's mind again and again. Everyone asleep under the tree, except Zo and Gryphon. Ram circling the perimeter of the giant fir like bloodhounds sniffing out prey. Zo taking his hand, pretending to be brave even though her eyes—they were always so easy to read—

proved it a lie. Her warm lips. The feel of her body pressed against his …

A shudder that had nothing to do with the cold ran up Gryphon's back. He'd been captured not far from the tree, trying to lead the Ram away from the people he cared for most.

If only he could ask Ajax if they were alive, though the chances were as likely as staying dry in this storm. Ajax had a family to protect, and the penalty for deceiving his captain was as deadly as deceiving Chief Barnabas himself. Dangerous.

Lightning struck not far away, brightening half of Zander's face in the fast-approaching darkness.

"*Come back to me*," Zo had said, just before she'd leaned into him, touching her soft lips to his.

Gryphon slid the key into the second lock.

He chewed on the inside of his lip until he tasted blood. He fought the urge to spit in Zander's face, to unlock the chains binding his wrist and strangle him with his bare hands. He was sure he could finish the job before he took a spear to the gut. It felt like the only way to quench the hungry blackness that consumed his insides.

Gryphon hung his head, remembering the promise he made to Zo before they separated. Whether Zo was alive or not, he needed to survive to warn the Raven Clan of an impending attack. Countless lives would be spared if the Raven had time to flee the Nest before the Ram arrived. Getting himself killed wouldn't serve them, even if it meant an escape from the overwhelming ache in his chest.

Thunder rolled again. Zander stared. Gryphon prayed for a miracle…and hoped he deserved one.

He turned the key.

The lock clicked open.

But his manacles clattered to the ground before he could catch them.

"WE'RE NOT WAKING HIM." Zo's head throbbed as she held Joshua's wrist to check his pulse for the tenth time in as many minutes.

The boy lay unconscious, but his heart beat a steady rhythm. Zo needed to feel that pulse; it was her tether to sanity. The sound of Ram fists connecting with Gryphon's body…the muffled grunts betraying his pain…they still echoed in her mind when she didn't check her thoughts. From her hiding place, she hadn't seen Gryphon's capture, but she had *heard*. She'd wanted to run out and fight alongside him. Even though she had Joshua and Tess to think of, her inaction tasted like betrayal.

Rain fell all around them, but they'd managed to stay mostly dry beneath the skirt of a giant fir tree. "This is insane," said Eva. She had the long nose of her Ram ancestors, set off by a thin mouth. "Do you have any idea what will happen to us if the Ram come back here?" Eva lay flat on her stomach—all leather and long legs—as she scanned the ground outside their fir tree haven.

Even with a full moon, it was impossible to see far beyond the confines of their shelter. "They have

Gryphon. They'll know you and Joshua are close." Eva ran her hand over her cropped hair, oblivious to the action. "If I were tracking us, I would have found us hours ago."

Eva was a Ram, just like the soldiers she feared. She'd fled the Gate with Zo for the sake of her unborn child. A baby who would have been killed at birth because it belonged, not to her betrothed, but to a man in the Ram's slave class known as the Nameless.

Zo gazed up at the tree trunk, hoping to inhale a bit of patience along with the strong scent of pine. "We wait until Joshua's ready, Eva. Not a moment sooner."

"But the Nameless will be miles away by now."

Zo conceded the point. At that moment, hundreds of escaped slaves traveled to get as far from Ram's Gate as possible to protect their newfound freedom. They didn't know how to find the Allied Camp. Zo had told Stone, Eva's lover and the leader of the Nameless rebellion, it was south of Ram's Gate, but that was the extent of their knowledge, and it wouldn't be enough to find the slot canyon that led to the Allies.

The Nameless needed her. So did her little sister Tess, Joshua, and even Eva. None of them would survive without Zo's ability to lead them to the Allies. But it didn't change the fact that all Zo wanted to do at the moment was sprint up the mountain to Ram's Gate—the place from which they'd just escaped—and demand the release of the young man she'd come to care for. The man who'd saved her life and the life of her sister, even though doing so had caused him to lose everything.

Gryphon.

Zo's little sister, Tess, sat like a watchdog beside Joshua's head, playing with the boy's red hair. In the low light, she looked even smaller than her eight years.

"Zo's smart. She knows what to do," said Tess. Dirt smeared across her nose and cheeks. Her blond hair hung in tangles. She glared at Eva with her giant blue-green eyes, almost daring her to contradict her big sister.

Zo hugged her knees to her chest, fighting a sudden surge of nausea, hoping Tess was right to trust her so completely.

"Someone's coming," Eva hissed. She pushed up onto her knees, wielding two deadly looking knives. At the same time, Zo yanked Tess to the ground and threw herself over her and Joshua's body. It was a futile effort to save them, but fear took over all rational thought.

Soft footfalls crept outside their shelter, each step marking the final moments of their lives. Zo glanced around for some kind of weapon or stick to help defend the two people—two children—for whom she was responsible. All she found in the darkness was a bed of dry pine needles and her medical satchel—nothing to defend them against fighters from the deadliest clan in the region.

The footsteps came closer, muted by the soggy earth. Eva moved from her knees to the balls of her feet, a compressed spring ready to fly into an attack. She adjusted her grip on her knives.

Hope fled. Zo couldn't catch her breath. Tess. Joshua. Eva.

The Nameless. Dying today under this tree meant the

deaths of so many others as well. Gryphon's sacrifice had been in vain.

Large boots stopped mere feet from Zo's hiding place. Boots she'd recognize anywhere. "Don't," she cried, trying to stop Eva before she attacked.

But her warning was too late.

Eva sprang, blades in hand, aimed at the intruder's chest.

CHAPTER TWO

Gryphon tensed when the manacles fell, but Zander didn't give any indication that he'd heard the clanking metal over the pouring rain.

Behind Zander, Ajax met Gryphon's eye.

He'd heard.

He'd likely been listening for the slightest sound of metal since he was the one to risk his life by giving Gryphon the key.

Gryphon had to remind himself to exhale and inhale at a normal rate, even though his heart thundered in his chest. Freeing his hands was only a small step on the path of not dying today.

When no one else seemed wise to Gryphon's partial freedom, he focused on the next step toward escape: the ropes binding his ankles. The men in his mess sat too far away for Gryphon to easily steal a blade.

Ajax stared up into the branches of the tree above

Gryphon's head. He gave someone in the branches a subtle nod. Then, without bothering to keep his movements quiet, he abruptly stood and walked away from Gryphon and the others, drawing Zander's attention for a fleeting moment before the mess captain realized Ajax only left to relieve himself.

But just as Zander looked away, a slight *thump* sounded next to Gryphon's hands. At first he thought it might have been a pinecone loosed by the rain. He felt around with his unbound hands, careful to keep his movement to a minimum, and then his fingers grazed something hard and familiar—the hilt of a small dagger.

How was it possible? He forced himself not to look up into the dark branches. Hope he hadn't dared feel surged through him. It must have been Zo's friend, Gabe, though why the Wolf would linger to help him, he didn't understand. He should have been running north to warn the Raven of the impending Ram attack.

Unless Zo put him up to it.

Ajax walked back to the mess and dared a glance up into the high branches of the tree over their heads. Rain pelted his face. He wiped it away before looking Gryphon in the eye. What his old friend tried to convey in that shared glance, Gryphon couldn't be certain. But he had a feeling it was important.

Ajax frowned and looked down at his hands as he repositioned himself on the wet ground. He grit his teeth and grabbed hold of his pant legs. He seemed to flex every muscle in his body. Then he nodded, jaw tensed in anticipation. The familiar zipping sound of an arrow flew down from the tree. The arrow sank deep into Ajax's thigh.

Ajax rolled and wailed, pointing in the opposite direction of the arrow. "Raven!" he half shouted, half growled.

"Link!" Zander called his men to order, as they all searched the trees in the opposite direction. Metal and wood scraped together as round shields were raised to form a perfect wall of defense.

I could kill Zander, thought Gryphon. *I could end him like he ordered Ajax to kill Zo.* He wanted to kill him as much as he wanted his freedom. But right now he couldn't have both.

Gryphon took his chance. Using the dagger gifted to him by the hidden ally in the tree, he sliced through the tight ropes around his ankles in one fluid motion and jumped to his feet.

Gryphon leapt over a bush and raced around a tree. Then another. He didn't get more than twenty strides before Zander shouted, "Stop him!"

Gryphon took off at a wild sprint into the dark forest. A spear shot past him within inches of his head. Arrows flew behind him, likely Gabe helping to cover his escape. Men shouted in pain. Gryphon didn't turn around. He ran as hard as he'd ever run, pushing through the absolute darkness as if the wings of hell beat at his heels.

After a couple hundred yards, the earth fell out from beneath him and he plummeted, rolling down the sheer side of the mountain. Rocks bruised his body. Brush and foliage scratched wicked gashes into his skin. He used his arms to protect his head as he tumbled, end over end, into the belly of a rocky gorge.

He landed hard in a freezing stream of mountain water that came up to his waist. In the distance Zander wailed with frustration. The ghostly sound cut through the pouring rain and echoed off the walls of the gorge. It was no small miracle Gryphon survived the fall. Now Zander's men would have to backtrack half a mile to a nearby ridge to get down into the ravine. He struggled to his feet then fell back into the water after his first step, clutching his head to clear away the dizzy spell that robbed him of precious time.

He lifted a hand to the back of his head and found a lump forming. He must have hit it in the fall but didn't remember.

He pushed himself up onto his battered hands and knees and crawled through the stream until the dizziness in his head cleared. Pulling himself out of the water, he collapsed on the black soil to catch a couple of breaths, then forced his weary body to stand. He kept his pace slow but consistent, heading northeast in the direction of the Raven settlement even though he wanted nothing more than to run back to the tree to see if Zo was alive and to check on Joshua and the others.

Until Zander and Chief Barnabas captured him or met their own end, Gryphon and the people he cared for would never be safe again. Their only chance for survival now was to follow the initial plan: warn the Raven. He'd promised Zo that he would help them evacuate the elusive Nest before the Ram raided and destroyed the clan.

He'd keep his promise and pray that those he loved were kept safe while he led his mess away from them.

From now on, Gryphon was a hunted man.

Zo scrambled out from under the tree to find Eva on the ground and a dripping gash on the intruder's arm. In the darkness it looked more like spilled ink than blood.

"Gabe!" Zo flung herself at the bleeding man. Gabe was more than a fellow Wolf fighting to bring down the mighty Ram—he was Zo's childhood friend and self-proclaimed protector. He'd gone to scout the wall for Ram movement before Gryphon was taken, but when he hadn't returned, Zo had assumed the worst.

"Where have you been?" Zo grabbed the front of Gabe's shirt, as if he'd somehow disappear if she let go of him. "Tess, bring me my kit," she called over her shoulder.

"It's not bad, Zo," said Gabe. He pulled her into a tight embrace.

Was she crying?

"Shhhh," he said, clearing her wild hair from her face and tucking it neatly behind an ear. "I'm here now. Everything will be fine."

But it wasn't fine. "The Ram took Gryphon," her voice cracked. "He tried to lead them away from the tree and they took him." She collapsed into a puddle at Gabe's feet. "I couldn't help him. The Nameless…Tess and Joshua…" She knew the words spilling out of her mouth didn't make sense. She'd made the right choice by staying hidden when the Ram captured and beat Gryphon. Too many people depended on her to help them reach the Allies.

It was the right choice. So why did it feel like betrayal? How could she survive the guilt of knowing Gryphon's death was on her hands when he, a Ram, had saved her? He was supposed to be her enemy.

"I'm going to go check on Joshua." Eva dusted herself off, scowling at Zo and Gabe down her long Ram nose. Her lips pursed together enough to accentuate her defined cheekbones.

In her excitement at seeing Gabe, Zo had almost forgotten Eva was there.

"Sorry about your arm. Decent block, by the way," Eva added over her shoulder, and then ducked back under the boughs of the tree, likely escaping their affectionate reunion.

Zo offered Gabe an apologetic shrug before Tess crawled out from under the tree carrying Zo's kit. Gabe ruffled Tess's hair and tapped her nose like he always did when they saw each other. Tess rewarded him with a beaming grin.

"I need to talk to Zo. Will you be all right if I take her for a minute?" he asked.

Tess offered one of her brave nods. "I'll stay with Joshua."

Gabe pulled Zo under a low-hanging shelf of rock, out of the rain. Blond stubble dotted his chin and the want of sleep hung heavy under his eyes.

"Take off your shirt," said Zo. She searched her satchel for the proper remedies, sniffing away a runny nose brought on by tears. When she looked up, Gabe stood half naked before her. His shoulders and arms were mounds of lean muscles, his stomach two neat columns of definition. Zo caught herself staring, blinked, and went to work repairing his arm.

It wasn't like she hadn't seen Gabe without a shirt before. When they were younger, he and Zo used to steal away to swim in a pond in the summer, when the sun made the cold water refreshing.

He'd looked different then, more gangly than anything. His time training under Commander Laden had changed him. She didn't see that same scrawny boy now. At nearly twenty years old, Gabe was suddenly a man. Somehow Zo had missed the transformation.

"I saw what happened." He rubbed his hands into his forehead and let them melt down his cheeks. "When Ajax came back, I hid in the nearest tree with an arrow aimed at his back. Lucky for him, he spared you. I followed Gryphon and his mess to the Gate."

"And?"

"And the Ram didn't let them in. The ladder was up and there was no movement on the wall."

Zo looked up too fast. A rush of cold prickled along her cheeks and neck, and dark splotches invaded her vision. It had been like that since healing Joshua. She held her head in one hand to fight the dizziness. "So Gryphon's not actually inside the Gate yet?"

Gabe frowned and stepped closer to her. His blond hair fell into his eyes as he scanned her face, looking for the source of her pain. "No, but..."

"We have to save him! We have to try!"

Gabe leaned away. Uncertainty lanced across his face as he regarded Zo. Whatever he discovered seemed a disappointment.

"I did try," he said.

He hadn't said he *would* try. He'd said he *did* try. Past tense. Zo's hope for Gryphon's survival shattered in those three simple words.

"Tell me," she whispered.

"No." He shrugged an apology. "You've been through too much. The Ram soldier helped us, but that doesn't change our goals. Our future. You and Tess need to get back to the Allied Camp."

Zo pushed Gabe's hands away when they rested on her shoulders, suddenly furious. "Tell me what happened to Gryphon!"

Gabe's lips pressed into a hard line. "After Ajax spared you, I knew I could trust him to help us. I confronted him before he rejoined his unit. He told me he'd give Gryphon the key to his manacles. Together we created a diversion to help Gryphon escape."

Gabe stared off into the distance as if lost to the memory. "I owed Gryphon as much after he spared my life and helped us leave the Gate."

"So he's alive?" She held her breath and hope in her chest. "Please, Gabe. Tell me he made it. That he escaped." She looked around, almost expecting him to pop out from behind a tree to surprise her.

Gabe frowned. He didn't answer for several moments, as if debating his answer.

"Gabe!"

"I tried to help him," he blurted. "Gryphon was outnumbered, and Ram spears never miss their mark."

Zo held up a hand to silence him. She bit into her lip and shook her head, forcing herself not to fall apart.

"I did everything I could," said Gabe. For some reason he wouldn't look at her. Why wouldn't he look at her! "I had to think about the Raven. I can't warn them about the Ram invasion with a spear through my gut."

She wanted to say, "*Forget the Raven!*" But that wasn't right. As much as she cared for Gryphon, as indebted to him as she was, it wasn't reasonable to risk the chance of Gabe getting caught when so many lives hung in the balance. She placed a hand to her stomach and staggered backward. An ache grew inside her, a void expanding, a candle that once provided warmth and light, snuffed out.

Gabe gathered her to him.

"Your arm," she whispered into his shoulder.

"It's fine, Zo."

Reluctant, but needing the contact of another person, she returned his embrace. Her arms fell a fraction of a second before his. She stood on clumsy feet, afraid she might topple over if she couldn't center her equilibrium. Falling, and proving her illness, her emptiness, would be disastrous. Knowing Gabe, he wouldn't leave her behind—even to save the Raven—if he thought she wasn't well.

Gabe gathered his pack and weapons. "Are you sure you can get back to the Allies? You don't look so good." His bright blue eyes seemed deeper than normal in the low light.

Healthy or not, Zo didn't have the option to remain on Ram soil. Too many people depended on her.

So much responsibility …

"As soon as Joshua is ready to travel, we'll follow the Nameless tracks. You know as well as I do that they won't survive long without the Allies' protection."

"Be careful. You know the dangers …" Gabe trailed off, possibly thinking of all of the ways this might end badly. Wild animals and wild men called Clanless roamed the mountainside, and there was also the added possibility of Ram troops tracking the Nameless.

Gabe reached out and took her blistered hands in his. "Go to Commander Laden and the Allies, and I'll meet you there as soon as I can. After this is over, I'm taking you away from this war. It's the only way we can be together."

Zo's head spun again. This time it was only partly due to the vertigo. She hadn't planned on surviving her time as a spy inside Ram's Gate. For so long there had been nothing beyond the need to avenge her parents' death. She never considered that Gabe would expect them to be together if she lived. She had to admit the arrangement made sense. They'd known each other all their lives, even before the raids began. And now they both worked for the Allies. Gabe already acted like an older brother to Tess. He was handsome with his fair features and easy smile. There was no question they could find happiness together.

Why did she feel so empty?

The image of Gryphon came to mind, his scruffy dark hair and the kindness in his eyes that turned to liquid fire when he was angry. She put a hand on her aching stomach and bit down on her tongue to keep from falling apart.

Gryphon was gone. She had to let him go.

Gabe bent down and kissed her frozen lips. Zo startled at the touch. Thunder rolled. With all their history together, Gabe had never tried to kiss her. His lips pressed into hers as rainwater trickled down her forehead and cheeks. Her stomach ached.

Gabe left her standing with her arms hanging helplessly at her sides and the betrayal of his kiss on her lips. The same lips that, only that morning, had belonged to Gryphon.

CHAPTER THREE

Wet boots.

Dripping cloak.

One small dagger that would hardly scratch a rabbit.

It didn't take long to inventory Gryphon's gear as he trudged through the night. The list of things he didn't have was much longer and—though it did him no good—occupied the majority of his thoughts.

Light.

Food.

Bedroll.

Shield and spear.

Joshua's million questions.

A map to the Raven Nest

A home.

A clan.

With every step away from the Gate, his spirits drooped lower and lower until he wasn't sure if his footsteps carried him toward his goal or away from it. He'd never traveled outside the Gate without a mess unit. His whole life until now was spent advancing in the hierarchy of his clan. Every goal that once drove him to improve, every day spent training to become the warrior he was today, meant nothing now.

If he wasn't a Ram, what was he? What was a man without a clan?

Gryphon headed north along the rocky bank of the river, where his tracks would be harder for Zander and his mess to follow. He had tonight to put as much distance between them as possible before his brothers searched for his tracks in the morning. They would study every blade of grass, every dent in the mud, until they confirmed his direction of travel and followed.

His clothes were soaked through from the night's rain, his nose and fingers felt like they'd fallen off long ago, and his wrists still ached from being bound. Blowing warmth into his cupped hands, he studied the wilderness around him.

The Wolf, Gabe, had told him to travel north for several days to reach the hidden Raven settlement. The chances of them finding each other in this vast stretch of mountain forest in time to warn and evacuate the Raven didn't bode well. That was assuming Gabe survived the night.

Hours passed. The sky turned murky gray in the low light before dawn. Gryphon searched the trees for Raven scouts and tried not to think about how easily they could hide in the dense fir and broadleaf trees surrounding him on all sides. One well-placed arrow from a legendary Raven bow could end him in an instant.

It was enough to make a man want to cower. But how could hiding serve him when he needed to be found by Gabe, and what was the difference between a Raven arrow to the chest and a Ram spear to the back? His only choice was forward.

By midday the stream bent eastward with the sloping land and Gryphon left its bank to keep a northern course. He hadn't eaten in more than a day. His legs shook. His feet tripped over rocks and brambles, but he kept moving.

After several hours of walking, the thick forest opened to a meadow of tall grass where tiny yellow and white blossoms speckled the ground. In the heart of the meadow, Gryphon spotted a leather pack tipped on its side. He scanned the trees surrounding the meadow and weighed the risk of exposure against the possibility of supplies. Food. A bedroll. In the end, potential comfort for the back and belly won out.

He darted into the meadow to retrieve the satchel, his mouth already salivating with hope of finding a hard biscuit or water skin. Wind rolled over the grass, making it bend and sway in confused directions while stirring the sweet aroma of wildflowers. Gryphon slung the abandoned pack over his shoulder and scanned the trees again. Chills crawled up his arms and along his spine. He reached for his knife and tried to look in every direction at once as he moved away from the center of the meadow, back to the protection of the trees.

An arrow struck the ground, inches from his foot.

Gryphon raised his hands behind his head. "Don't kill me. I have a message."

The peace of the meadow evaporated as at least fifty men stepped out from behind the trunks of trees and dropped from branches. They wore black feathers on leather strings around their necks and animal hide on their bodies. They all had raven-black hair with eyes to match, and wore wood-slatted armor on their chests.

A man with long hair and red war paint around his eyes stepped forward. As he did, fifty bows stretched to guard him in case Gryphon attacked.

"A Ram without a flock." The red-painted man had a full string of feathers around his neck, marking him as the high-ranking leader of the group. He carried a hatchet with a rope tied to the hilt. As he approached Gryphon, he swung the hatchet around his wrist by the rope and caught it. He walked a full circle around Gryphon, swinging the blade and catching it. Swing. Catch. Swing. Catch.

Gryphon stood tall, looking over the heads of the men surrounding him.

"You are a long way from your wall, Ram," said the leader. All the clans in this region spoke different dialects of the same language. The Raven and other lesser clans of the north dragged their tongues when they spoke, pronouncing each word with precision.

Gryphon nodded, still touching the back of his head with his fingertips in surrender. "I've come to warn your people of an invasion."

A smile cracked the corner of the leader's careful mask. "Your lies will do nothing to spare your life, Ram."

Gryphon felt the rage of the men surrounding him, their hatred as tangible as the arrows that would soon pierce his heart. With their bows drawn, his life depended on these men not extending two fingers.

"One of your men was recently taken prisoner by my mess," said Gryphon. "Barnabas' interrogators broke him, and now my chief knows the location of your settlement. He's sending at least ten units for your grain stores and he'll kill anyone he encounters in the process."

The men in the circle broke into nervous conversation. Ten mess units equaled about two hundred of the most deadly warriors in the region. That many Ram could easily wipe out a thousand Raven in open combat.

The leader approached Gryphon, standing so close their toes touched. His smirk diminished to a thin line. His nostrils flared and color flooded his cheeks to match the red paint around his eyes. He spoke loud enough for his entire flock to hear, his tone not matching the jovial cadence of his voice. "Thank you for the entertaining story, Ram. But I can think of a better way for you to entertain us." He gestured to two of his men, and they stepped forward. "Why don't we let this Ram see how far he can get before we kill him?" He put a finger to his lips, as if pondering some great puzzle. "It won't be fun unless the Sheep has a head start." He

threw up his hands and faced his men. "What do you say?"

Through their cheers, Gryphon wondered how long they had waited for the chance to kill a Ram. For decades his clan had ruthlessly hunted the Raven in search of their grain stores. How many brothers and sons had fallen to Ram spears over the years? The number had to be staggering.

Gryphon dropped his hands to his side. "I'm telling you the truth. You need to evacuate the Nest." Gryphon knew at once that his words wouldn't be enough.

"It's time to run, little lamb."

Raven bows stretch back into firing position. A smile plastered the leader's face. His sneer hardened like a promise. "Your blood will not be enough to satisfy the crimes your clan has committed against my people. But it's a start." He smacked Gryphon on the back twice. "We'll give you a five second lead. Ready, go."

Gryphon stayed rooted in place.

"One. Two."

He closed his eyes. The faces of the people he cared for most flashed through his mind. Joshua, Zo, Ajax, his mother, little Tess …

"Three. Four."

He tensed every muscle in his body to prepare for death.

Then a man tore through the line of Raven and into the meadow, gasping for breath before shouting, "Stop!"

Gryphon turned to see Gabe and nearly collapsed in relief. How had he escaped the Ram? How had he found him? His shirt was ripped, a bloody bandage tied around his arm.

"Put down your weapons." Gabe stripped his pack and pulled his shirt over his head to show the mark of the waxing moon on his upper back. "I represent Commander Laden and the Allies." Gabe bent in half with palms resting on knees drawing air into his rasping lungs.

Bows stayed trained on Gryphon's chest as men looked to their leader for orders.

"Is that you, Wolf?" The Raven leader walked up and attacked Gabe with a giant hug. "I thought you were captured."

"I was." He clapped Gryphon on the back. "But this Ram helped me and a host of Nameless escape the Gate. Did he tell you about the invasion?"

The energy in the air shifted as Gabe's words registered on the faces of the Raven, melting their former reverie like wax from a dripping candle. Even though he'd just narrowly avoided execution, Gryphon felt bad for these men. "I've disabled the pulley system to the only exit of Ram's Gate. It will buy us some time to evacuate your people, but we don't have long."

Gabe nodded. "You must take us to your chief and let us convince him to flee to the Allied Camp. It's the only place your families will be safe."

The Raven leader shook his head, pointing a finger at Gryphon. "If I take this man into the Nest, he will never be allowed to leave."

"Your clan secrets are the least of your worries, my friend," said Gabe.

The Raven leader turned to Gryphon. "No Ram has ever been welcome in the Nest. I cannot guarantee your safety."

Gryphon swallowed, thinking of the promise he made to Zo to warn the Raven. If he left now, was that promise fulfilled? How could he ever face her again if he didn't see this through?

He picked up the abandoned pack and hefted it onto his back. It likely belonged to one of the Raven, but he figured he'd earned it. "Lead on."

THE NEXT DAY, Joshua still didn't wake, even while the sound of marching Ram soldiers echoed in the distance. Zo had hoped the gate would have taken longer than a day and a half to repair. But it seemed Barnabas didn't intend to let Gryphon's heroics alter his plans.

When she lived as a spy and Nameless slave inside the Gate, she sent stoppered bottles filled with information about Ram numbers, supplies, and troop movements down a river that ran under the enormous city wall to a group of Allied men. Gryphon and his mess captured one of the Raven working with the Allies and interrogators broke him for information about the location of the Raven Nest—a secret that had been preserved for centuries, despite the Ram's best efforts to find it.

Zo hoped Gabe managed to warn the Raven in time.

Eva sat with her back toward the others, hugging her legs to her chest. She refused to eat and only drank when Zo insisted she do so.

Zo knew the Ram girl was desperate to track the Nameless. Eva had lost everything: her family, her clan, even the father of her growing child. But what could they do other than wait? Overwhelmed by her own grief, Zo struggled to find compassion for the other girl. She put a hand to her aching head and fought another wave of nausea brought on by vertigo.

Tess frowned. "You still haven't recovered from the healing? Have you tried—"

"I've never been any good at healing myself, bug. Don't worry about it. I'm sure I'll be fine by tomorrow morning."

"Maybe I could try—"

"I said, don't worry about it." Zo didn't mean to snap. This wasn't Tess' fault.

Eva didn't turn around, but in an uncharacteristically small voice said, "Gryphon was a good man. I mourn his passing too."

Zo pressed her hands into the sides of her head and tried to make the world stop spinning.

Please don't talk about him!

How was she ever going to get Joshua, Eva, Tess, and a host of Nameless refugees to the Allies if she couldn't even lean up against a tree without her vision spinning? She couldn't save them and mourn for Gryphon *and* kick this illness all at once. Especially not while Gabe's confusing kiss still lingered on her lips. How could she continue to be strong for others while she was becoming weaker all the time?

That night, when everyone else slept, Zo pulled the cold night air into her lungs and let the smell of pine and lemongrass sooth her aching head. She took in another breath, and as she released it, resolved to put the pain of losing Gryphon away. Eventually she would mourn his death and face the guilt she felt for getting him involved. Until then, she would cage her feelings in a dark corner of her mind. If they spilled over, she'd fight to push them back.

It took most of the night grappling with herself until she secured the vault of her heart and all thoughts of Gryphon were thoroughly laid to rest in the back of her mind for a time when she had the luxury to grieve.

The task before her was different from her mission inside Ram's Gate. No one—not even she—had expected her to survive her time working as a spy for the Allies. The consequences of her failure then would have ultimately only affected herself. If she didn't find a way to control her grief and kick this sickness soon, hundreds of innocent people, including her own sister, would pay the price.

She massaged her fingers into the muscles at the base of her skull with all her force, pushing Gryphon and the truth of his fate away.

CHAPTER FOUR

Staring down an entire flock of Raven scared Gryphon less than learning what had become of Zo and the others. He was fairly certain that Ajax spared Zo's life, but what if Zander sent someone to verify he'd done the job? What if she was really gone? He kept looking over to Gabe, waiting for the right opportunity to ask, terrified by what his new friend might tell him.

They kept a fast pace, trotting with the Raven surrounding them on all sides. It turned out that Gabe and several of the feathered warriors were old friends. Gabe asked after their families and exchanged light banter, although the tension on the faces of the men was thick as clay.

The Raven avoided Gryphon, almost pretending he wasn't there. He couldn't blame them. The Ram had targeted their people ever since the Kodiak clan had been raided. For years his people sent mess units, his included, on excursions to discover Raven food stores. Raven warriors were cunning and deadly. They swooped in like a birds of prey and attacked from the trees with their arrows only to disappear again. Despite their agility, many "birds" had fallen to Ram spears over the years, and men don't easily forget a lost brother.

Gryphon, Gabe, and their Raven escort jogged up a steep climb along the edge of the cliffs that dropped into the frothy ocean below. Pine trees and rocks bore a carpet of lichen and the brine of the sea burned the inside of Gryphon's nose as he pulled air into his lungs.

The trail narrowed, forcing him and Gabe to walk side by side. If he didn't take this opportunity to ask Gabe about Zo and the others, he was a coward.

"Tell me."

Gabe would know what he wanted. The two had come a long way from being enemies to find friendship. Their connection through it all had been their common interest—they both cared for Zo and would do anything to keep her safe.

Gabe frowned and met Gryphon's gaze for a brief moment before looking ahead at the rocky trail. "Are you asking about Joshua, or about *her*?"

"Is there a difference?" snorted Gryphon, ready to punch Gabe in the face.

Gabe scowled. "Just because you went against your nature and spared her doesn't mean she was ever yours to protect. She was my responsibility. Mine."

Was?

His throat tightened into knots. *No no no no no …*

"Joshua was still asleep when I left them, but Tess

said his heart sounded fine and his breathing was normal. I set them up with plenty of provisions. With Eva's help, they'll have an easy time tracking the Nameless once the boy is awake."

Yes, if they survive the wilderness and the wild men that inhabit the mountain.

The trail ended at the foot of a rock wall that soared at least thirty feet above the ground. Gryphon wasn't surprised when the Raven began to scale the rock. They reached for hand and footholds with the ease of a child climbing a generous tree.

"What about ..." Gryphon couldn't even utter her name. He clamped his mouth shut and fought the paralyzing tightness in his throat. He and Gabe were the last to start the climb. Gryphon felt his body go through the motions of gripping the rock with hands and feet as he pushed with his legs and pulled with his arms to scale the rock. Gabe kept pace next to him.

Clinging to the wall, fifteen feet in the air, Gabe stopped climbing. The corners of his mouth drooped. He stared straight ahead at the rock, as if ashamed. "I'm sorry." A pause. "It never would have worked between you and Zo. You would have always reminded her of the soldiers who raided her home and killed her parents." The muscles in Gabe's neck flexed.

Gryphon's arms shook from supporting his weight.

The thin hope that Zo was still alive snapped. Reality hit Gryphon like a blow to the stomach. Ajax had actually followed orders and killed her. He likely hadn't had a choice. Gryphon tried to swallow, but he couldn't force down the lump in his throat. His eyes clouded, distorting his vision as he reached for the next handhold. He blinked away a tear that leaked down the corner of his face, and searched blindly for a grip. His fingers slipped and he fell.

His body relaxed in the air, accepting the impact of the ground against his back like a gift. His head smacked against the rock with a hard *thump*. He gasped and sputtered, blind and foolish, like an infant learning how to draw breath in the wind.

Gone. How could she be gone? The cold fact didn't fit within the structure of his reasoning. It cut a fissure into the crust of his consciousness. Gryphon buried his fists into his eyes and yelled at nothing and everything. He rolled onto his side, pushing away an offered hand and ran at the trunk of the nearest tree. His chest and shoulder connected with the tree first. His arms wrapped around the trunk, his feet dug trenches into the ground as he pushed and pushed against the thick wood. Rough bark bit into his skin. No matter how hard he pumped his legs, no matter how hard he tried to rid himself of the truth, the tree wouldn't budge. Not even an inch.

That was the cruelty of life. No matter his efforts, he couldn't make the wind blow a different direction or the waves stand still or the mountains part. So many of his problems could be solved with a little more force, an extra training session, or sheer strength of will. But Gryphon couldn't control this, couldn't fight it away, not even with all his substantial strength.

He collapsed on the ground, grabbed two fistfuls of hair, and wept like a child with Gabe at his side and the Raven warriors watching in confused, silent awe.

Zo was dead. Nothing but his grief mattered.

WHEN MORNING FINALLY CAME, Joshua opened his eyes for the first time in days.

"He's awake! He's awake!" said Tess. She knelt next to him, bobbing up and down on her knees like a bumblebee tethered to the ground.

Joshua groaned and pushed up to rest on his elbows. "What happened? Where am I?" His wiry chest was bare. The scar on his abdomen was still crusted over, but the skin around the wound bragged a healthy peach hue. "Where are Gryphon and Gabe?" He looked at Eva then over to Zo. "What is Eva doing here?"

Zo and Tess didn't bother answering any of his questions before wrapping him into a hug. Tess openly wept, and Zo found herself jealous for the chance to express her relief without falling apart.

She pressed her forehead into Joshua's and held it there as she looked into his eyes. "I see you, Joshua."

"Umm." Joshua grinned. "I see you too. Quite well, actually."

Tess rolled around in a fit of giggles.

"What am I missing?" said Joshua.

Zo pulled away and tapped the end of the boy's nose with the tip of her finger. "Sorry. It's an old Wolf custom. Eyes are the windows to the soul. I was greeting your inner light. Acknowledging your spirit." Zo shook her head and smiled. "It has been so long since I've been able to be a Wolf. I couldn't help myself."

Thirteen-year-old Joshua fingered the two-inch scar on his stomach and a violent shiver rolled over his skin. "All I remember was fighting you in the ring, Zo. I didn't know how to protect you." He paused and swallowed a lump in his throat causing his Adam's apple to jump. He'd stabbed himself in the stomach to save her life, a rash decision made because only one person could leave the ring alive. "Why didn't I die?" He reached out and held Zo's hand. "How did you save me?"

Zo didn't really understand everything herself. After Joshua tried to take his own life in the ring, Zo had been desperate to use her skills as a healer to save him. In the healing blessing, heat like fire formed beneath her hands and rolled up her arms and into her chest. If someone hadn't helped her sever the connection, she might have been consumed by the heat.

For Joshua, Zo was willing to take the risk, but it had cost her something that went beyond simply feeling dizzy all of the time. The muted energy she relied on to heal others didn't seem to hum beneath her skin as it once had. She'd never realized the energy was there until, after healing Joshua, the heat was gone—leaving only emptiness behind.

Zo held Joshua's hand as she explained their flight out of the Gate. She pushed away the image of Gabe half-carrying Joshua while Gryphon stayed behind to disable the Gate's pulley system. She'd trusted Gryphon completely—he didn't know how to fail. It had made Zo feel invincible knowing Gryphon was on their side.

Zo cut off the train of thought before it grew into something she couldn't control. She told Joshua about the hundreds of Nameless refugees that now roamed the dangerous hills without resources and without a guide to the only place they would find safe refuge—the Allied Camp.

"So Gryphon and Gabe are off to warn the Raven?" said Joshua.

Eva said, "Actually—"

"Yes," Zo cut in, ignoring Eva's stern expression. Gryphon was Joshua's mentor and the closest thing he had to family. She couldn't bear to watch him suffer, not after everything he'd endured. They'd tell him the truth eventually, but not yet.

"I should be with them. They'll need my help evacuating the Raven," said Joshua. His voice frequently changed octaves despite his efforts to prove his Ram manhood.

"I'm sure Gryphon," she stuttered his name, "thought we'd need you here."

Joshua nodded, his pale skin a little too translucent for Zo's liking. "You're probably right."

Zo checked his pulse and listened to his heart. Her vision tilted to the right and then the left, as if she were on a rocking ship. Meanwhile Eva began rolling blankets and securing packs. "What are you doing?" said Zo as she pinched the skin on the back of Joshua's hand to check his hydration level.

"The boy's awake. We'll be leaving soon," said Eva.

Joshua raised a hand in question. "Did she just call me a boy?"

"He just woke up. He needs more time." What Zo really meant was, *I need more time*. This tree was special.

Under these boughs Gryphon had held her. Kissed her. It was her last connection to him and she didn't want to give it up.

Lock your heart, Zo.

"I don't need more time," said Joshua. "I actually feel kind of amazing."

"You're sure?"

Joshua turned over and did a quick set of push-ups on his fists to illustrate his point. "I just hope you ladies can keep up." His grin spread the length of his face.

Joshua had endured so much. Zo needed to protect him from learning the truth about Gryphon. At least for a time.

Eva shook her head in disappointment, and crawled out from under the tree with the others, leaving Zo with only her deception for company.

***

GRYPHON SHOULD HAVE KILLED Zander before making his escape. Revenge demanded it. But his vengeance wouldn't end there. Zo was so innocent, and so much better than Zander, that the old adage of a life for a life didn't apply.

Ajax. His brother. His best friend in this world. The man who'd helped him escape death. He needed to die as well for following Zander's orders.

How quickly adoration turned to hatred.

As soon as he kept his promise to Zo and helped the Raven evacuate their hidden home, he'd track Zander and Ajax down. The hunter would become the hunted and justice would be served.

Gryphon kept pace with the rest of the men, barely aware of his surroundings. He followed, but his desire to save these savages who hated him didn't seem to mean as much without Zo. With her death, he realized something disappointing about himself: he was selfish.

Zo's mere existence made him challenge everything he believed about people outside Ram's Gate. One look from her and he wanted to be better than he was. He wanted to prove that his people weren't the monsters she believed them to be. Not all of them. Not him. Now he didn't know what to believe.

They ran for the better part of three days. Gabe and the Raven didn't seem to ever tire. By the time they stopped at the base of an enormous tree, Gryphon nearly collapsed at their feet.

"These Birds know how to travel," Gryphon wheezed beside Gabe. They hadn't spoken since Gryphon had learned about Zo. Neither wanted to discuss their loss. Or their future.

"They're smaller than you. Lighter. Faster. You might beat them in a fight, but you have to catch them first," Gabe said, panting

Gryphon nodded because it used less air to do so. He pointed at the line the Raven had formed to climb a tree using man-made pegs spiraling up its thick trunk.

"What's up there?" Gryphon gestured to dense canopy above.

Gabe smiled. "You'll see."

Gryphon climbed the tree last. The pegs were made of sturdy wood and so natural looking he doubted he would have spotted them on one of his routine excursions with his mess unit. The curling climb went slowly. The higher he ascended the more the ground seemed to spin, jumping up and back with nauseating inconsistency. His legs shook by the time he broke through the thick canopy high above the ground and dropped to a platform made of wooden planks. Branches of the monstrous tree jutted through the floor. "I think I might be sick," said Gryphon.

Around him, nearly fifty Raven smirked at his condition, and even Gabe nudged him with a stupid grin on his face. "You're sort of pathetic," he said. "I think it does everyone good to see you this way. The mighty Ram as green-faced as a tree nymph."

"Remind me again why I'm doing this?" Gryphon groaned as he pushed up into a seated position. "Whoa." Whatever smart remark he was about to make dissolved on his tongue as he stared out at the network of bridges connecting the thick forest of trees, bridges invisible from the ground below.

The leader of the Raven Flock offered Gryphon a hand to help him stand. His grip was almost too firm, as though he'd rather yank him over the side of the platform than anything else. "We travel above ground the rest of the way. It's the only way to reach the Nest." He pulled Gryphon closer, glaring. "This is your last chance to turn back. I promise you, once we reach the Nest you will never be permitted to leave alive."

Gryphon considered climbing back down the tree. He'd warned the Raven. Why force his help upon people who'd likely kill him for trying? If he hurried, he might be able to track down Zander and Ajax. After exacting his revenge, he'd be free to seek out Joshua and the rest of the Nameless at the Allied Camp. He'd need to arm himself with more than a small dagger …

Gryphon dropped his head, thinking about Zo. About her panic at hearing the Ram's plans to attack the Raven. Leaving now would be giving up on her desperate drive for peace. He was the only one with Ram experience. If the Raven Chief didn't take Gabe's warning seriously, a massacre would ensue.

Gryphon swore under his breath and met the Raven's question with a firm nod of the head. "I came to help, Bird. I'll finish the job."

The Raven appraised him once more. A few of the lines around his mouth smoothed and his grip on Gryphon's hand loosened a fraction. "You're a strange man, Gryphon." He clapped his back and gave orders for his men to move.

Gryphon stepped out onto the first of many roped bridges. The planks shifted and groaned like ice beneath his feet. They weren't built to carry someone his size. He closed his eyes and sighed. He'd do this for Zo, protect these people when he'd failed to protect her. Even in death, she made him a better man.

But afterwards, when the Raven were safe, he'd have his revenge.

THE NAMELESS REFUGEES had two full days' head start on Zo and her small company of travelers. They gave the massive wall of the Ram a wide berth as they worked their way south to find the tracks of the Nameless.

"Shouldn't we be concerned about running into Ram scouts?" asked Joshua. He hadn't stopped asking questions since waking up that morning. "I mean, don't you think Barnabas will send a mess unit after the Nameless?"

Tess looked between Joshua and Zo, biting down on her lower lip. Zo blinked away another dizzy spell and leaned on her walking stick like an old woman. "The Ram have been too busy fixing the Gate and preparing their attack on the Raven to bother with the Nameless," said Zo. "Don't you think so, Eva?" Zo eyed the Ram girl and encouraged her answer with a nod.

Eva frowned. "Barnabas might not send a full mess, but I think it will be a miracle if we don't come across one of his scouts. And let's face it, this group," she gestured at the four of them, "doesn't stand a chance against a full Ram warrior."

Tess whimpered. Zo reached back and slugged Eva in the arm.

"What?" said Eva. Her small mouth twisted and her eyes pinched as she narrowed her gaze. "Would you rather lie to the girl?"

"To spare her needless fear? Yes, I would."

Eva let her long strides carry her in front of the others. She looked over her shoulder and a chunk of her butchered hair fell into her eyes—hair cut by the knife of her unwanted betrothed inside the Gate as part of an engagement ceremony. "There's no such thing as needless fear. Without fear, you can't be brave."

Zo shook her head and let her gaze drop to the tracks left by the Nameless under her feet. There was no use in explaining human decency to a Ram.

Joshua snatched Tess's hand out of the air and held it as they walked. He was so much taller than her that he almost had to slouch to make it work. "Wanna play a game?" His voice jumped and dived between man and boy.

Tess's blond hair bounced with her step. "What kind of game?"

"Gryphon and I used to play it when I was younger. It's a game where you practice not leaving any tracks as you walk. Gryph called it 'Rabbit Foot' because rabbit tracks are so hard to find unless there's been a good rain."

Tess nodded and Joshua led her off the trail where he and Tess wove between branches and bushes, keeping to the balls of their feet. Every so often he scooped her up on his shoulders and ran a hundred feet ahead of Zo and Eva to give Tess time to practice and travel at her slower pace. Once Joshua deemed her ready, he tested her by letting her get ahead of him while closing his eyes. After a minute of waiting, he'd open his eyes and start walking, but the moment he saw a trampled plant or a snapped twig that marked Tess's passing, he sprinted toward her with fingers outstretched, ready to tickle.

Zo felt like crying every time a laugh escaped Tess as she ran from Joshua. Even after surviving months of slave labor inside the Gate, Tess's spirits hadn't fallen.

She and Joshua both carried with them a beautiful kind of innocence that made Zo violently protective. A part of her looked at Joshua as a piece of Gryphon that she could keep when the real man had been ripped from her side.

"You know that Ram scouts are the least of our problems," Zo said to Eva, taking advantage of the younger members of their little group being out of earshot.

"I've heard stories about the predators on the mountain," said Eva.

Zo's gaze fixed on Tess, her voice an urgent whisper. "The bears and mountain lions are one thing, but I'm more worried about the Clanless. Ever since your people invaded the Kodiak Caves the number of wandering men in these mountains has grown. The Kodiak chief, Murtog, refused to rally his men against the Ram after the raid. Many of his people were taken into the Gate as slaves. And many Kodiak deserted the clan in protest. The rest of the Clanless are robbers, thieves, and murderers banished from the other clans in the region. I hear they're vicious."

Eva nodded. She thumbed her boiled leather vest and weighed the dagger in her hand. "So am I."

The small group traveled a few hundred yards off the Nameless trail to build a fire and rest for the night. Zo, Eva, and Tess gathered wood while Joshua set out into the forest with his sling to hunt for fresh game.

Eva dropped an armful of knobby, dry branches into the growing pile and continued collecting wood closer to Zo. "Why don't you tell Joshua the truth about Gryphon? He deserves to know."

Zo's head swayed, and a bout of dizziness rushed her so fast and hard that she dropped to one knee and clutched the sides of her head. "He's been through so much. I want to make sure that he is completely well before I tell him what happened." Zo gritted her teeth and tested opening her eyes, but regretted the decision.

What is wrong with me?

"I think you're afraid to tell him because you haven't accepted Gryphon's fate yourself. You avoid the topic because saying that Gryphon is *dead* out loud will make it more true."

Zo flinched and clutched her stomach. The dizziness overpowered her and she vomited.

Eva's voice softened. "You're going to have to deal with this, Wolf. I know Barnabas. Gryphon is gone forever and the boy deserves to know." She walked away to gather wood near Tess, leaving Zo to wipe the bile from her lips in peace.

Eva was twenty, only three years older than Zo, but she'd seen a lot in her life. At times, Zo wanted to hate the Ram girl, with her blunt comments and cold analysis. But the truth was, they shared a lot in common. They both gave their hearts away to men not of their clan and, unless Stone managed to escape after the Nameless revolutionaries attacked inside the Gate, there was a good chance neither would see the man they loved again.

Joshua came back just before dark carrying two dead rabbits by the ears and a giant grin on his face. "Dinner is served." His smile shone as brightly as his red hair did in sunlight.

Eva pulled a thin knife from her waistband and made

quick work of Joshua's kill. The animals cooked on a spit over the fire, the red flames licking the meat as if they too were starving from a long day's hike. Dripping fat sizzled in the fire. Zo's mouth watered and her stomach rolled with hunger.

Exhausted, they all stared at the fire in a daze until Joshua broke the spell of silence. "If it weren't for my sling, we'd all go hungry tonight." He stretched out his legs as he leaned against a tree with his arms tucked contentedly behind his head. "It's a good thing Gryphon left me to take care of you girls."

"Yeah, I'm sure the fact that you were unconscious had nothing to do with it," said Eva with a harmless grin. Tess snorted then rolled into another fit of giggles.

"That's it." Joshua jumped up and attacked Tess with wiggling fingers, stealing her breath with hysterical laughter. Zo might have joined in were the circumstance different. Still, she allowed herself a smile. "Be quiet, you two."

Joshua looked thoroughly chastened and slightly embarrassed, as he remembered they weren't the only ones on this mountain. He ruffled Tess's hair and settled back into his spot against the tree—only he slipped and his hand came down on a sharp rock.

"Ouch!" He sucked the wound to keep the slow stream of blood from running down his finger.

"Don't use your mouth." Zo dug into her medical satchel for ointment and a thin strip of dressing. "It's like you want an infection."

She took his hand in hers and dressed the wound, making sure to quiz Tess on the proper herbs to help with this kind of minor wound. He didn't really require a blessing of healing, but in the interest of teaching Tess, Zo held Joshua's injured hand and repeated the words of the blessing. She waited for the warmth to surface on her skin and for the energy of her touch to transfer into Joshua's wound…but it didn't.

Zo knew she wasn't herself, but to not be able to produce any energy? This wasn't even a serious injury.

She looked up to find everyone around the fire staring.

Josh asked, "Are you all right?"

Zo smiled. "Sure, kid." She turned to Tess and said, "This is the perfect kind of wound for you to practice on. Why don't you do the blessing?"

Tess knelt next to Joshua. She studied him with such a serious expression, Zo had to force herself not to laugh. "I'm going to give you a healing blessing. It might feel uncomfortable at first, but it will help you get better much faster."

Joshua gave Zo an "Is this kid serious?" look. He pursed his lips together, and managed, "I would like that very much, young healer."

Tess swatted his arm. "Be serious."

"Go ahead, Tess," said Zo.

Tess wrapped her fingers around Joshua's hand, closed her eyes, and sang the blessing. Zo usually kept the melody soft and to herself. Not Tess. She sang out the ancient words, the melody carrying great power.

When the simple song ended, Zo pulled Tess into her own lap and hugged her. "You're getting really good, bug. Mother would have been proud." She cleared the emotion from her throat and let Tess hop off her lap. Their mother would have been proud. She should have been the one to teach Tess the healing songs. Not Zo.

"We need to discuss our defenses," said Eva, pulling out three knives: one from a sheath at her back, one at her hip, and one small knife strapped to her calf beneath her pant leg. "If we're attacked, we need a plan of action."

It was such a Ram thing to say, but Zo had to admit that Eva was right. "You're the ones with the Ram training." Zo gestured toward Eva and Joshua. "Be my guest."

Joshua frowned. "Usually we start by listing our assets. You know, what we have to offer the group. Then our liabilities."

Eva nodded. "I have three knives that I know how to use better than a spoon or fork. Like all women of my clan, I know how to fight. Beyond that, I'm determined to reach the Nameless and find Stone, and I'll do anything to make that happen."

"Good," said Joshua. "And liabilities?" It was easy to see the boy's training surface. Zo wondered how many of these lessons came directly from Gryphon, his mentor.

"I'm pregnant and prone to sickness in the mornings and sometimes at night. Nothing too bad." Eva fidgeted. "I'm also desperate." She laughed a little at herself and stared back into the fire.

Joshua leaned over to Tess and whispered, "Her desperation might hinder her judgment. Her honesty is a sign of trust. A compliment."

Tess nodded, as if she were mentally taking notes.

"I'll go next," said Joshua. He pulled out a small

shield, a sling, a bow, a quiver of arrows, and a knife. Gryphon had packed him a bag of supplies before their escape. No extra clothes, only weapons. "I'm decent with the bow and knife, but I can hunt small game better than most with my sling. I'm stronger than anyone here."

Eva opened her mouth to protest, but must have thought better of it. It was easy to overlook Joshua's size and only see the thirteen-year-old boy, but the kid likely had them all in weight.

"I've also been apprentice to Gryphon, and he's probably the best Striker the Ram have ever seen." The boy's chest was so full of air he might have lifted off the ground. "As for liabilities, I don't do well on night watch, and I need to eat a lot to be full. I have no idea where we're headed, and I'm inexperienced in fighting in real life."

"Fair enough," said Eva.

Zo cleared her throat and pulled out her one unimpressive dagger. She wasn't used to spilling her strengths and weaknesses, preferring instead to keep her talents hidden and her weaknesses buried. But for Joshua and Tess's sakes…"I'm a trained spy and healer, and the only one here who knows how to get to the Allies."

"Liabilities?" Eva raised a brow.

Joshua nodded encouragingly.

Zo sighed. "I'm sick. There's something wrong with my head when I stand up too fast. I have frequent dizzy spells where my head pounds. Sometimes it's bad enough to make me nauseous. I'm not great in combat. In fact," she swallowed, "I don't think I could kill a person even to save my own life. I don't do well with that sort of thing."

No need to tell them about her struggle with healing. She was sure whatever was affecting her would pass with time.

Eva and Joshua shared a look.

"My turn?" asked Tess. She looked around and snatched up a rock sitting close to the ground. "I have this. I could probably throw it at someone." She twisted up her lips in deep thought. "I'm also good at hiding."

Zo put up a hand. "Great job, Tess. You don't need to go on."

Tess' liabilities were glaringly obvious. She was slow and weak, without any real ability to defend herself.

Eva and Joshua took turns using the strengths and weaknesses they had all shared and devised a plan. Eva unstrapped the knife around her calf and fastened the small sheath to Tess's belt. "When I was your age, I already had three years of training with weighted weapons. Your lessons will begin tomorrow."

Zo thought to protest, but given the circumstances, it made sense to teach Tess everything possible to defend herself if she got in a bind. And who better to learn from than a Ram who was bred to kill from the time she could walk?

They ate their meal and doused the fire. Even though the blaze would have helped them stay warm and keep animals at bay, it wasn't worth the risk of exposing their location to Clanless and, more likely, Ram scouts. Just as the last wisps of smoke carried on the night breeze and the coals of the fire turned to a weak, flicking glow, a bird called not far away.

Eva sat up then Joshua followed her lead, like deer

lifting their heads to listen for a predator. Zo clutched her knife to her chest. She knew that call. Commander Laden taught it to her as part of her training. She let out a small "caw" sound, mimicking the call.

Both Eva and Joshua whipped around and stared at Zo. She could imagine their questions. They weren't used to working with other clans. Where there is hate there is also fear.

Out of the darkness, two figures stepped from the trees into their camp.

CHAPTER FIVE

Two days traveling the Raven rope bridges was enough to make Gryphon miss even Zander's company.

"I think I'd like to reconsider your offer to turn back," Gryphon said to the Raven leader. Gryphon had learned the multi-feathered leader was called Craw. He also had learned Craw was oddly friendly when he wasn't ordering his men to take part in the merriment of Gryphon's death.

"You've come far enough now that I'd have to kill you if you tried to leave. You've seen too much."

"Please do." Gryphon groaned. His hands were filled with splintered wood and rubbed raw from sliding along the spun ropes. He'd traded the comfort of his hands for peace of mind. But now, even the muscles in his shoulders and neck ached from constantly tensing them.

It was no wonder his clan hadn't discovered the location of the Raven until now. Ram mess units had likely run right under these bridges without ever realizing they existed high above the forest floor. The bridges were obviously well maintained. The railings surrounding each platform were carved with symbols Gryphon had never seen before, as well as images of birdmen and women in various settings —planting grain, talking to trees, bending in prayer.

Gryphon made the mistake of looking down again. He cursed under his breath as the ground swayed, then jumped up to meet him. "What will you do after all this?" Gryphon said to Gabe. He tried to keep his attention trained on the back of Gabe's head instead of the distant ground.

Gabe shrugged. "I'll return to the Allies, make sure Tess is cared for, and fight your bloody clan until I either get a spear through my heart or die an old man. Whichever comes first."

Gryphon nodded even though Gabe couldn't see him. Wolves and Raven and even the brutish Kodiak could work together and live in relative peace, but never the Ram. The thought made Gryphon slow his wobbly pace. Was this entire journey pointless? Even if they did evacuate the Raven in time, weren't they just putting off the inevitable? The Ram would eventually wipe out all the clan in the region. Even the Allies and the valley-dwelling Wolves. Was there really a point in resisting them?

Zo's death, above all else, proved there wasn't.

"You've been quiet, Gabe," said Gryphon. He assumed it was because of Zo. As painful as it was to talk about her, Gryphon longed to hear someone else say her name. To make her real, if only in memory.

"You miss her," said Gryphon. "I'll listen."

But Gabe kept walking, not bothering to so much as shrug a shoulder. It was as if they were strangers again and Zo—their common ground—had never existed.

Zo had had a foolish temper that led to poor decisions, not to mention she was supposed to be Gryphon's enemy. But beneath it all, she was the most human person he'd ever met. Life without her would be completely deficient. Didn't Gabe—Zo's childhood friend—feel that?

Gryphon dropped the subject. As much as he wanted to talk about Zo, it was probably too painful for Gabe. Gryphon had no choice but to respect Gabe's need for silence and give him time.

The crash of ocean waves spurred the Raven forward at an increased pace. Through the thick branches, Gryphon made out an endless expanse of blue, a sight he'd grown used to while sitting atop the sheer cliff that marked the edge of Ram's Gate.

He used to study the waves, pondering his goal to restore his family's honor, imagining what it would feel like to command his own mess. Now he snorted at his own foolishness. What was pride without honor, and what was honor without a clear conscience? As much as he loved his people, he could not serve them now or ever again. His chest tightened at the thought. *I'm so sorry, Mother.*

The foliage opened as they crossed the final bridge leading to a platform large enough to accommodate the entire flock of Raven warriors as well as Gryphon and Gabe. Gryphon glanced over the edge of the platform. The ocean crashed into the rocky ravine hundreds of yards below, the sound ricocheted off the rocks like dozens of voices fighting to be heard.

Not fifty yards beyond the cliff was a forested island that sat like a gigantic pillar that stood apart from the mainland, surrounded completely by cliffs and, eventually, sea. The towering walls of the island were sheer and plateaued even higher than the canopy platform upon which they stood. Were Gryphon standing on the ground, he'd have to crane his neck to see it.

How could anyone reach such a place?

Craw, with his feathered necklace catching the breeze and whipping about his painted face, cupped both hands to his mouth and crowed at the large island. The high screeching sounded anything but human.

"What is he...?"

Gabe silenced Gryphon with a look and stepped next to Craw. Like the Raven, he cupped his hands to his mouth and arched his back a little as if to throw the howl that poured from his lips.

Craw walked over to Gryphon, resting his hand on the Ram's shoulder. "The horn has never blown from this platform. If we want any chance of delivering your message, it's best to keep it that way."

Now that his people knew the location of the Raven Nest, in only a matter of days, Ram horns carried around the necks of every mess leader Barnabas sent would blare from this platform. A thrilling voice of strength to the ears of Ram warriors, but terrifying to everyone else.

The Raven parted from the trunk of the tree to form a V formation. Gryphon nudged Gabe's shoulder, a question burning on his tongue. But he didn't have to wait for long. An arrow whistled through the air and lodged with a quiet thud into the trunk of the tree, not far from Gryphon's head.

Gryphon instinctively reached for his shield, but the Raven had taken that and every other weapon from him the day they surrounded him in the meadow. A few of the Raven shared smiles.

"With the wind, it might have hit any one of you," Gryphon grumbled. He knew the Raven were legendary bowman, but even they couldn't predict a gust of wind. Another whistle cut the air and this time Gryphon dropped to the ground, covering his head with both arms. The arrow *thumped* into the tree, inches from the first.

Gryphon cursed and climbed to his feet. Even if it meant taking an arrow through the neck, he would not move an inch at the next whistling sound. For the sake of his pride, if not his rear end.

But the V formation broke, and two men rushed to the arrows, pulling them with some effort from the tree. A thin, shimmering string dangled from each arrow's shaft, so slight Gryphon might not have noticed it if it didn't catch the faint light of the overcast sky.

Gabe broke his long silence with arms crossed over his chest, his cape dancing in the breeze. "Lion's Silk." He nodded toward the men, who'd formed two lines, and, with gloved hands, heaved on the thread-like material. "As light as a spider's web but strong as the mountain lions that roam the region."

"What is it made from?" Gryphon collected the arrow with silk from the ground as the Raven still pulled against an invisible weight. The string was cold to the touch and seemed to be made of hair-thin strands of metal. But it couldn't be metal, because as Gryphon tried to break the Lion's Silk, the woven strands held strong. "Magic?" Gryphon asked, still trying to break the strands. He'd heard about the Raven and their mystical practices.

"Resourcefulness," corrected Gabe.

For some reason, Gabe never looked Gryphon in the eye anymore—not since they escaped the Gate together. Was it possible that Gabe blamed him for what happened to Zo? The injustice of the thought made Gryphon want to break the Wolf 's nose.

Across the gap, a massive rope ladder with boards stacked along the frame lifted off the face of the island wall, pulled higher and higher as the Raven heaved on the Lion's Silk. It had to be more than fifty yards in length, with no hand railings to help support the flimsy frame. When the rope ladder stretched horizontally between the island and the tree platform, the Raven tied off the silk around a thick branch.

Without preamble, the feathered men walked, one by one, across the gaping divide to the island. The ladder gradually slanted upward to the island. Since there were no railings, they held their arms out wide for balance as they crossed the treacherous catwalk hundreds of yards above the ocean. The fall would kill them; there was no question. But they were graceful in their steps—so confident that Gryphon had to wonder if they thought, like their namesake, they could fly to the island.

Craw slapped Gryphon on the shoulder, startling him. "I hope

you're ready, little lamb. It's your turn."

TWO STRANGERS STEPPED from the shadows. It was just light enough to see the feather necklaces and the paint smeared on their already dark skin. They kept a safe distance from Zo and the others, holding up their hands to show they held no weapons.

"We saw the smoke of your fire," said a man whose face was cast in shadow.

The young woman at his side stepped forward. Her skin was the same warm tone as her companion's. Her eyes slanted just enough to make her look exotic. "We're tired from traveling and hoped you'd have news of the clans."

Zo jumped in, before Joshua or Eva spoke and gave away their Ram accents. "Who are you?" It was customary for the intruder to make the first introductions.

The two figures took a couple of steps forward to let the lingering light of the fire embers touch their faces. The man was smaller than the Ram and Wolves, but his lean form was still potentially dangerous. His dark eyes swept over the camp and settled on Zo. His head was shaved at the sides, leaving a stripe of black hair down the center. The woman at his side let her hands hang casually from the strap of her pack. Though she was even smaller, and her lips fuller, the resemblance between the two was unmistakable.

"I am Talon and this is my twin sister, Raca. We are traveling home to the Raven after a long journey south."

Zo wondered if they came from the Allied Camp but didn't want to reveal too much about her knowledge of Commander Laden and the Allies. Enemies of the cause would kill for that kind of information—especially the Ram.

The Raven girl called Raca hitched up her pack and smiled. "We usually avoid smoking fires, but I made Talon stop when I saw your group. It isn't every day you find other women outside of the protection of a clan."

Talon took another step forward. "We mostly just wanted to make sure you were all right."

Zo looked to Eva, who shook her head from right to left. "No," she mouthed, while keeping a firm hold on both of her knives. Joshua was more relaxed, looking to Zo for his cue to attack. His confidence in her was terrifying. No matter their talks of assets and liabilities; in that moment it was clear that they all saw her as their leader. A poor decision.

Zo had no other choice but to follow her gut instinct. If these people were Raven then they needed to know about the Ram's plans to attack their clan. "You are welcome at our fire."

Talon and Raca relaxed and walked over to their circle.

"Tell me," said Talon in his slow-paced Raven accent, "how do two young women, a boy, and a child find themselves outside of clan protection only a day's journey from Ram's Gate?"

Eva waved her knife in front of Talon's nose. "This is our fire, *Bird*. You have no business asking questions."

At hearing Eva's harsh Ram words, Talon immediately drew his own blade, with Raca and Joshua following suit.

Zo's hands shot out to calm the circle. "Enough. Eva, put that away. Joshua."

One by one, the circle rested their weapons in their laps, though none went so far as to sheath them.

"You're a Ram," said Raca to Eva. "I've never met a Ram woman before. For some reason, I always imagined they grew beards and had thighs the size of tree trunks. You're actually kind of pretty."

"A compliment? Charming." Eva twisted the knife in her hand.

Joshua snorted, and the dying coals of the fire crackled.

Talon studied Zo. "We don't mean to be rude, Ram. It's not every day you see a pair of Ram and a pair of Wolves enjoying the same fire."

Joshua said, "How did you know that Zo was a—"

"Wolf?" finished Talon. "Well, look at her. Long neck, elegant lines, the feminine curve of her jaw. It's easy to spot."

"You can stop staring," said Joshua in a hard tone at odds with his usual affable nature. "She is not yours to look at."

"Joshua!" The last thing Zo needed was Joshua picking a fight with this Raven.

"No, he's right." Talon rubbed the back of his neck and looked up at the deepening blue of the night sky. "I didn't mean to stare." He glanced back at her, and one side of his lips curled into a half smile. "You're very pretty." He cleared his throat. "And that is why I'm concerned about you all. I doubt you'll make it to the Wolves alive, if that's where you're headed."

"We aren't traveling all the way to the Valley of Wolves," said Zo. "We're tracking a group of Nameless. They had two day's head start on us after we all escaped Ram's Gate."

Raca and Talon exchanged a long look and, without a word spoken between them, snatched up their packs and stood. "We better be moving," said Raca with an apologetic smile. "It was nice meeting you all." She said it like a eulogy. As if there was no way a group of defenseless women could escape the Gate and live to see another day.

"Wait!" said Zo, "There is something you should know. I have news of the Raven."

She took a deep breath and told them that the Ram had discovered the secret location of the Nest and were marching there now. As she spoke both Raca and Talon sank back to the ground as though the weight of a boulder rested upon their shoulders.

"I don't want to believe you," said Talon.

"Our companion, Gabe, knew the way to the Raven settlement. He left a day ago to warn your people. He'll get there at least a day or two before the Ram, giving your people a chance to evacuate."

"Gryphon is with him. He'll make sure they get out in time," said Joshua, with so much confidence Zo's chest tightened and she felt the need to rest her head on the ground and curl into a ball.

Fight the grief, she urged herself.

"Who's Gryphon?" said Raca in a quiet voice, looking at Zo with her brows knit together.

Zo tried to keep her expression even, but her devastation felt completely transparent.

Joshua spoke up before she had to answer. "Gryphon is a Ram Striker. He's my mentor and the one who helped us all escape the Gate." He met Zo's eye with a proud smile. "He's also in love with Zo."

CHAPTER SIX

Aside from Craw, Gryphon was the last to cross the ladder.

"I don't understand," said Gryphon. "How will you get across without leaving the ladder in place?"

Craw wiggled his bushy black eyebrows and said, "I am a bird. I will fly."

These people were crazy. Gryphon shook his head and took a deep breath. Before he stepped out to follow the others, Craw stopped him. Even though Gryphon was taller, there was something in the way the Raven carried himself that made him feel as though he was looking up to the Bird.

"Your Ram upper half is much larger than your lower. Keep your center of gravity low. Crawl if you must. No one will think less of you for it. The wind is strong today."

Gryphon nodded, determined to surpass the Raven's

expectations of him. No way would he crawl like a beggar to the Raven Nest. He might be a deserter, but he hadn't lost all of his pride.

Gryphon stepped onto the first wooden plank of the horizontal ladder, determined not to think about the thread-like material supporting the wobbly structure. The board sank with the pressure of his weight. Gryphon crouched low, threw his arms out wide and traded the sturdiness of the platform completely for the ladder. The whole ladder shook along with his knees, so much so that Gryphon couldn't find the balance to lift his foot and take another step.

"Drop to your knees. You must keep moving."

With his jaw clamped so hard his teeth might shatter, Gryphon forced himself to take the next step. Then another. Then another. On the rope bridges he'd been able to hold onto the railings and look ahead to the next platform. Here the gaps in the wooden planks were spaced more like a ladder and required him to look down to find the next footing. But it was a long, long way down —the distance so extreme, so deadly, that Gryphon fought a tremor that raced up and down his spine, churning his stomach to the point of needing to be sick.

When he was nearly halfway out, a gust of wind hit Gryphon and the ladder so hard the entire structure lifted several feet in the air then fell back down again so rapidly that Gryphon's feet lost traction on the wood before gravity brought him swiftly down. But it was too late for Gryphon to recover his balance and footing. He missed the plank with one foot and hooked the ladder in between boards with the other.

The horizontal ladder bounced up and down, the strain on the Lion's Silk made obvious by a metallic, high-pitched whine. Gryphon gripped the wood with both hands and a leg, terrified the Silk would snap.

Hearty laughter boomed from both the men on the island and from Craw—the last Raven left on the platform—while Gryphon struggled to pull himself back onto the ladder. Though his heart felt as though it might leap from his chest, he couldn't help but offer a shaky smile. Almost dying could be exhilarating. He supposed.

"What am I doing here?" he grumbled to himself. It was a fair question, one he'd asked himself a hundred times over.

The wind calmed and the ladder stopped bouncing enough for Gryphon to pull himself up. A mild breezed cooled the sweat running down the sides of his face. He knelt on the ladder and commanded his arms and legs to stop shaking. Maybe crawling wasn't such a bad idea after all.

He reached out for the next rung of the ladder when a spear launched from the ground below Craw's platform. It struck the board where his hands rested, splitting the wood in two. Instinct took over. Forgetting his fear of heights, Gryphon grabbed the spear before it dropped to the ocean and, somehow, found himself in a low crouch on the teetering bridge. He dodged a second spear before identifying his attackers.

A group of men dressed in boiled leather with large circular shields stood beneath the canopy of trees and the platform. Gryphon's people. The Ram. A volley of Raven arrows soared down to meet them, but the Ram linked their shields in perfect unison to deflect the attack. The fluidity of their movements startled him. He never realized how precise, how beautiful the dance of war could be. The moment the arrows stopped, a spear—like lightning—launched from the shields toward Gryphon's chest.

Gryphon flattened himself against the wooden boards, the spear jetting only inches above his head. The Raven answered again, only this time Gryphon didn't squander the cover their arrows provided. He stood with spear in hand and sprinted the remaining twenty yards across the chasm, numb to the deadly drop below.

The arrows stopped. The Ram retreated back into the cover of the trees.

"They're climbing!" Craw called from his place on the platform. He reached for his knife and began to saw at the Lion's Silk.

Orders from the Raven soldiers surrounding Gryphon had the men running in all directions, reloading their quivers, and scrambling for position. Arrows launched toward the base of the tree but flew blind through the thick foliage. Craw sawed through a strand of Lion's Silk, rendering one side of the horizontal ladder limp.

Gryphon clenched his fist around the spear in his hands, willing Craw to work faster at the second strand of Silk than he had the first. Gryphon saw a flash of metal at the edge of the platform. The Raven archers must have as well—at least fifteen bolts soared in that direction.

Gryphon relaxed some, knowing the Ram would not

be foolish enough to attack the platform with a host of Raven providing cover. But Craw couldn't stay there forever, and eventually one of Gryphon's compatriots would brave the platform for the glory of the kill.

Craw stopped his sawing just before the spindles of the woven Silk broke. He ran and dove onto the ladder, catching it in mid-air as he flew across the chasm. With deadly speed, he swung into the side of the island cliff, somehow managing to hang onto the lowest rung of the ladder with one hand.

The Raven crowed victorious. But Gryphon knew better than to underestimate his own clan. He checked his grip on the spear and scanned the tree line for Ram. What was a mess unit doing here now? Barnabas wouldn't want the Raven to learn about his planned attack until the full Ram force was present.

"They targeted you." Gabe stepped up next to Gryphon. The Wolf had been so quiet on their journey Gryphon forgot he was even there. "They didn't attack until you were on the ladder."

But why?

Craw neared the top of the ladder. Gryphon knelt on the edge of the cliff and extended his hand to the Raven leader, surprised by the relief he felt for the man. Craw reached up and clasped Gryphon's forearm. The Raven smiled, his breath labored. "Not bad, little lamb."

A spear flew from the edge of Gryphon's vision. Time slowed. Gryphon pulled with all his strength to lift Craw to safety, but the spear struck the Raven in the back. Craw's mouth and eyes each formed a circle, shock frozen on his face that slowly melted into agony as his body hung limp in Gryphon's grasp.

Gabe and the others helped Gryphon pull Craw's body onto solid ground.

"Gryphon, son of the deserter!" Zander's voice boomed from somewhere in the trees across the chasm.

Gryphon might have called the man a friend only days ago. Now he wanted nothing more than to return his spear. He should have assumed Zander hadn't giving up on tracking him; it wouldn't suit the mess leader's ambitions to return to the Gate without his prize. But that meant Ajax was there as well—his best friend, the man who'd freed him, but also the man who'd killed Zo. His heart ripped in half: one half cared for Ajax and his young, struggling family, and the other despised him in the darkest, blackest way possible.

Zander yelled, "We will hunt you down with the rest of these Birds. You are a traitor and a coward to leave your mother to bear your shame along with your father's."

Gryphon growled and ran to the edge of the cliff. He hitched up his front leg before launching the spear in the direction of Zander's voice. It shot across the ravine and into the trees. A man cried out in pain, and a sense of dread filled Gryphon. Whom had he hit? Was it Zander? Ajax? A different mess brother who was simply following orders?

Gryphon turned back to the crowd of Raven warriors. Those who weren't bent over Craw's lifeless form stared at him in wonder—likely marveling at the powerful throw directed at his own people.

Craw gagged and bucked on the ground. His own men gathered around him, pushing Gryphon and Gabe to the back of the crowd.

Standing out on the edge of the cliff, Gryphon looked across the divide to the trees that hid Zander and his old mess unit. "I will kill him," he said. "I will kill him."

ZO GAPED AT JOSHUA. "Don't say that."

The thought of Gryphon loving her had sounded too wonderful. Too sweet. Joshua didn't know that with his words he was offering poisonous berries to a starving person—a painful lie.

Talon pulled his shirt over his head to show Zo and the others a crescent moon tattooed on his back. The symbol of the Allies. Zo bore the same mark.

"We were sent by our chief as ambassadors to Commander Laden. Our clan has been invited to join the Allied forces, though we do not believe our chief will accept Commander Laden's offer. Our people endure the northern climate and the close proximity to the Ram because we are tied to our land. It's deeply woven into our heritage. Many of the Elders believe if we leave the land, our people will lose their souls."

"But with the coming invasion, your chief will reconsider," said Zo.

Raca picked up a rock and weighed it in her hands. "I doubt it."

Zo couldn't help but think of the night her parents

died in a Ram raid. The fear that engulfed her as she and Tess squeezed into baskets to hide in a corner of their home. The chilling sound of the Ram war horn blaring in their ears as people were slaughtered.

"You need to help convince your chief. If your people don't evacuate, hundreds will die. The Ram have pledged that they will not discriminate between a Raven warrior and his family. The children…"

Talon's expression hardened in the low light of the dying fire. "You do not need to remind us to consider the children of our clan, Wolf."

Raca reached out and placed a placating hand on Talon's arm. "She's only trying to help, Brother." Raca turned to us. "His wife and two small children are anxiously awaiting his return."

Zo reeled, her mouth dropping. She wanted to catch up to the Ram forces and hold them off with her bare hands. "What will you do?" She shivered against the cold.

"We will run," Talon snarled. "All night and all day until we reach our home."

Talon and Raca secured their packs, and Zo embraced each of them, silently muttering a blessing of vitality and courage. She frowned when the familiar tug of energy didn't come. They would need all the help they could get if they were to reach the Raven stronghold before the Ram.

"Safe travels," said Zo.

Raca leaned in and pressed her cheek to Zo's. "May you find your Gryphon," she whispered.

Zo swayed on her feet. Her head throbbed.

They were gone before Zo had the chance to correct the woman. Even if Gryphon were still alive, he had never been her Gryphon.

That night Zo took the first watch. In spite of her exhaustion, she didn't think she could sleep. Not after their encounter with Raca and Talon. She sat awake watching the trees while her imagination took hold. Every rustle of leaves was an enemy approaching, every cricket chirp a distant scream. She clutched her knife to her chest and stayed in that position until the first signs of dawn were upon them.

She reached over and shook Eva awake.

The Ram looked confused by the dim light coming from the Eastern sky.

"I couldn't sleep, so I didn't wake you for your watch," said Zo. "I think I'll try and rest now though, until the sun is up."

Eva rubbed her eyes and nodded.

Just as Zo curled on the ground next to Tess and Joshua, Eva whispered, "You need to tell Joshua what happened to Gryphon today. He can't go on thinking that everything is fine. He deserves to know."

Zo lay still with her back to Eva and her eyes closed. "What if I can't tell him?"

"Then I will."

CHAPTER SEVEN

"Where is my brother?"

The voice carried over the gathering crowd of Raven. A man wearing several rows of feathers walked forward. The Raven bowed as they stepped out of his path.

The chief knelt next to Craw and reached for his hands, then paused, seeming to think better of it. His expression darkened as he turned away from his brother. "Cover him and prepare him for burial." The chief 's voice was void of emotion.

As two of the chief 's men stepped in to remove Craw, Gabe leaned over and whispered to Gryphon. "They fear the body. They believe if they outwardly mourn for their dead, the deceased can never be released to join their ancestors in the underworld. The chief loved his brother, but he will not weep for him."

Everyone turned away from the body as it was taken to be readied for burial. The chief, who Gryphon knew was called Naat'áanii, or Chief Naat, stood and looked out across the cliff toward the mainland. His lips moved as though he was speaking but no words came. When his silent prayer ended, he turned a cold eye on Gryphon and said, "Feed the Ram to the sea. Let the fish and birds eat his rotting carcass. His presence desecrates the land of our ancestors."

Craw's men who had escorted Gryphon to the Nest shifted feet. Gabe stepped forward, bending into a bow with arms raised like wings at his sides. "Please, Chief." Gabe stared at the ground while holding his bow. "I represent Commander Laden and the Allies. I ran with Craw and his men outside Ram's Gate and was taken prisoner by the Ram. I escaped with Gryphon's help days ago. We've come to deliver a warning."

Gabe held his awkward position, waiting for the chief to cut him off. When he didn't, Gabe pressed forward with his plea. "Ram soldiers captured one of your scouts and broke him for information regarding the location of your clan."

Gryphon squirmed. He and Ajax had been the ones to capture the scout. Gabe had actually told him about the enemy camp where they found the young Raven scout in exchange for Zo's protection inside Ram's Gate. The Raven Chief wouldn't appreciate that little detail.

"Gryphon has forsaken his clan to help us. He initiated a rebellion that allowed hundreds of Nameless slaves to flee Ram's Gate and now has traveled here with me to warn your people that at least two hundred Ram warriors are marching toward the Nest as we speak. We expect them to arrive in less than two days' time."

More and more Raven joined the crowd, creating a half circle around Gryphon and Gabe.

"How do I know that this Ram," he spat the word, pointing at Gryphon with a furious hand, "isn't still loyal to his clan? What if he intends to have us evacuate our homeland so that his people might slaughter us in our escape? Or at the very least, pillage our grain stores?"

Gryphon said, "You have my word that—"

The leader leapt at Gryphon, a hatchet somehow materializing in his hand. He held the blade to Gryphon's throat, breathing hard, prepared to drag it across skin. "Your word means nothing to me, Sheep."

It took all of Gryphon's self-control not to fight back. Striking a chief was the surest way to foul the situation. Gabe stepped in and slowly rested a hand on the Raven leader's arm. "Please, Chief. You must listen to us. For the sake of your children and clan."

"My brother is dead." For an elderly man, the chief's hold on Gryphon was solid, his skill wielding the hatchet apparent. "I will hear nothing more from you or this beast." The Raven Chief pressed the blade into Gryphon's throat, forcing him to step backward toward the cliff's edge.

"Father, stop!" A boy no older than Joshua pushed his way to the front of the crowd. He wore a leather braid around his forehead with long black hair flying loose about his face. Something about the youth seemed familiar to Gryphon, but he couldn't place it.

"You cannot kill this man," the boy said plainly. He folded his arms in front of his chest and looked Gryphon directly in the eye, hardly blinking.

"Not now, Sani."

"This man spared my life, Father. If you kill him, you kill me." He hesitated only a moment, filling his chest with air and letting it out slowly. "I am his 'Atiin."

The Raven leader loosened his hold on Gryphon and looked at the boy beside him as if he were seeing him for the first time. "You're mistaken, son. Many of the Ram share this man's look."

And then Gryphon remembered. It was the day he'd first been named Striker and Zander's second. A flock of Raven warriors had attacked them while they were scouting for Raven grain stores not far from this very spot. Gryphon had been launched into the flock of retreating Raven with orders to kill. When he discovered the young Raven boy struggling to string his arrow he was reminded of Joshua. He'd intentionally missed the mark to spare the child. His conscience didn't permit killing the innocent.

Gryphon studied the boy before him with new eyes. He was short but carried himself with calm pride rarely found in one so young. Very different from Joshua's easy smiles and desperate desire to please.

"I was with your son when we attacked the Ram mess," Gabe said. "I add my witness that this is the Ram soldier that spared the boy's life. He is different from the others, Sir."

Gryphon flinched. He might disagree with Barnabas and other leaders in his clan, but at his core, he still considered himself a Ram. Without his clan, what was he but an untethered castoff? A Clanless.

The Raven Chief lowered his hatchet but mistrust

still stained his expression. "Bind him, and bring him to the Gaagii Court. The Elders will determine his fate." Then to a man at his right with an impressive collection of feathers he added, "Send out a team, your best, to hunt down those Ram. They've seen the Nest."

Chief Naat leaned in to Gryphon, staring him directly in the eyes. "Whatever heathen gods claim your allegiance, you might want to start praying to them. The Elders will not be merciful."

"I'm meeting with the chief and the elders first. When you're asked to join us, don't say anything they can use against you." Gabe spoke out of the corner of his mouth as they passed a sweeping village built into a network of redwood trees.

"They should be making preparations to flee this island," Gryphon hissed back. "The Ram know their location. What am I compared to ten approaching mess units? These people will be slaughtered."

As Gryphon, Gabe, and their Raven escort walked through the village, women gathered their children and rushed up ladders leading to homes built high in the trees. A statue of a carved wooden bird with outstretched wings guarded the base of each tree.

"They're meant to scare evil spirits away from our homes." The boy, Sani, appeared as if out of nowhere. "My people believe birds carry power on their wings. Power strong enough to protect them even from men as mighty as you, Ram."

Gryphon nodded, grateful for his young guide, but still restless with the need to get these people moving.

"Wooden birds will not save your people from Ram spears."

Gabe squeezed Gryphon's shoulder. His brows pulled together, and his lips formed a hard line. With only the slightest movement, he shook his head.

They approached a wall of thin wooden logs bound together to create a large circle. Mud plaster filled the gaps in the wood, making it impossible to see inside. Just outside of the circle stood a small square platform. An engraved plaque hung on a tall frame of wood. Gryphon still didn't know how to read, and wished Joshua had taken time to teach him. From the frame dangled two lengths of thick rope with slipknot loops to serve as handcuffs.

"You will await your judgment here," one of the guards ordered. Gryphon stepped onto the wooden platform. When the guard moved to place Gryphon's hands into the cuffs, Sani waved him off. "It is my right to attend to this man." Though small in stature, Sani carried himself like a grown man. The guard bowed and backed away from Gryphon to make room for the chief 's son.

Sani held up the cuffs, only slightly flinching when the Gryphon willingly raised his hands.

Gryphon glared at Gabe. "We don't have time for this. They don't have time for this."

Gabe scratched the back of his blond head. "I'll do my best."

"Be sure that you do. I didn't leave Joshua and..." Gryphon swallowed hard, stunned to realize he'd forgotten that Zo was actually gone. His whole body rejected the idea that he would never see her again. It didn't feel right. "I didn't leave them to die along with the Raven. If these people don't agree to leave, our efforts are for nothing."

Gabe nodded and walked into the plastered circle of logs along with a number of elderly men who all carried a stone the size of their fists.

"Why did you spare my life, Ram?" Sani asked. The boy pulled on a rope connected to a pulley, raising Gryphon's cuffed hands high above his head. The rough fibers of the rope cut into his skin as the slipknots tightened around his wrists.

"Had I known you were the chief 's son, I might not have." Gryphon groaned against the strain on his wrists.

Sani's eyes were deep, black, and haunting. He regarded Gryphon with such intense focus that Gryphon feared he'd tumble into those eyes and be lost forever. "I don't believe you." The boy tilted his head to one side. "I think you view your mercy as weakness. That is why you are so sad."

Gryphon closed his eyes and let his head fall back. If he ignored the boy, he might stop talking to him. After a few moments, smoke from the fire a few feet away assaulted his lungs. It smelled of cedar and made Gryphon cough and sputter. Unable to shield his face from the strong-smelling smoke, he opened his eyes long enough to see Sani fanning the fragrant cloud toward him.

"What are you doing?" Gryphon coughed again as Sani lifted the lid of a basket by the fire and pulled out three bundles of herbs. On by one, he dropped each bundle into the fire, continuing to fan the smoke in his direction.

"Mugwort to cleanse you, lavender to restore balance, and sweetgrass to drive away bad influences," said Sani.

Gryphon wiped his watering eyes on his shoulder as best he could. "I don't need your witch doctoring."

Through his tears he thought he saw Sani shake his head. "It is customary to prepare the accused for punishment. We believe the smoke will cling to the bad in you and pull it away, leaving behind the good."

Gryphon's head rolled forward, exhausted. When the smoke didn't hit him full in the face he could actually breathe.

"I thought you said they wouldn't hurt me because you are my '*Atiin*.'"

Another wave of smoke hit him before Sani answered, "They will not kill you, but that doesn't stop them from selecting other forms of punishment."

Gryphon hung from his ropes, assaulted by smoke, thinking of Zo and worrying for Joshua, Eva, and little Tess. What would become of them if they didn't make it to the Allies? Why hadn't he just abandoned these people who seemed too fixed on their hatred of him to even help themselves in a time of crisis?

The smoke stopped and the door to the wooden chamber creaked open. Sani lowered the rope connecting his bound hands, his gaze intense as ever. "You're ready."

By midday, Zo's head expanded and contracted over and over with throbbing pain. She leaned heavily on her walking stick and let Tess lead her with her tiny hand.

"I just don't understand why you aren't getting any better." Tess adopted a mature tone whenever she tried to sound like a healer. "Your reaction to healing Joshua doesn't seem normal." She looked back and raised one brow, ashamed to have to ask, "Does it?"

Tess's round eyes fell in and out of Zo's focus. "No, bug. It doesn't." The vertigo, the nausea, the headaches…her body should be recovering after healing Joshua. Worst of all, she still couldn't tap into her healing energy.

"I can carry you," said Joshua. He fell in step with Zo and Tess, letting Eva lead as they followed the obvious tracks of the Nameless. "Gryphon used to make me carry huge rocks up the mountain to build my strength." He held up his hands to show just how big the rocks had been.

"Thanks, Joshua, but I'm all right."

"You don't think I can do it, do you?"

Before Zo had a chance to respond, Joshua swept her legs out from under her and hoisted her onto his back like a child. "Told you."

Zo laughed. "You've made your point. Now put me down!"

Joshua pretended to ignore her and set off after Eva with Tess trailing at his heels. After struggling to free herself, she finally gave up and closed her eyes. He was maybe an inch taller than her, and still carried the build of a stretched-out child. He wouldn't last long with her on his back.

After several minutes passed, and seeing the neutral look on Joshua's face, Zo said, "You've got to be tired, Ginger. Put me down."

"You're light as a bird, Zo. This doesn't even compare to training."

Joshua's strength was a grim reminder of the power of the Ram. If even one Ram scout happened upon them, there would be little they could do to stop him. It was hard to imagine that at that moment two hundred of these bred killers were marching on the Raven, hunting Talon's family and the families of countless others.

Please save them, Gabe.

At dusk, they filled their water skins and rested by a stream, letting their tired feet soak in the rushing water. Joshua reached above his head and stretched, then pulled his sling from his pack.

"I think I'll try to find us some dinner." He moved to stand, but Zo pulled him back down by the arm.

"Rest, Joshua. There is still plenty of time for hunting."

Joshua only shook his head and rose to his feet again. "Until Gryphon gets back, it is my job to take care of everyone."

Zo's vision tilted as she watched Joshua disappear into the forest. Eva's grumblings about Zo lying to Joshua were lost in the wind. She lay with her back to Zo, her hand resting protectively on her stomach even though it was still too early in her pregnancy to see any sign of the baby growing within.

"Do you think Stone is waiting for us with the Nameless?" she asked. "Do you think he was able to escape after we left?"

"I hope so," said Zo.

If anyone could escape the high walls of the Ram's Gate, it was Stone. Not only was he the leader of the Nameless rebellion, he was madly in love with Eva. Zo couldn't imagine him failing to find her again. Not when the couple had risked so much to be together.

Crossing clan lines to find a mate was looked down upon by every clan, even the Wolves. It was one of the reasons it was so easy to differentiate between them.

Zo pressed her fingers into one of the Nameless tracks. "We can't be more than half a day behind them now, if that."

"You're dodging my question, Wolf. I asked for your opinion, and I don't want you to lie to me like you have the boy."

Both Eva and Zo turned as Joshua stepped into the clearing. His whole body seemed to sag under the weight of what he'd just heard.

"You're lying to me?" His face was so open, so trusting, Zo had to look away.

"It's nothing, kid," she said.

Eva threw the knife she'd been holding into the trunk of a tree. The blade sank deep into the target. "The Wolf keeps secrets from you, Joshua."

Joshua staggered back a step. "No she doesn't. She wouldn't."

Zo climbed to her feet and black dots invaded her

vision. "I'm only trying to protect you, Joshua. You've been through so much—"

"No!" This time he shouted and Zo flinched. He stood like one of the rabbits he hunted, ready to flee.

"Tell him." Eva folded her arms. "Both of you need to hear the words spoken out loud."

Zo dropped to her knees and held her head. "I...I can't."

"Do it, Zo," said Eva. "You must."

Tess dropped down next to Zo, her little hands draped around Zo's shoulders. A weak stream of energy flowed through the little girl. Comfort. Courage. Peace.

"Joshua, don't be mad!" Tess chastised. "You're making it worse."

Zo pulled Tess into a hug. "He has a right to be mad, bug." She didn't realize tears had formed in her eyes— the first she'd shed for Gryphon. She wiped them away and took a deep breath.

"Gryphon was taken by his mess unit while trying to lead them away from our hiding place in the tree. He's... he's dead, Joshua. I'm so sorry."

Joshua's face, his entire body, constricted. He was so rigid he could barely shake his head. "I don't believe you." His face turned red to match his hair. "Gryphon wouldn't leave me. He fought them. He got away."

Zo clutched her stomach and groaned. "Gabe saw everything. He said Gryphon tried to escape, but Zander and the rest of the mess had spears."

"No!" Joshua screamed. "Did you see his body?"

"No, but—"

"Then you don't know what you're talking about. He's alive. How do you know he's not wounded somewhere in the woods, waiting for me to come and help him?" He pointed a damning finger at Zo. "You gave up on him." His control broke and he burst into a sob. "You left him!"

Zo put a hand to her face, as if slapped. Her careful wall of unfeeling crumbled. Tears streaked her cheeks. "We made a promise to each other. I swore to him that I would go after the Nameless if he would warn the Raven. We were going to meet at the Allied Camp." She took a few deep breaths to collect her emotion. "I can't let these people"—she gestured to the Nameless tracks—"die when I could lead them to safety. I left because I'm their only hope and because it was what I promised Gryphon I'd do." She panted from the exertion of yelling, surprised that her head had stopped spinning.

A twig snapped not far away. Zo scanned the trees in that direction. Though her imagination ran wild with possible evils lurking in the trees, she didn't see anything.

Eva tugged Tess and Joshua forward, giving Zo a pointed look. "Too loud." She pushed them ahead of her on the trail and, thoroughly chastened, Zo followed.

The back of Joshua's neck was bright red as they walked. His shoulders shook and he occasionally rubbed tears from his eyes, but he didn't make a sound and never turned around. Poor Joshua. So alone in the world.

Crying made Zo tired. Her head pounded harder with every step traveled. She reached back to take her water skin from her pack and saw a flutter of movement in the trees behind her. Forgetting her water skin, Zo looked straight ahead and whispered to Eva. "We're being followed. Get ready to run."

Eva didn't offer any indication that she'd heard other than her hands moving to the knives on her belt.

Before she had time to think up a plan, running footsteps charged them from behind. A man wearing a boiled leather vest caught two of Eva's knives in his shield before tackling Zo to the ground. He rolled with her secured in his arms until she lay on top of him as a human shield.

He slowly climbed to his feet, bracing Zo's head in his hands as though he might snap her neck if she tried to run. "You're supposed to be dead," said the Ram, his cheek pressed into Zo's ear.

Adrenaline pumped through Zo. Her fingers curled into claws as she tried to break free of his grasp.

The Ram pulled her back a few steps to keep eyes on both Eva, who held a new knife in each hand, and Joshua, his bow already nocked and drawn. Tess was missing.

"I have no business with you two," said the Ram. He smelled of body odor and beef stew. "When our scouts didn't find the girl's rotting carcass, Chief Barnabas ordered a search. He wants her back alive." He snickered then licked his lips. "For questioning."

"Release her or die," said Eva, calm as ever.

The scout took a few more steps back. "Aren't you Taurus's betrothed?" The Ram paused. "What are you doing out here with this Wolf?"

Eva cocked her throwing hand behind her ear. "I said, release her."

"Don't pretend you could kill me, girl. I'm only one of several men combing this mountain for the girl. I'm doing you a favor by letting you live."

Zo jammed her heel into the man's boot, but he didn't show any sign that he felt her assault. His deep laughter shot hot, sour air into her face. "If you're interested in a little fight, Wolf, I'd happily accommodate."

The Ram backed further away from Joshua and Eva, still holding Zo as a shield.

A *thump* sounded against the man's skull. With Zo still in his grasp, he whipped around to find Tess only a few feet away, clutching a rock. She twisted up her face and reached back to hurl another rock at him.

"You little—"

Another *thump* sounded, this time bringing the Ram to his knees with Zo in tow. He reached back and pulled one of Eva's knives out of his shoulder with a roar.

His grip on Zo slackened. She threw her elbow into his nose, but he quickly regained his hold of her. "I am a Ram," he grunted in her ear. "I don't feel pain." Two more thumps sounded. This time, the strong arms binding her fell away. Zo scrambled out of reach before the Ram dropped face-first to the ground with a knife and arrow sticking out of his back.

"Nice work, little mouse." Despite obvious effort, Joshu couldn't produce a smile for Tess. "Lesson number one: never show the enemy your back." He dropped to the ground and clenched two fistfuls of his red hair. "Gryphon taught me that."

CHAPTER EIGHT

There were no chairs inside the circle of the Gaagii Court. No podium or stand for the Raven Chief, just the wooden wall surrounding them and bare ground. Elderly men stood in a loose circle, the chief among them. They wore black paint on their faces in the shape of a bird whose wings were outstretched to act as a mask across their eyes. Like the chief, they wore necklaces of feathers, marking their prestige within the clan.

But it was the stone they each carried that captured most of Gryphon's attention. Sani joined the circle and clasped his thin arms behind his back, calm as a spring morning.

"We have heard the words of the Wolf and believe that the Ram are marching toward us. Scouts have returned confirming the number of men you warned would come," said the chief, in his oddly accented way.

Gryphon blinked then looked up at the sun. Was it

really almost dusk? How many hours had he been tied to that platform? It had only felt like minutes. What else had Sani been burning and how had he not accounted for the passage of so much lost time?

"We have questions for you, Ram. Questions only one of your kind can answer."

Gryphon nodded for the chief to continue.

"Your people have hunted us for the location of our grain stores. If we told your chief where to find them, would they continue their attack?"

Gryphon closed his eyes, filling his lungs with the smoke that still clung to his clothing. "My people have hunted for the location of your clan for years. Yes, Barnabas is in desperate need for a replenishment to Ram food stores, but he also wants to rid you from the land. He will keep some of your people as Nameless, but those he sees as a threat, and those who wouldn't be able to work would be considered a burden. Another mouth to feed." Gryphon swallowed. He couldn't bring himself to go into more detail. "Your only option is to flee this place. Abandon your homes and take to the ocean where the Ram don't have resources to follow."

Several men in the circle turned a few shades whiter. Others flared their nostrils, flexing their hands around the stone they carried. All looked to their chief for response.

"We are tied to our land, Sheep. It is the source of all our power. We have been here since long before the Ram, the Wolf, and the cave-dwelling Kodiak entered the region. Fleeing for us means surrendering everything that defines our people. Many of us would sooner die fighting with honor than prolong a struggle that would lead to the same end. What you suggest simply isn't possible."

A Raven Elder with dark gray hair and a face weighed down by the lines of time dropped his stone to the ground, gaining him the surprised attention of the group. His eyes were clouded with a milky white film. He spoke in a strange language and pointed vehemently at Gryphon. He then turned his sharp gesture on the rest of the men in the circle as he spoke.

Gryphon and Gabe exchanged confused looks then went back to watching the weathered man finish his heated rant. When he finally stopped speaking, the chief, who'd been shifting his feet in the dirt the entire time, bowed his head to the old man and dropped his stone to the dirt as well. Everyone else in the circle followed his example.

The chief turned to Gryphon and frowned. "There is to be a *Hai*, or test. If you pass, our shaman says it is a sign that our people should follow your council and leave tomorrow morning."

Gryphon didn't like the sound of that. "And if I don't pass this test?"

The chief ran his hand along one of the feathers adorning his neck. "Then you will be the first Ram sacrificed in defense of our homeland."

"Why did those Elders carry the rocks?" Gryphon asked

Gabe as they rested in a little tent, awaiting Gryphon's mysterious test.

Gabe lifted and dropped his shoulders without saying a word. "You don't want to know."

"Try me."

Gabe rolled onto his side to look at Gryphon. "Just an old tradition. Raven Elders always carry stones into a trial in case the person on trial is found guilty. Stoning allows for more people to exact justice."

"You're joking." Gryphon whipped his head back in the direction of the Gaagii Court, as if he could actually see it through the fabric of the tent.

"Don't act so surprised. Your people are twice as brutal." He lifted his hands to show his missing pinkie fingers. "Or have you forgotten?"

The Wolf had a point, but he still couldn't believe he willingly walked right into a possible stoning. "About this test…what exactly happens in a *Hai*?"

Gabe's voice grew quiet. "I've never witnessed one before, but …" he turned away from Gryphon to straighten his pack. "Whatever it is, it will not be easy. You heard the chief. Many of these people would rather die than leave. They're betting—hoping, really—that you won't be able to beat the obstacle they set before you."

Gryphon wasn't immortal, but if this was to be a physical test, he couldn't help but be encouraged. His whole life up until this point had been training. He was strong, fast, and agile. Whatever his other failings, his body was sound. If it was possible to survive the *Hai*, he would find a way. Not just to save these people from the Ram, but for Joshua and, in a small way, for Zo as well.

Sani pulled back the tent flap. Ash was smeared along his cheeks and forehead making him appear ghostly; his expression level as ever. "It is almost time, Ram." He looked down at the small vacant space just inside the tent. "May I sit with you?"

Gryphon gestured for the boy to sit, and Sani let the buckskin flap of the tent door fall closed behind him. "Hold out your arm." Sani untied a beaded leather bracelet from his wrist. Polished stone beads of vibrant shades of green and blue rattled together as Sani fastened the bracelet to Gryphon's wrist.

"Why?" asked Gryphon as he fingered the cold stones.

"Protection. As your *'Attin*, it is the most help I can offer you in the *Hai*."

They sat in silence together. Gryphon assumed Gabe and Sani didn't know what to say to a man they assumed was about to walk to his death. Still running his fingers over the bracelet, Gryphon asked Sani, "What language was that Elder speaking during my judgment? I've heard tales of clans outside of our region speaking in strange tongues, but always thought the local clans spoke only the language of the Ram."

Both Sani and Gabe snickered at that. "What?" Gryphon asked. "Why is that funny?"

Gabe clapped Gryphon on the shoulder. "Do you honestly believe we all speak the language of the Ram?"

Gryphon did. It's what he'd been taught since childhood.

Sani said, "My people were the first to inhabit this region. We were born out of the trees and soil, the water and wind. We cared for the earth and the earth cared for us. We called ourselves the Raven because legend says the First Chief spoke to the wise Raven and the Raven called him brother."

Gryphon glanced over to Gabe, wondering if he actually believed the crazy story. He'd never heard of any such history and always been told the Raven, like the other clans, had moved into the Ram region, pilfering its resources and robbing the Ram of the clan's livelihood—even taking and mutilating the Ram language.

"What you heard in the judgment was the language of our first fathers," said Sani. "The language of land and sky…of the Raven. It is the language of our holy text and the root of the language we speak today."

"Are you claiming the Raven were the first to dwell in this region?"

Gabe winkled his brow. "How can you not know that? Do the Ram not have stories of the migration? Where do you think the clans got their animal names?"

Gryphon had never considered the fact that all the clans carried the name of an animal. He'd always assumed the Ram had taken on the name as a symbol of power. He'd felt pride in the name.

"As wandering clans pushed into the region, my people welcomed them so long as they were peaceful," said Sani. "The clan that settled in the south was the most social, and began the tradition of trading and working together to protect the region. Because of them, the three clans came together once a year."

"The meeting was called an Ostara. All of the houses

of the Wolves still hold the meetings and Kodiak and Raven still attend when they can," said Gabe.

Sani nodded. "My people named the clan after the beasts who hunted and lived in packs. Wolves. Another clan settled in the Eastern part of the region. They were large in stature and preferred stone to tree and kept to themselves like the mighty Kodiak who kept to the Kodiak Hills."

"And the Ram? You mentioned three clans, but there are four. Do you believe my people were the last to arrive to the region?" asked Gryphon.

Sani shook his head.

"Actually," said Gabe. "Your people came at the same time as mine. The stories say we used to be one clan. Two brothers whose families had families, and so on."

"Impossible."

"It's true," said Sani.

"We were large and spread out like the Wolf packs of today. Your forefather and mine, brothers, had a disagreement that blossomed into a feud that eventually divided our one clan into two."

Sani said, "You pushed your way north, deeper into Raven territory, but by then your numbers were large and my people did not have the means to stop you without war. You were named after the mighty Ram for that reason. We were a peaceful people, and eventually conceded to give you the land where Ram's Gate sits today. For many years the region lived in peace. But hatred festered among your people. The Ram were hungry for war, desperate for revenge. They built and trained a might army and secreted slaves from the other clans. The massive wall of Ram's Gate wasn't built until after the first raids."

Gabe shook his head. "By then the Ram were too strong to be stopped," finished Gabe.

Gryphon thought back to his time in Chief Barnabas's house. The scrolls which carried the histories of old. The Historian who had scoffed at his inability to read. She'd called him ignorant, even though most of the Ram couldn't read—it was considered a fluffy gift with no benefit. A waste of time that could be spent training.

Had Barnabas and the chiefs before him intentionally kept the people ignorant? The thought made him dizzy…and angry.

The tent flap opened and a stout Raven with gray ash smeared along his face, similar to Sani's, said, "It is time."

But before Sani and the elders could lead Gryphon away, Gabe grasped his shoulder. "You're a good man. Zo would be proud."

Gryphon's throat tightened.

"There's something I should say." Gabe shook his head, as if struggling with some unseen demon. "I never told you…Thank you for sparing my life in the Gate. Thank you for helping Zo and Tess." Sorrow and something else crossed his face. Guilt?

"This was my decision, Wolf. I promised Zo I'd come. I have no regrets."

The lines around Gabe's mouth deepened. "I didn't deserve your mercy," he whispered.

Sani pulled back the tent flap before Gryphon could

respond. "We must hurry. The ritual must begin right when the last light of day departs from the sky."

Gryphon ducked out of the tent, wishing he'd had a chance to ask Gabe what he meant. With head high and fists clenched, he prepared himself as he might if he were about to engage an enemy. Through his training with the Ram, he'd learned how to retreat within himself to the point where he almost couldn't feel pain. Whatever the Raven had for him, he'd survive. It was the Ram way.

The procession of elders and Gryphon, with Sani bringing up the rear, walked along a dirt path lined with Raven burning torches to ward off the encroaching night. Old, young, male, female—all gathered to watch Gryphon take the walk that would determine their fate.

They stopped at the base of a large tree. The elders stepped aside to reveal a ladder that spiraled from the ground up into the canopy. This ladder was different from the one Gryphon encountered on the journey here. There was a handrail, and instead of knobs for steps, broad wooden planks made for a comfortable ascent. In the low light, Gryphon craned his head to see a small, enclosed house near the top of the tree.

"I'm to take you up," said Sani, accepting a torch from a neighboring guard. Sani bowed to his chieftain father, taking to the stairs in front of Gryphon.

"How old are you, Sani?" Gryphon asked as they climbed. The boy looked ten but acted twenty.

"I am thirteen," said Sani.

The same age as Joshua, but the boys couldn't be more different. Joshua was tall and awkward, still growing into his newly acquired height. Sani was short and lean. Joshua was loud and often clumsy, while Sani was quiet and precise in his actions—graceful, even.

Tree sap from the railing stuck to Gryphon's hand. The smell was powerful and somehow relaxing. They climbed for several minutes until the stairs stopped at the base of the tree hut. Sani tugged on a rope, bringing down another staircase that led into the aerial room.

Gryphon pulled himself into the circular space, and searched the area for a potential threat. What he found were five totems carved into the shapes of various birds, all staring into the center of the room. All terrifying. A chill rolled up his arms and legs, coalescing up his spine in one giant wave.

Sani used the torch to light five candles, one at the base of each totem. When he finished, he handed Gryphon a knife and, with some difficultly, draped a leather necklace over his head adorned with one white feather.

"What is this?" Gryphon ran his fingers over the feather.

"The white raven is a very rare and sacred animal among my people. Its feathers bring protection and good fortune." Sani lowered himself down the ladder in the floor of the small room, and stopped before closing the latch. "For the sake of my people, I hope to see you in the morning."

"What am I supposed to do?" Gryphon called after him. "There's nothing here!"

The door in the floor closed and locked.

Gryphon glanced around the room. The flickering

light cast wicked shadows across the birds, whose mouths opened as if shrieking in anger.

So this was it? Gryphon was to sit in this treetop room without windows or doors until morning? He couldn't help the relieved laughter that escaped him. He'd been prepared to fight a lion or worse. This was nothing.

Footsteps sounded on the roof of the enclosed room. Other movement surrounded the hut. Gryphon backed away from the walls to stand in the center of the room with knife raised. Something bitter tickled his nose. Smoke rolled from the mouths of the five birds in a continuous, loud exhalation. Gryphon dropped to the floor to avoid the smoke, but within minutes, the entire room was cast in a clouded haze.

Gryphon held his breath as the smoke reached him. His lungs burned in pain and he had no choice but to inhale the smoky air.

Only moments later, his screams shook the entire tree.

***

Joshua carried Tess on his shoulders so the group could travel at a faster pace. A hard wind picked up leaves and dirt as it blew north, against them. Having a Ram scout come so close to taking her brought the danger of their situation back to the forefront of Zo's thoughts. She guessed the others shared her fears.

Ram scouts usually traveled in pairs, as insurance in case one was killed. That meant the Ram who'd tried to take Zo had a companion. And he was close. Joshua and Eva had dragged the dead Ram's body into a thick patch of grass and covered it with branches. There wasn't time for a burial, not that a Ram would extend the same courtesy to another clan.

They'd been lucky the Ram hadn't expected them to fight back. But if the second scout found the body of his friend, he'd want blood.

Joshua refused to meet Zo's eye. He wouldn't even accept the water skin she handed to him when they stopped to hydrate.

"We've got to be close," said Eva after taking a greedy draw of water. Beads of sweat dotted both her and Joshua's foreheads, and Tess looked ready to fall asleep standing. The terrain grew rockier the higher they climbed. Skidding on loose gravel and climbing over boulders added to their exhaustion.

"Can't we rest?" said Tess. She slipped her hand into Joshua's and leaned against his side.

"Why are you complaining?" Joshua flicked her nose. "I'm the one doing the heavy lifting." He tried to smile at Tess, but his lips barely curved at the sides. His hero, his mentor was dead, and Zo had lied to him. Joshua wore his pain like one might a ragged shirt. It hung on every dent and crease in his freckled face for the entire world to see, no matter how ashamed he might be to appear affected.

"I know, but I don't *want* to ride on your shoulders anymore,"

Tess whined, placing another hand on his arm.

Zo knew her sister well enough to sense the healing

blessing she was covertly giving Joshua. Her "I'm tired" plea, was just an excuse to touch him with her healing hands. With hair blowing into her face, Tess flashed Zo a sad grin.

Tess had trained as a healer with Zo for only a year before they entered the Gate. Zo looked forward to continuing her sister's education. A healer had to love the person they healed, and watching little Tess will her compassion into Joshua during his time of denial and anger made Zo more proud than she had any right to be.

Tess was special. She'd make a much better healer than Zo.

Without waiting for her approval, Joshua snatched Tess and threw her back onto his shoulders. She let out a strangled cry and Joshua battled a smile that under normal circumstances would have come easily. The girl may have been a liability in every tactical way, but at that moment, Zo considered her the most valuable asset of their little company. If nothing else, while she sat on Joshua's shoulders, Zo knew he wouldn't do anything drastic, like sneak off to look for Gryphon on his own.

Zo tightened her grip on her pack and medical satchel and followed after them. The trail took on a steeper grade approaching the summit of the small mountain. Patches of snow dotted the ground, even though spring had settled in the valley. The cold wind burned Zo's cheeks as they fought against it and the rise of the mountain.

Eva matched Zo's stride, falling in step with her behind Joshua. "He's going to be all right." She looked straight ahead as she spoke. "So are you."

Zo shook her head thinking about Joshua's future. The image of her, Tess, and Joshua living with Gabe—making a life together—didn't settle properly in her mind. Would they set up a farm near the Valley of Wolves? Maybe keep sheep and a few goats? She imagined Gabe's lips on hers, adoration filling his touches with warmth as little children laughed at their sides. Gabe would be a good father. It should have been a happy thought. But every touch would seem like a betrayal to Gryphon in Joshua's eyes. And in a way, hers too.

Zo wiped her tears and forced Gryphon from her mind.

As they crested the summit of the mountain, a glorious sight made them all halt on the trail. Joshua helped Tess down from his shoulders, his chest pumping from the effort of carrying both of them up the steep climb. "I don't believe it," he gasped between breaths, looking to Zo for the first time since she'd told him the truth about Gryphon.

A large group of people—at least a few hundred men, women, and children—had set up a makeshift camp. Families huddled in circles against the wind, while others combed the area for firewood and items to help provide a temporary shelter. A group of small children no older than Tess chased each other in circles before collapsing in a fit of giggles from the effort.

Tess must have recognized several of the children, because she ran out to greet them with giant hugs.

"I can't believe we actually did it," Zo said, mainly to herself. She turned to share her joy with Eva and found the girl frozen in place with her hands pressed firmly against her stomach, the wind pulling her short hair a hundred different directions. "I don't see him." Her voice was small, not matching her usual roar.

The odds of Stone escaping Ram's Gate were poor at best. He was the leader of the rebellion. He would have stayed to fight, providing time for as many Nameless to flee as possible.

Zo rested a hand on Eva's shoulder, but the Ram girl shrugged it off. "Don't pity me," she hissed. "I don't need it."

Color had left Eva's face and she swayed on her feet. This girl gave up her whole life for Stone, carried his child, and left her family for this crazy man. Zo understood Eva's loss and had to chew on the inside of her cheek to keep her composure.

Zo took hold of her wrist, and this time Eva didn't resist. Zo whispered a blessing of hope and peace then dropped her hand to give Eva the room she needed to grieve.

The blessing did nothing. Zo was still too empty to offer a proper healing. But at least she'd tried.

Then someone shouted on the opposite side of the camp. "Guess what we found!"

Zo and Eva startled at the burly voice. The owner was tall, with a dark, shaved head. He wore a leather vest, leaving his muscled arms exposed to the cold. He held an unconscious man over his shoulder. Judging by the limp man's fur-lined boots and boiled leather armor, Zo had to assume it was the second Ram scout.

"Stone," Eva staggered in his direction, but fell after only two steps. She pushed herself back up to her feet—

this time with more control over her limbs—and sprinted toward Stone.

The Nameless leader didn't see her among the crowd of people who came to greet him. He dropped the Ram onto the ground with an unceremonious bump. Then he rolled out his shoulders while laughing at something another man said. Eva was halfway to him when—as if there were some invisible line that existed between them —he turned and spotted her across the clearing.

"Move!" Stone ordered. He nearly trampled a man, dividing the crowd with his big arms. He sprinted toward Eva, as though running from his own death.

Zo held her breath, gripping Joshua's sleeve for support as the lovers reached for each other. When Stone pulled Eva into his arms, he sank to his knees and held her close. Stone openly wept while kissing every inch of her face, cupping her cheeks with his calloused hands. In between kisses, he whispered words only Eva could hear. His hand moved to her stomach in such a tender way that Zo had to close her eyes to block the pain that accompanied the joy of seeing at least someone's world put to rights.

She ached with jealousy, and the imagined life of raising sheep and growing vegetables with Gabe wasn't enough. Because no matter how hard she tried, she couldn't will herself to see Gabe the way Stone saw Eva.

She covered her mouth to quell the sob that erupted from somewhere deep within and ran from the clearing so as not to mar Eva and Stone's reunion. She dropped to the ground, surrounded by the cover of two large trees, ashamed she hadn't the courage to face Eva and

Stone. She really was happy for them; her pain just seemed so much easier to endure when she'd had Eva to share it.

The idea that other people would move on after Gryphon's passing—that they would find love, make children, become a family—was too difficult to imagine when it wasn't possible for her.

I'm so selfish.

"Zo?" Joshua peeked around a tree. His fists were tight and swayed at his sides in an uncomfortable manner. His gaze shifted between Zo and the ground, as if seeing her cry was like Zo seeing Eva and Stone in the clearing. "I'm sorry for what I said." He cleared his throat to keep his voice from jumping between bass and tenor. "I know you were trying to do the right thing by coming here." And then all fidgeting left him, and he dropped to his knees next to her. "I know you miss him, too."

Zo wiped at her running nose and watery eyes. "I'm a mess, Ginger." She ruffled his hair and yanked him into a hug that made them both fall.

When they sat up Joshua pulled a soggy leaf out of Zo's hair and she returned the favor. "Do you love him?" He tilted his head to one side like he used to do when Gryphon gave him instruction. It was his listening face.

Zo smiled and plucked another leaf from Joshua's hair. "I don't know. I didn't have a chance to find out."

And I never will, she thought.

"We should go back." She climbed to her feet and pulled Joshua up with her. "I have a feeling Stone will want to know what I can tell him about the Allies."

CHAPTER NINE

The birds around the room flapped their wings. Their little eyes condemned him to an awful death: their shrieking cries rattled his head until he had no other choice but to cover his ears and curl into a ball on the floor. Smoke filled his lungs and burned his vision as the room spun in rapid circles.

He lost his grip on time and space. He was suddenly falling. Up was down, left was right, and somehow he knew there was no way he would survive this terror. The birds shrieked even louder than before. He tried to run but kept colliding with walls. He used his fingernails to scratch at wood and his own face, desperate to peel away the crawl of panic on his skin, feeling certain if he didn't break free his heart would explode. The smoke pushed him back down to what he hoped was the ground, but even with eyes closed, his head spun. "Someone kill me!" he heard himself scream. He spun faster and faster, his mind fraying into thousands of pieces. Insanity: its own brand of pain.

Then everything went black. Images flickered in his mind. His mother's face. His father's shield. The forest by his home. Flashes of his life burned bright against the back of his eyelids then dimmed again to utter darkness.

The flashing stopped and he was eight years old, hiding behind a tree in the woods while his mother cried again. Weeping because of Father. She always cried in the mornings when she thought Gryphon had left for training. It felt wrong not to watch her. Such sadness demanded a witness, even if it meant receiving lashes for being late.

Gryphon hated his father. Hated him. Mostly because he made his mother cry, but also because of the way his instructors treated him. He was always selected last in every drill. Always forced to do extra work.

"For your father's mistake," his trainers would say while Gryphon struggled to lift or push or pull whatever they were training with that day.

And Gryphon would do whatever they asked, knowing that someday he would be the strongest, fastest, and most skilled warrior the Ram had ever produced.

For your father's mistake.

Gryphon ran to morning practice, determined not to be late today. It was the last day the boys and girls he'd been training with over the past three years would be together. They were splitting them up: boys would go one way and girls another.

Upon entering the cleared field that served as their training ground, eight-year-old Gryphon bent over, hands on knees, collecting his breath while the rest of the kids arrived. He was getting faster. The thought made him smile.

For your father's mistake.

Gryphon's instructor was a young woman. Her hair was a warm brown and whenever she smiled, a strange heat always filled Gryphon's cheeks.

"Gather 'round," his instructor said. She was not alone today. A man and a woman, each wearing boiled leather armor and stern expressions, stood behind her. Their legs were spread wide, their hands clasped behind their backs, eyeing the children as they might a potential meal.

Gryphon stood as tall as he could, keeping his chin high and holding eye contact to show he wasn't afraid of them, even though he was.

"Today," his young instructor smiled, "marks a day of advancement. You should all be very proud of yourselves."

Gryphon refused to smile, though he felt the urge.

"The girls may follow their new instructor." Several girls waved as they ran to keep up with the female instructor. Once they were out of sight, his instructor continued. "Before I send you to work with your new instructor, every one of you will receive a special gift from me. Something that will make you stronger."

Gryphon couldn't help the grin that stretched across his face. Whatever the instructor's gift, he wanted it desperately.

"Who would like to go first?" she asked.

Gryphon's hand shot into the air, even though he

knew he would be chosen last. He looked around to realize his was the only hand in the air. Did the other boys know something he didn't? He turned back to the woman who'd trained him for the last three years and found her smiling.

"Follow me, Gryphon, son of Troy."

Gryphon flinched under the weight of his father's name. To have it attached to his was cruel. The other boys snickered to each other as Gryphon walked away with both instructors at his side. They opened up the door to a large shed that housed blunted training weapons. The man shut the door behind them and crossed his large arms in front of his chest.

Gryphon didn't want his "special gift" anymore. He just wanted to leave this room.

"Today is your eighth-year beating. You will receive one every year to help you learn how to conquer pain." The woman smiled, and lifted a blunted sword off the rack. "You will not resist or fight back. Do you understand?"

Tears gathered in Gryphon's eyes. He didn't want to feel pain. He didn't want to have to stand there and let the pretty young woman hit him. But he was a Ram, and as with everything else, he needed to prove to them that he was better than his father. "I...I understand," he said, forcing his voice to come out steady.

The man at the door—his future instructor—cocked his head to the side, appraising him. Gryphon balled his little fists and clenched his jaw as the first blow came. The sword flew through the air, and the flat of it connected with the side of his face. The force of the blow knocked him off his feet. He wanted to cry as he climbed back to his feet to receive another gift, but he didn't. Instead he looked his warm-haired instructor in the face and commanded his features to remain neutral.

"Good for you, Gryphon," the woman said, swinging the blunted sword back to strike him again. But there was something evil in her expression that contradicted her praise. The words she intoned rang like a bell in Gryphon's mind. *"For your father's mistakes."*

The scene shifted to another beating. Then another. Each more violent than the next to mark his growth in skill and size. Gryphon didn't want to be in the shed any longer. Didn't want to see his mother's tears. Didn't want to have to think about his father and the shame that he'd inherited from the man.

A new face walked into the shed, this man bald with large round eyes that didn't quite sit inside his skull. He recognized the man, but had only seen him at a distance.

"After seeing your progress, the Seer asked me to administer your twelfth-year beating. Your training has been impressive, young soldier."

Gryphon nodded his gratitude to Gate Master Leon. He didn't care who hit him, even if it was the Seer's favorite advisor. He just wanted it to be over.

The Gate Master smiled in an unnerving sort of way. He turned back to lock the door to the shed, which was odd because none of the other instructors had bothered.

"I'd like to see what you're really made of, if you don't mind."

"Excuse me, sir?" Gryphon's spine stiffened.

The Gate Master dropped into a fighting stance with

legs wide, both hands up and ready to strike or block. "No weapons. I just want you to fight me, boy. Show me why they think you're so *special*." He spat the last word.

When Gryphon just stood there, the Gate Master reached out and slapped him across the face. "Fight me!" he growled. He went to strike him again, but Gryphon's hand flew up to block the attack.

The Gate Master's lips pulled into a tangled smile that revealed rotting teeth. "Oh, this is going to be fun." He grabbed Gryphon by the hair and threw him into the side of the shed before jumping on top of him. The first few punches to his ribs invigorated Gryphon. He broke free of the Gate Master's hold and landed one solid fist to his jaw.

Liquid fury seemed to fill the man as he attacked. Lacking both size and skill, Gryphon managed only two more hits before the Gate Master dropped him to the floor again. Only this time he didn't get up. Gryphon willed himself to pass out as the Gate Master administered his blows, but the man was merciless and only brought Gryphon to the edge of unconsciousness before moving from his head to punch his sides, arms, legs, and back. Through bleary vision, the Gate Master seemed to grow black feathers. With each hit he crowed at such a pitch, Gryphon abandoned blocking everything but his ears. By the time he was through, Gryphon couldn't even rise from the floor of the damp shed.

He pinched his eyes shut. This couldn't be happening. This wasn't real. He wasn't twelve years old. This was a dream. Just a painful, painful dream.

When he gained control of his breathing and with

eyes still closed, he told himself, "I'm going to wake up now. I'm going to wake up."

The crowing stopped, the void of sound a heavy silence.

Gryphon dropped his hands, pulled one more breath through his nose, and opened his eyes.

But what he saw terrified him.

Gabe watched him from only a few yards away.

"What did you do to her?" the Wolf asked. His voice ricocheted off the black nothing that surrounded them.

Gryphon didn't realize he was carrying someone until he looked down. Cradled in his arms was Zo, hanging lifeless with limbs spilling over his arms. Blood rolled from an unseen cut down her forearm and dripped off her fingertip. Each drop hit the black ground and broke the quiet with a thundering boom.

"I don't understand." Gryphon's voice echoed in the black drum of in-between space. "What happened?"

"You did this," said Gabe, pointing at Zo.

Another drop of blood collided with the floor. On impact, a *boom* shook the ground beneath his feet.

"No." Gryphon sunk to one knee, trying to force Zo's head up so he could look into her eyes and see life. But his efforts were like sand slipping through his fingers.

"You left her. She didn't have a chance without your protection, and you left her."

Gryphon shook his head over and over again. "She made me promise to help the Raven. I wouldn't...I couldn't..."

Suddenly Zo vanished, and Gryphon found himself

hugging empty space. He swiped at the air around him, but it was too late. She was gone.

A foreign sob rumbled from his throat. He'd never made that sound before, didn't know it was possible. He couldn't lose Zo. Not again. She meant too much. Without her, the darkness slid closer to him. Somehow Gryphon knew that if the darkness came too close, he would be lost to it as well.

Gabe stood right next to him, his hair turned black and feathery, eyes dilated to tiny black orbs. He held out his hand and offered Gryphon a familiar knife. "This is the only way to make the pain stop, Ram."

Gryphon accepted the blade, testing the weight of it in his hands.

"End it now, before you hurt someone else." Gabe rested his hand over Gryphon's, turning the point of the knife toward Gryphon's chest. Sorrow weighed down the lines of the Wolf 's face as he nodded encouragement. "That's right. Do this for Zo. It's what she would have wanted."

Gryphon didn't want to die, but when had he ever refused Zo anything? Wounded Raven and Kodiak warriors appeared at his feet. First five, then ten, then twenty. They all clutched spear wounds, moaning like the waking dead from pain. Their anguished, bloodshot eyes looked up to him with the simple question, "Why?"

Gryphon redoubled his grip on the knife. Pressure built around his temples, pain so real he nearly collapsed.

"Just end it." Gabe's voice turned darker as he helped the knife break skin. His eyes lost their almond shape, growing more round and protuberant. Like the Gate Master. Then it changed again to

Zander. Then to Barnabas.

Zo wouldn't want me to do this. Gryphon shook his head as if trying to wake from a dream. The tip of the knife dug deeper into his chest.

Then Tess appeared, walking around the fallen Raven and Kodiak like a tiny blond dancer. Her little hands rested on Gryphon's cheeks. "I don't want you to die."

Hadn't she said those words to him already? In another time? Another life?

Tess' bright greenish-blue eyes were slightly different in color but identical to Zo's in shape. The little girl leaned forward and pressed a kiss to Gryphon's forehead. "You. Are. Good," she whispered.

Then everything fell away. The dying men, Gabe, the Gate Master, Barnabas, Tess, and even the blackness. A different pain replaced the throbbing in his head.

A pain in his chest.

He looked down and saw the knife an inch deep in his own flesh. His biceps cramped with the effort of killing himself.

With great difficulty, Gryphon forced his muscles to relax. The knife Sani gave him clattered to the wooden floor of the tree hut. He dropped to his knees, blood-stained hands grasping his chest where the knife penetrated. The wound wasn't deep enough to cause serious damage. Just enough to prove how close he'd come to killing himself. The smoke in the room was gone, and a few slivers of light fought their way into the wooden dungeon.

The trap door in the center of the room fell open, and Sani peeked his head over the floorboards. "We're saved." The normally reserved boy pumped the air with his fist before cupping his hands around his mouth. He crowed using varying pitches down to the people below before turning back to smile at Gryphon. "The Ram are here. It's time to get off this island."

STONE HELD Eva's hand in two of his, and they all sat around a fire to eat a meal of boiled venison and wildroot. Zo had spent the last hour explaining how to find the Allied Camp using a map of twigs, grass, and small rocks.

She leaned in to adjust the two twigs that represented a slot canyon. "The final stretch is narrow and will not be easy for someone your size to cross, but you can do it." She looked up to see Stone bring Eva's hand to his lips.

"We're going to make it, love," he said.

Zo blushed and looked away. The dozens of fires that dotted the clearing drew her attention. Many of these people wore nothing but rags to fight the chilling nights on the mountain. They ate what food the land provided and, according to Stone, had sometimes gone whole days without a morsel to eat. Still, the people smiled and laughed around their fires. Perhaps still in shock from the trauma of escaping their slavery.

Freedom. It was such a peculiar thing. You could give

a person food, water, and shelter, but take away their free will and they could never truly be happy. "If we die on this mountain," Stone had said, "then we die free. And I can live with that." He'd smiled his crazy smile, where his eyes turned to saucers and his grin reached his ears.

Zo remembered the first time she met Stone up in the treetop hideout—a headquarters for the Nameless insurrection. Stone had ordered her capture. They dangled her over the edge of a platform high in the trees (some Raven construction) to get her to disclose her work as a spy for the Allies. She hadn't exactly liked the man, but his passion for freedom could not be questioned.

As Eva and Zo rinsed their dinner bowls in a nearby stream, Stone shouted orders to "Circle up!" This sparked a flurry of movement among the people. They gathered their supplies and arranged the company so that the men slept on the outer rim of the circle, protecting their women, children, and supplies within. Zo noticed that every man also slept with a stick sharpened to a point like a spear. A Ram weapon.

Several men reported to Stone and received orders for night watches. Joshua turned to Zo. "This guy's a good leader. The Nameless follow his orders without question."

"We resent the term 'Nameless,' boy." Joshua startled when Stone appeared behind him. "We have names and we'll never be forced to live without them again."

"Stone," said Eva, taking the Nameless leader's hand. "Joshua didn't mean any harm."

Stone didn't look so sure as he eyed the boy. "I just don't love the idea of a Ram in my camp."

Eva threw her head back and laughed, drawing the attention of many of the company. "And here I thought I'd be sharing your bedroll tonight." She made as if to walk away, but he snatched her around the waist. "Point taken." He turned to Joshua. "You're welcome here, boy. But you'll refer to us as 'Freemen' from now on. Understood?"

"Yes, Sir," Joshua said.

Zo kept Tess close as they lay under the dark sky. The wind died, leaving them to enjoy the charcoal night dotted with stars in peace. Tess smelled like campfire, sweat, and salted venison. Zo committed to scrubbing the girl for a solid hour once they reached the Allies. She could use a bath herself.

Thoughts of warm water heated over a fire, her straw-stuffed mattress, and the protection of Commander Laden's men carried her into a dreamless sleep.

Until a man's cry of pain startled her awake.

CHAPTER TEN

By the time Gryphon and Sani reached the bottom of the tree stairs, the entire Raven Clan was in chaos. People ran in all directions, preparing to leave their homes, while others shouted warnings that the boats would be leaving within the hour. Some Raven looked to Gryphon as if he were a hero, while others— mostly the older set—scowled in his direction.

"What did you do to me up there?" Gryphon stumbled over an exposed root but still managed to keep pace with Sani. "Why did I see those things?"

"I'm to bring you to the edge," said Sani, ignoring his questions.

Gryphon grabbed the boy's shoulder and spun him around. He refused to take another step until he understood what had just happened in that tree. "Tell me," he demanded.

Sani sighed. "In our ancient language, the word Hai

means winter. Only our shaman understand the secrets to the smoke, but I do know it is prepared and blessed by their holy hands and that it forces men to face the cold and darkness inside them."

"It sounds more like torture than a test."

Sani shook his head impatiently. "That's why you're given the dagger. Only a person with enough good, or light, inside them can survive the trial. Anyone whose darkness is greater than their light kills himself. This way the Elders can stand blameless in punishment."

Only then did Gryphon notice the ash rubbed all over Sani's skin. He wiped his finger along the boy's arm, smearing the chalky soot. "Burial ritual for your uncle?" Gryphon had heard they covered their bodies in ash to protect themselves against the dead.

Sani shook his head. "For you."

Gryphon couldn't muster a response.

"Come," said Sani, pulling him along behind him. "We're needed at the edge."

He shook as he staggered after Sani. His arms tingled without Zo dangling from them—as disturbing as that had been. Now that his brain was clear of the drugged fog, he knew that he had not killed Zo. The glorious truth seeped into his soul just as one weeds visions from reality after waking from dream-filled sleep.

Gryphon wasn't Zo's murderer. Zander had given the command. By killing Zo, Zander had robbed the world of so much goodness. Robbed Joshua and Tess of someone they loved. Robbed Gryphon of a future happiness he cringed even now to consider. Zander would pay for his crime.

They moved through the main dirt road that ran directly down the center of the island. Gryphon expected to hear the sounds that usually accompanied war, but all was quiet as they reached the cliff separating the Raven home from the mainland.

People stared at the blood staining Gryphon's shirt, their questioning eyes wandering to his face. They backed away as he and Sani neared the chief and the small group of men surrounding him. Gabe broke free from the group and ran to Gryphon, folding him into a giant bear hug. "You're the luckiest bastard I've ever met, you know that? If we survive this, you owe me a story."

Gryphon patted his back, doubting the Wolf would be interested in hearing about the vision of Zo's bleeding corpse. The details were blurred, fading from the grasp of his memory like a dream. The more he tried to remember, the further away the details of his hallucinations slipped.

"What's happening?" Gryphon asked as they pushed their way through a flock of stoic Raven warriors to the front of the group at the edge of the cliff.

"See for yourself," said Gabe.

Gryphon stepped to the edge and peered across the chasm to the mainland below to find hundreds of Ram warriors in mess formation. Their calm stance exuded arrogance. At the head of the army stood Barnabas, legs planted wide near the edge of the cliff. His cape caught the breeze off the ocean. Rarely did the Ram Chief venture outside the walls of Rams Gate, but these were hardly normal circumstances. The Raven had eluded the Ram for years. Today marked a major victory for his people and apparently Chief Barnabas didn't intend to miss it.

The wrinkles on Chief Naat's already heavily lined face deepened when he spotted Gryphon. "You." If that one word were an arrow, Gryphon would have been pierced through the heart. "I don't know how you survived the Hai, but you have cost my people their souls! Instead of fighting alongside the spirits of our ancestors, my people are fleeing, leaving their heritage and livelihood behind."

The man had no idea what he was saying. "I didn't force you to do anything." Gryphon growled. He was done taking blame for risking his life to save this ungrateful man and his people. He pointed at the Ram army. "You don't know what they're capable of! They will murder everyone within range of their spears. Leaving was always your only option."

Sani went to his father's side. "We are evacuating the people into boats anchored on the other side of the island. We have five large vessels with room to take the entire clan."

Gryphon nodded at Sani, grateful that at least one of the Raven wasn't completely crazy.

The chief pinched the bridge of his nose. "What we lack is a heading. Those ships are fishing vessels. We don't have the supplies to store enough water and food for my entire clan. After a week at sea we will be in a great deal of trouble."

"I can help with that," said Gabe. "Your clan has been friendly to the Allies. I know that Commander Laden would welcome your entire people to the Allied

Camp if your men will join in the fight against the Ram. You'd have to sail south for several days before we'd make the hike inland, but the Ram will not know to pursue us there, and your ships will travel faster than the Ram could on land."

"You will lead us to the camp?" A spark of hope entered the chief 's voice. Then he bowed and shook his head in obvious defeat. "We shouldn't be leaving at all. The Nest is impossible to attack. Without the bridge their forces are useless."

"But father, the *Hai*," said Sani. "The spirits have made their decision. We can't just ignore their wishes."

The sound of chopping wood called everyone's attention. Gryphon peered down at the mainland to find men swinging axes at the bases of the giant redwoods. Each mess crowded around a different tree with shields raised to protect those wielding axes.

"Not the trees," Chief Naat moaned, clutching his stomach as though he might be sick.

"The redwoods are sacred to them," whispered Gabe. "They believe the trees are tunnels that allow their dead to travel to the underworld. They also believe all blessings come through the trees, gifts of livelihood sent by their ancestors."

"Trees?" Gryphon asked, amazed.

Gabe shook his head. "To them the trees are family."

"Kill them. Stop them!" shouted Chief Naat.

The Ram had plenty of time to link shields and the chopping didn't cease. The massive trees were tall enough that, if felled properly, they could act as a bridge to the Nest.

Ashen and beaten, Chief Naat turned to Gabe. "I accept your offer, Wolf." He looked over at Gryphon. "On the condition that this Ram stays behind with a group of my best warriors to hold off his clan and destroy what we can't carry of our grain stores."

Gryphon wanted to hit the man. "I need to meet my apprentice at the Allied Camp. He'll be waiting for me there."

"Then you can travel with my warriors once you complete this task."

"I do *not* belong to your clan, Chief. You have no authority over me." Gryphon's hand flexed around a non-existent spear. The longer he went without a weapon the more naked he felt.

"Maybe so, but I will not allow a Ram on my ships. Even if you are a Clanless now."

Gryphon winced. The word Clanless made the hair on the back of his neck stand on end. There wasn't a lower class of person than someone who wasn't claimed by *something*.

Gryphon looked out at his people across the chasm. *Not my people anymore*. He didn't know how they planned to take the island, he only knew that they would find a way.

"It's settled then," said Gabe as he shook the Raven Chief 's hand. Gabe didn't really have a choice but to accept the Raven's terms, but his readiness to do so stung Gryphon.

As Chief Naat and his entourage walked back to the heart of the island, Gabe turned to Gryphon. "I'm sorry, my friend. You can't expect a man who's about to lose his home not to hold on to prejudices."

"I know what it feels like to lose a home, Gabe," Gryphon snapped. He pressed the heels of his hands into his forehead and sighed. "I will follow whatever Raven survive to the Allied Camp. They know the way."

Gabe studied the ground, shifting his weight from one foot to the next. "Have you considered what you'll do after all this is over?"

I'll hunt and kill Zander and Ajax. "I've tried not to think about it."

"Well, I know you have no interest in joining the Allies, but what about Joshua?"

Gryphon frowned. "What about Joshua?"

"He's a good kid, Gryph. Don't you think he deserves a chance with a clan?"

"There is no way I will ever be accepted in the Allied Camp, Wolf, and you know it."

"But Joshua is young and orphaned. Commander Laden would let him join up. He'd have a home with the Allies. A future."

"What are you saying?" Gryphon whispered. Gabe was, of course, right. But that meant …

"Joshua will follow you anywhere, Gryphon. If you come back, there will be no leaving him behind."

"You think I shouldn't travel to the Allies with the Raven?"

His silence was a way of offering Gryphon another knife.

When Gabe finally spoke, Gryphon wished he hadn't. "You know him better than anyone. Do what you think is best for the boy."

ZO BLINKED AWAY the sunspots in her vision as fire lit up the dark night. A child next to Zo sat up from her blanket and wailed. Zo pulled her and Tess under the wings of her protection. A woman cried out for help a few yards outside the circle, clutching the foot of what must have been her husband as he was being dragged away by two men with long, wild hair and tattered clothing.

Joshua, who'd been lying fast asleep at Zo's side, sprang to his feet, and with one quick motion launched his spear into one of dark figures. The second man released his hold on the husband and barreled toward Joshua.

"No!" Zo screamed.

Metal from the wild man's knives flashed in the torch-light as he pounced, but Joshua ducked out of the way and in the same motion turned and thrust his fist into the man's side.

The dark man released a labored growl and turned back to face Joshua. Only then did Zo consider his immense size, his arms stretched out wide like a massive bear standing on hind legs. His knives were his claws. Joshua, his prey.

The giant's back was to Zo, and she didn't waste the opportunity. She leapt from her place on the ground and tackled the man from behind. He fell almost too easily. Joshua and the Nameless husband each jumped onto one of his arms to detain the monster. The man bucked and fought, making it impossible for Zo to keep her seat. More men jumped on him, binding his arms behind his back. The man with the spear in his stomach lay motionless beside them.

Stone's orders thundered across the clearing, and soon everyone in camp was awake and crowding tighter into the protective circle. Men raised their makeshift spears, and the soft sob of children carried on the breeze. Everyone's attention stayed fixed on the black trees and bushes surrounding the clearing.

"They weren't human," someone hissed. "Demon animals that walked on two legs," said another.

Zo hooked Joshua by the collar as other Nameless men dragged the captive away. "What were you thinking?" Zo spun him around. "You can't just go and fight a wild man. You're young, Joshua. You could have been killed!"

Joshua tugged free of Zo's hold and took a step back. "I'm not a kid, Zo."

Zo eyed the space between them with disgust. She wanted nothing more than to hug the boy, but even though he was a kid, Zo saw a glimpse of the man within.

"Gryphon trained me to react, and that is exactly what I did. It's who I am. It's who he wanted me to be." Joshua's voice shook just enough for Zo to know he was fighting emotions that had nothing to do with tonight.

Zo closed the distance between them, and when he tried to push her comfort away, she batted his hands and threw her arms around his neck. "I just..." A sob ripped from her throat. "I just can't lose you, too."

Joshua stood still as a plank of wood, but eventually melted and put his arms around Zo, patting her back.

"I'm sorry, Zo," he said, but she could tell he wasn't apologizing for fighting that man tonight.

Once Zo could speak without breaking her composure, she whispered, "You were amazing. He would have been so proud of you."

This time, Joshua's resolve to be strong broke and he was thirteen again. Zo looked down to find Tess hugging him from behind. Her little lips moved in the form of one of her blessings.

"This is the boy!" someone shouted.

Zo and Tess stepped away as Stone marched up and clasped one of Joshua's hands. Zo hoped for Joshua's sake that no one saw the boy's tears in the darkness.

"Good man," said Stone. He turned to Zo. "We lost three others, and would have lost a fourth, if it weren't for your boy here." He slapped Joshua on the back.

"Do you want to tell me what that was?" asked Stone.

Zo wanted to sink to her knees in exhaustion. She placed her arm around Tess and dragged the girl more firmly to her side. "That was a Clanless attack."

CHAPTER ELEVEN

A few hundred yards from the edge, Gryphon and a small company of Raven warriors assembled to take orders from the commander whom Chief Naat had left in charge. The new leader was middle-aged and stood almost as tall as Gryphon, making him a giant among his people. His head was shaven and white paint ran in long lines down his face, as though smeared by his own fingertips.

He stared out at the twenty or so men who wouldn't be joining their wives and children as they boarded ships on the other side of the island.

"Rati, supplies. Kyi and Peti, your men are on traps. Veta, your bow and a black arrow. Meet us at the pit. Two minutes," the commander rasped. At his word, men shot like arrows out to fulfill their tasks. The clipped orders provided Gryphon almost no hint of their plan, only a strong sense of foreboding which made his heart pound in furious time with the distant rhythm of Ram axes.

To Gryphon the commander said, "You will come with me." He thrust a melon-sized barrel into Gryphon arms, lifted another barrel onto his own shoulder, and took off at a run toward the heart of the village. Gryphon didn't asked questions. He just tucked the barrel under his arm and followed.

When he first saw the illustrious pit filled with enough barrels of grain to solve the Ram's food shortage, he had to blink a few times to be sure it was real. He'd been on many excursions over the last two years searching for the Nest— for the grain. He'd begun to think it only existed in myth. When the Raven leader descended a ladder, Gryphon followed. He used his knife to spear a hole into the lid of the barrel then threw the blade to Gryphon for him to do the same. "Diluted pine resin." The Raven answered Gryphon's question before he had a chance to ask. Spread it over the top of the barrels along the perimeter of the pit."

Gryphon obeyed, walking around the edge of the pit and pouring a wavy trail of resin over the barrels. The Raven leader followed behind him sprinkling shiny black powder over the sticky barrels.

"The trees!" someone yelled from above the pit. "They're about to fall!"

Gryphon ran the rest of the perimeter; emptying his bucket over the barrels with the Raven leader right on his heels. When he finished his task, Gryphon tossed his bucket onto the ground and flew up the ladder and out of the pit.

Though he hadn't been told the purpose of the resin and powder, a sinking dread filled his stomach. He glanced over his shoulder one last time to take in the sight of all of those barrels. Grain meant flour, and flour meant bread and full bellies. No small miracle in their hungry region.

The young bowman met them fifty yards from the pit carrying an arrow with the tip covered in a black, porous substance. "I have everything ready, sir." He lifted an oil lantern with a nod.

"Good," the painted leader said. "Hold your arrow until it will do the most damage."

"Yes, sir." The young man sprinted up a set of stairs that spiraled around a nearby tree.

"The rest of you, get into position," the leader shouted.

Gryphon and the twenty or so Raven who'd been left to prepare for invasion sprinted to the edge of the island to meet the Ram. Climbing the backside of one of the island redwoods, he pulled himself onto a platform with the other men. Strangers, all of them.

A brief thought—*What am I doing here?*—flitted through his mind. He didn't know these men. They shared the common goal of wanting to escape the island alive, but that was all. The men of his Ram mess trusted one another with their lives. They were men he'd die to defend and who would willingly return the sacrifice.

He thought of the archer and his black-tipped arrow, and his stomach rolled, more conflicted than ever.

Gryphon lay flat on his stomach, watching the Ram take axes to the mammoth trees that stood at the edge of the cliff. The Raven surrounding him seethed and winced as the Ram hacked at their ancient heritage.

There was no sense in the Raven using their bows against the Ram shields that protected the men working the axes. The Raven conserved their arrows and waited.

Lying on the platform felt like waiting for death. "There has to be another way off the island," he said. Wood-slatted armor rattled as the Raven at his side turned away from him. But Gryphon didn't care. He'd risked everything to help these people and dying wasn't part of the plan. Especially not when he had a favor to return to Zander.

Everyone startled when Sani dropped onto the platform from a branch above. The boy dusted his hands on his pants and crawled over to Gryphon and the others. "The chief filled all of our smaller fishing vessels with supplies to be towed behind the big boats," he said. "Our only option is to cross the logs after the Ram come over. If we're lucky, the Ram will follow us, giving our people the time they need to distance themselves from shore."

"You're supposed to be on a boat," Gryphon growled at Sani. The last thing he needed was another kid around to remind him of Joshua.

"I told you before; I'm your *'Atiin*. I'm honor-bound to serve you until I have paid back my debt."

"You're a fool. None of your people would condemn you for not following through with this whole *'Atiin* thing. One less Ram in the world would be a blessing in their eyes."

"But they wouldn't have to live with the shame. I would." He studied Gryphon more closely. "Where is your armor?" He looked down the row of warriors and frowned. "Did no one bother to find you some?"

The other Raven had the decency to look sheepish.

Sani pushed up onto his knees and went to remove his own armor. He was instantly tackled by one of the warriors. Another removed his own wood-slatted chest plate and forced it into Gryphon's hands. The man was so narrow, Gryphon had no hope of strapping on the armor, but he was too stunned by Sani's rash decision and the effect it had on the men to do anything but hold it stupidly in his arms.

Little Sani, a boy Joshua's age, was the clear leader of their suicidal band. Gryphon shook his head in wonder and handed the armor back to the warrior who offered it. "No, thank you," he said. Then he turned to Sani. "You don't belong here, boy. Or have you already forgotten the ruthlessness of my clan?"

Sani clasped two hands in front of him and shrugged. "The boats have left. This conversation is pointless." He turned his attention back to the mainland and left Gryphon gaping.

The redwoods groaned as the last splinters of wood snapped under the weight of the giant conifer. When they fell, it was as if a portion of the sky fell with them. The tree Gryphon and the Raven warriors perched in shook as the wooden carcasses connected with the island to form a bridge.

The Raven murmured curses, their hatred for Gryphon's people almost as tangible as their agony over the loss of their trees. Their ancestors.

"I'm sorry." Gryphon whispered when the sound of

breaking branches and shifting ground ceased. It needed to be said, even though the apology wasn't nearly enough to balm the pain of losing so much.

The twenty Raven warriors each nocked an arrow but stayed low and out of view. Gryphon was more accustomed to seeing Raven from the ground as they fired upon him. This new vantage point gave him a deeper appreciation for the discipline of the Birds.

The Ram couldn't keep formation as they climbed over and under branches of the felled trees to get to the island. One of the Raven warriors stretched his bow, practically shaking with the desire to kill.

"Don't," said Gryphon. "You'll give away our position." The man looked ready to turn his bow on Gryphon, but didn't. They all knew their only chance of escape was through stealth.

Ten Ram made it to shore. Then twenty. Thirty. They linked back into formation, holding their shields aloft and spears at the ready. They scanned the trees, each man protecting his brother's back as the army advanced along the road that led deeper into the island.

Men he'd known his whole life approached the Raven's first trap—a trip wire made from Lion's Silk triggered to set off a slew of automatic crossbows. The deepest form of betrayal was to sit and watch his clansmen walk unknowingly to their deaths. The desire to call out to them, to warn them, filled his lungs.

He could save them. It would be so easy. By doing so, he might earn back his place in his clan. Zo was gone, and Joshua had a better shot at happiness without him in his life.

If he helped the Ram—his people—he might be allowed to the go back to his family home and to his mother. She'd be happy to have him, even after his betrayal. Ajax still needed help concealing his new son's birth defect from Ram authorities, and it would be nice to get back to training with his mess brothers—with the exception of Zander, of course.

Gryphon shook his head and pushed his clenched fists into his forehead. Logic raged against the convictions of his heart. How could he go back and serve in Barnabas' ranks? How could he sit by and let his people die? No matter what damage the Raven traps did today, the Ram were too strong to be defeated, even by the combined forces of the Kodiak, Raven, and Wolves. What use was there going against the winning player in the region's power struggle? Why not preserve himself? It would be so much easier.

Gryphon recalled a training session he'd designed for Joshua when the boy was only ten years old. He'd set markers in the field in front of his family home for Joshua to run sprints. Joshua, always eager to learn, nodded his head vigorously as Gryphon explained the drill. Later, when he looked out the window to check on Joshua's progress, he saw that the boy had moved the markers closer together to make for a shorter run.

Gryphon remembered the lecture he'd given Joshua as if it were only yesterday. *The easy path is for cowards*, he'd said.

Gryphon clamped his jaw shut and forced himself to watch what was in his power to prevent. His decision made.

His people walked blindly into the Lion's Silk. They were so concerned with protecting themselves from an aerial assault they didn't notice the trip wire. It all happened at once. The Lion's Silk let off a metallic whine as it stretched. The trigger released fifty arrows shot at an upward angle from the ground—something the Ram hadn't anticipated. Men cried out in pain. At last half of the first two mess units dropped to the ground. Any other group of men would have fled, but the Ram regrouped. The survivors of the two units merged into one, and the marching continued with more vigor than before.

Gryphon's whole frame shook with sorrow as his people stepped over the bodies of their clansmen to continue deeper into the island. Ram faces blurred in Gryphon's vision as they filed past. A small hand touched his shoulder when the last of the Ram left the tree bridges for island soil.

"It's time," said Sani.

Gryphon nodded and pushed up to his feet a changed man. A Ram no more.

"They're called Clanless," Zo said a second time. A crowd had gathered around her and Stone, all wanting the same answers Stone demanded. It was still hard to believe that she was the only one, besides maybe Tess, who knew anything about the people wandering the mountain without the protection of a clan. She reminded herself that most Nameless live their whole lives inside the walls of Ram's Gate as slaves. They were like children when it came to life outside the Gate.

"They're nomads. People without a clan who wander the mountains."

Stone ran a hand over his shaved head. "Why haven't we seen them before?"

Zo shrugged. "They give Ram's Gate a wide berth. No one wants to tangle with the Ram."

A Nameless man broke through the circle. Blood ran down the side of his face. "They took my wife. How do we get her back?"

Zo scanned the group, looking for someone to take charge of this situation. Someone like Gryphon, who knew how to lead. But even Stone awaited her answer.

Zo stumbled over her words. She wasn't a leader and had no desire to be responsible for these people. For some reason, she thought she'd be able to sink back into the crowd of Nameless and let Stone handle things from here. But no one else had traveled this terrain. Her opinion carried weight.

A terrifying thought.

"Th…they like to barter," Zo said. "They like to kidnap and ransom the prisoners for food and supplies."

"But we don't have supplies," Stone growled.

Zo looked around at the haggard bunch. Desperation stripped the joy of escape from their faces. They were captives again.

And Zo couldn't stand it.

"We'll get her back," Zo blurted. "But nothing can be done until the morning." She attempted to fill her lungs with slow, deep breaths, but still couldn't manage to get enough air. "Where is the man Joshua helped capture?" she asked with a voice shakier than the confident tone she'd intended.

Stone's eyebrows lifted. "He's over by the—"

"Double your night watch and take me to him," she said. "The rest of you need to sleep. Tomorrow is a big day." She knew the families of those taken by the Clanless wouldn't find any rest tonight, but they had to try. Zo turned back to Tess and Joshua. "You two need to stay with me. Do you understand?" Tess chewed on her bottom lip, but nodded while Joshua stood behind her, resting his hands on Tess's shoulders. "We will." He looked down at Tess then back up at Zo and puffed out his chest. The gesture spoke volumes. He would look out for her. Be Tess's protector if she needed one.

Zo nodded, choking down the emotion Joshua's response elicited in her. They were a family, the three of them. Joshua and Tess were both too young to be required to be so brave, but still they looked at Zo as if she held all of the answers of the universe and would have no difficulty solving this and all other problems.

She knew they were wrong, but hoped what she had to offer might keep them alive.

Stone led them toward the center of the circular camp, where the smell of unwashed bodies reminded her of her time spent sleeping in the Nameless barracks inside Ram's Gate. At the center, a man lay on his stomach with arms bound behind his back. His head lay in the dirt, his eyes closed as if he were asleep.

"Wake him," said Zo.

Stone grabbed the man's bound hands and pulled

him up so he sat on his knees. Then Stone took a handful of the prisoner's tattered shirt. He curled a fist like he might strike him, but he turned back to Zo, waiting for instruction.

"What is your name?" Zo stood next to Stone and the Clanless man.

He grunted something unintelligible. His hair and beard were so full she had trouble finding his face beneath the mess. No wonder the rest of the Nameless thought he was an animal.

"Answer me," said Zo.

The man looked straight ahead, refusing to make eye contact.

Stone threw his fist into his face. "You will speak to her or you will die. Choose wisely."

Zo shook her head and noticed something on the man's face. She nudged Stone out of the way. "Someone bring me a torch."

With more light, Zo saw a cut on the man's cheek that had been reopened by Stone's fist. The wound was red around the edges and oozed pus. "My kit," Zo called over her shoulder to Joshua. The boy sprinted off into the darkness while Tess inched closer to the wounded man. "It's infected, isn't it?" she said.

At the sound of Tess's small voice, the animalistic man turned his head.

"Yes, kid. How would you treat this?" Zo asked, all the while studying the man, who seemed to relax in Tess's presence.

Tess rattled off her list as though she was back in the Allied Camp, reciting one of her daily lessons in the Healer's Tent. "Clean it. Pack it with wool soaked in witch-hazel and garlic. And a blessing of purification."

"Very good," said Zo.

"Healers," the man said in a raspy voice. His Ram accent was so heavy Zo could barely make out the word.

He looked over at Zo and smiled. "Pretty healers."

Stone stepped in to strike the man again, but Zo held him back. "Please. Give us some space."

"Pain," said Stone over Zo. "I've lived with the Ram long enough to know how to make you wish you were dead, Clanless."

Zo sighed. They wouldn't get anywhere with Stone spouting threats every other second.

"Do you want to treat him?" Zo said, ignoring both men and giving her attention to Tess, "Or should I?" She wouldn't be able to manage the blessing, but the herbs would help him well enough.

Tess was usually overeager to practice her budding skills as a healer, but this man, with all his hair and filth, made her pause. She finally tilted her head to one side and asked him, "What's your name?"

The man squinted at her through the curtain of his wild and matted hair as if deciding whether answering the child would cost him. He finally grunted and said, "Name's Boar." His voice sounded like rocks rubbed against each other.

"Will you hurt me, Boar?" asked Tess.

It was such an honest question, some of the fight in the man's body visibly slipped away. His mouth fell open a fraction of an inch and, when Boar's gaze dropped to the ground, Zo knew the man had met his match with Tess.

Unless this was all an act.

"I—" the man struggled to clear his throat, "I won't harm you, child."

Stone made to protest, but Zo silenced him with a look.

"I found it!" Joshua said. His red hair matched the torch's flame as he approached carrying Zo's medical satchel.

Zo rested it on the floor in front of her little sister and stepped back.

"I'll need hot water," said Tess, as she bravely crouched in front of Boar.

Healing was a difficult skill to master. Not just anyone could do it. There were, of course, certain things that could be taught. Zo's mother had written down all of her recipes for various remedies, powders, oils, and concoctions. But healing wasn't like baking. So much of a person's ability to heal came from their ability to find love and compassion for those they treated. One also had to tap into a spiritual energy that very few had the ability to control. The skill was heredi-tary, which is why most healers learned the art from a parent.

Tess didn't see the hard set to Joshua's shoulders as he hovered behind her. A pot of steaming hot water was set at her side. She took a deep breath, dipped a clean swath of cotton into the water, and lifted it to the man's cheek. "How did you cut yourself?" she asked.

The man flinched under her ministrations. "Knife."

As usual, Tess bit her bottom lip while she worked. "Were you running with it?"

Boar snorted, making Tess flinch until she saw the man's yellow smile. "Wasn't my knife what done it," he said.

Tess tossed the soiled cotton aside and searched Zo's kit for what she needed. She sighed. "I'm so tired of people fighting. Why do people have to hurt each other?"

"Food," said Boar, wincing this time as Tess applied her medicines.

"Were you fighting over food when you got this?" asked Tess.

Zo had trained her sister to keep her patients talking as a way of distracting them from pain, but she'd never expected her sister to feel so at ease with someone like Boar. It reminded her of their mother. She never cared who it was she was healing, only that the job was done well.

"Is that what you're after? Food?" Zo sat next to her sister with her legs tucked underneath her.

Boar eyed her with about as much trust as he might a snake. "Something like that."

"She's my sister," Tess whispered. "She's good."

How could the word of one little girl wield so much power? But then, Tess was so pure, so innocent, that if she bestowed her trust, then perhaps he should too.

"I'll talk. But you must give your word to let me free."

Zo should have talked the decision over with Stone, but said, "Agreed. So long as you help us get our people back."

Stone sounded as if he was gagging on a tough piece

of meat, but Zo ignored him and gave Boar every ounce of her attention.

"We're starving," the Clanless said with a shrug of his shoulders. "When we can't find animals to hunt, we take people."

"I don't understand," said Tess. She secured a bandage to his cheek and sat back with arms folded. "How would stealing people make you less hungry?"

"Meat," was his only reply.

Stone stood up and walked over, rage vibrated off his skin. "You filthy, disgusting—"

"Joshua," Zo snapped, jumping up to hold Stone at bay. "Take Tess to bed. It's been a long day."

"But—I didn't do the blessing," Tess protested as Joshua scooped her up and threw her over his shoulder like a sack of flour.

"I'll take care of the blessing," Zo lied.

Tess parted the blond hair that fell into her face and waved a "goodnight" to Boar.

Boar's eyes tracked her as she left the campfire with Joshua. "She's so innocent," he said. "Are all children so…pure?"

Zo ignored the question.

"Are you telling me that these people you took tonight are meant to be a *meal?*" She must have misunderstood him. Humans didn't debase themselves to that level.

Boar's whole demeanor shifted. He stared down his nose at her and said, "You have no idea what it's like. Having to fight for every little thing in life. A bit of bread, a handful of berries, a morsel of meat." He scoffed, "Even a soft spot to lay our heads comes with a price."

"But to eat…*people?*" Zo held the back of her hand to her mouth and fought a violent gag reflex. She trembled to think that she'd let Tess near him!

Stone landed another fist to Boar's face, this time knocking him onto his back. Then he kicked him in the side twice before Zo stopped him. As disgusting as Boar was, killing him wouldn't bring Stone's people back.

Boar groaned and spat a mouthful of blood at Stone's boots. He turned to Zo. "Have you ever been hungry, healer? Really hungry?"

"Hasn't everyone?"

Boar's chest filled with wind and he barked, "No! No one but the Clanless really know what it's like to feel like Ram spears are jabbing at your innards ALL. THE. TIME. It's all we can think about. Look at me," he demanded. "I wasn't always an animal. I have no family. No home. Nothing to love. Nothing to protect but myself. And I'm so *tired* of being hungry."

Zo studied the man with a more critical eye, beyond the tattered clothes and messy hair. His eyes were sunken, his arms and legs, though wired with some muscle, were bare of any excess fat. The gums around his yellow teeth were pale instead of a healthy pink.

"Are our people dead?" asked Zo, solemnly.

The man shook his head. "We felled an elk a week ago. We're still living off that for a time, but people don't usually travel through these parts, and our leader didn't want to waste…resources, just in case. Spring comes late in the mountains. We're desperate."

There was no justification for trading your humanity. Whoever these men were, they were the darkest kind of evil. Zo had never heard of the Clanless banding together in large groups. How many of them were there? Enough to terrorize this group all the way to the Allies?

"I've heard that the Clanless like to barter. Could we make a trade?" she said.

Boar studied her and then looked over at Stone. "S'possible. Depends on what you're willing to part with." Boar licked his lips, as if the idea gave him pleasure.

Stone crouched in front of Boar and jabbed his knife into a patch of grass at the bound man's feet. "Let's make this happen. How do we arrange a trade?"

CHAPTER TWELVE

Gryphon, Sani, and the rest of the Raven warriors slid down from their hiding place in the trees to cross the Ram's barbaric bridge. They kept to the shadows, their fluid movements swallowed up by the echo of crashing waves below and the destruction of Raven homes behind them.

It wouldn't be long before Barnabas' men discovered the island empty and the grain stores wasted.

At the head of each felled tree bridge stood a Ram sentry, left to ensure no one escaped—a tactical mistake on Barnabas' part. One mess unit should have been left behind, not single men spread apart without the protection of a phalanx. It wasn't like Barnabas to be so careless guarding his rear.

The Raven at Gryphon's side stretched their bows and each took aim at a different sentry. Gryphon searched wildly through the thick foliage for any sign of danger. "Something's not right," he whispered to Sani.

On some unspoken cue the arrows flew, hitting their marks with deadly precision. Before the sentries' bodies hit the ground, the Raven, with Gryphon and Sani, flew toward the tree bridges at a dead sprint. Sani wasn't as fast as the other men, and Gryphon matched his pace to ensure the boy made it to the trees.

From behind them, a spear flew, striking the Raven in front of Gryphon. He reached for his shield to protect him and Sani from the next attack, but of course it wasn't there.

Gryphon swore. The first Raven men reached the tree bridge, gaining added cover from the branches. If they could just make it that far, they'd have a chance.

"We beat your healer whore before she died!" a familiar voice shouted behind Gryphon.

His legs stopped working and, trembling with rage, he turned to face Zander.

"She begged us to stop, begged for mercy. But we bruised her, cut her, bled her, until her face looked like ravaged meat. She wasn't pretty in death," Zander's voice trembled with hate. He stood—chest heaving—flanked by a handful of his mess brothers, including Ajax, whose face was a blank slate.

Sani tugged on the back of Gryphon's shirt, trying to pull him away from Zander, but Gryphon ignored him. The frame of Gryphon's vision turned red. His fingers ached to grasp his spear. He needed to make Zander hurt the way he did. He couldn't imagine a greater pain than the one Zander's words inflicted. He reached for his dagger—the only weapon in his possession—and flung it at Zander's head.

The knife sunk into the wood of Zander's shield. The lazy smile on the mess leader's face brought Gryphon back to the reality of the situation. He looked down at Sani, still tugging at the back of his shirt, and gaped at the magnitude of his mistake. The rest of the Raven were on the tree bridge, crossing to the mainland.

"Kill the boy and bind Gryphon," said Zander.

Every instinct in his body screamed to charge Zander and break his neck. But Gryphon pulled Sani behind his back and together they inched toward the fallen tree. He would avenge Zo's murder, but not at the risk of Sani's life.

Gryphon's mess brothers formed a half circle around him, preparing to tackle him as a group. Sani muttered a chant in the Raven's strange language, his head buried into Gryphon's back. Gryphon met eyes with Ajax, and his old friend frowned in misery. Ajax had a family. He followed Zander's orders for the sake of his wife and child. Even when those orders included killing innocents —killing friends—Sara and the baby came first.

Arrows flew over Gryphon and Sani's heads. Zander called for his men to link, but two of Gryphon's mess brothers went down before the wall of shields could save them.

Gryphon practically threw Sani onto the fallen tree bridge and barreled after him with the frustrated shouts of Zander nipping at their heels. When they reached the halfway point on the tree bridge, a Ram horn sounded.

"Move!" Gryphon hissed. "Quickly." The other Raven warriors positioned on branches of the tree stowed their bows and ran.

Sani jumped up and grabbed hold of a branch of the tree bridge, his lithe form swinging through the air only to grab another. The other Raven traveled in similar fashion, quickly outpacing Gryphon, as if the laws of gravity had no hold on them. Behind Gryphon, the *thunk* of spears connected with wood. When his feet finally hit solid ground on the opposite shore, Sani and the rest of the Raven ran at least fifty paces ahead of him.

Gryphon put his head down and sprinted as fast as he could into the forest away from the cliff. Ram shouts behind him pushed him faster. He caught up to Sani and took hold of his arm, pulling him along.

Eventually their pace ebbed, but death was too close to their heels to stop running. The Raven took turns casting hate-filled glances at Gryphon. He'd almost gotten their chief 's son killed. They were right to be angry with him. But Gryphon couldn't be moved to care about anything beyond his hatred toward Zander.

"She wasn't pretty in death."

Gryphon had been so careful not to allow himself to wallow in the possible details of Zo's death. But hearing Zander taunt him with her pain had been too much. Gryphon sprinted away from Zander to save his life, but it felt as though he moved in the wrong direction. For the hundredth time, he vowed to kill Zander.

"You will stay back with the rest of the women," Stone said to Eva.

"But Zo's going with you!" she protested.

"Boar trusts her and insisted she be there when the trade is made."

Morning brought with it the chaos of people working together to pack up camp. Fire pits smoked, finally resting from a long vigil to protect the people as they slept.

"Zo has some experience with these savages. She must go. You," he cupped Eva's cheeks and kissed her forehead, "will stay with the rest of the camp, under the protection of armed men."

Eva produced two daggers in the time it took Zo to blink. One pressed into her lover's side. "If anything, I will be protecting them." She smiled and pressed her full lips to Stone's neck then sauntered away, leaving Stone to gape after her.

"I love that woman." A grin as broad as a Ram's shoulders stretched across his face. He shook his head, as if to clear his mind, and turned back to the small band of men who'd volunteered to meet with the Clanless.

"Everyone ready?" he asked.

They had released Boar early that morning after he promised to deliver Stone's message that the "Freemen" would make a trade in exchange for the people stolen by the Clanless. Boar seemed convinced that his leader would agree to meet them if Stone came prepared to give his band something of equal value.

While the Nameless couldn't offer them food, they did have an impressive collection of weapons stolen from the Ram. Short swords, bows, spears, and even a few of the coveted round shields. Any group of people trying to survive this uncivilized region would be desperate for such an offering.

Zo scanned their surroundings as they marched out of camp and into the forest. Light filtered through the trees, casting life in either brilliant sunshine or harsh shadow. She tightened her grip on a knife she carried—one of Eva's—and tried to relax.

Cannibals. They were on their way to meet cannibals. She'd let Tess administer to a man who chose to eat other people instead of starve. She shook her head, still overwhelmed with disgust as they approached a massive boulder that served as their meeting place.

Stone had told Boar to have his leader and the Nameless prisoners meet an hour past sunrise, but no one waited for them as they approached the boulder.

"They could just be late," offered Zo. "He might not have found them in time to meet." They had only released Boar a few hours ago. His people could be anywhere.

"I'll kill him," Stone growled. He turned a full, impatient circle. "We shouldn't have placed our trust in a—"

"Clanless?" Boar and a ragged group of men emerged from clever hiding places around the boulder, effectively surrounding Stone, Zo, and the rest of their little company. They, like Boar, wore rags for clothing and had twigs and leaves sticking out from all angles to help them blend into their surroundings. "You are late, Nameless. We have been here for some time."

The fact that Boar called Stone a Nameless wasn't lost on anyone. Clearly, Zo hadn't been the only one questioning captives last night.

"You failed to mention that you escaped Ram's Gate," said Boar. The men of his company crowded behind him, marking Boar as their leader.

"And you failed to mention that you were the leader of your Clanless band," said Stone.

Boar's men dragged three Nameless to his side. They each had their hands bound, but otherwise appeared unharmed. "You said last night you wanted to make a trade, healer." Boar sought her out amid the crowd of Nameless. "What can you offer me?" His eyes brightened, his brows jumped up and down as he scanned her body.

Stone stepped in front of Zo, blocking her view of Boar. "We have weapons." He instructed the five men who carried sacks over their shoulders to open them. Several blades *clinked* against each other in the process. Two others dropped a pair of Ram shields into the offering pile. Circular shields framed in valuable metal and inlaid with impenetrable snakewood, ensuring a beautiful death to any that went up against it.

The shields alone made a generous deal for the Clanless.

Boar picked up a blade and stared down the length of the sword, checking for balance. He tested the weight of it in his hands. "There really is nothing quite like a Ram sword." His gaze locked on the shields and he seemed to salivate. "I once owned a shield like this." He reached for the leather straps secured to the back of the shield. "Barnabas took it from me before my banishment."

All of these men—these Clanless—once belonged to

one of the four clans. Many, judging by their looks, were Kodiak, but there were a few who could have been Raven or even Wolf.

Stone gestured to the pile. "These blades are yours in exchange for my people. The shields," he said, "are insurance that your men won't come near our camp again."

Boar smiled and casually tossed the shield down into the pile of weapons. Zo flinched at the sound of metal hitting metal. "No deal."

"What?" Stone balked. "I've offered you a generous trade. What more can you want?"

Boar's wild gazed zeroed in on Zo. "I want her."

CHAPTER THIRTEEN

Gryphon traveled at the rear of the flock of Raven with Sani just ahead of him. He couldn't decide if the Raven warriors ran so fast out of fear of the pursuing Ram, or because they meant to lose Gryphon. Either option seemed equally probable.

Legs burning, sides aching, lungs screaming, Gryphon wanted nothing more than to stop and give his body time to recover from their nightlong sprint. He and his mess had run many excursions throughout the mountainous region—he certainly wasn't a stranger to pushing himself beyond physical limits—but these Raven were inhuman. They floated across the ground it seemed, their legs barely having to push against the earth to propel their weight forward. Even Sani seemed to have little trouble keeping pace.

Gryphon's sheer mass slowed him. His head pounded with every meaty stomp of his legs. Even if the Ram managed to find their trail in the darkness, there was no chance his people would catch up to these Birds. No wonder they'd managed to hide themselves from the Ram for so many years.

Humbled and frustrated by his body's limitations, he used what little breath he could spare to call, "Please… stop."

Sani signaled the men ahead of them with a shrill whistle that Gryphon would have mistaken for an actual bird.

Gryphon's legs cramped up as he stumbled to a stop. He dropped to his hands and knees and sucked as much air into his burning lungs as possible. When he couldn't catch his breath, his body fell into a fit of coughing and sputtered gasps.

Gryphon looked up to find Sani's face blank of expression while the ten Raven warriors stared down on him with amused smiles. Their chests rose and fell with want of air—something that did little to appease Gryphon's dented pride as he rolled to sit on his backside in the dirt.

"Finally," said one of the men between breaths.

Gryphon turned to Sani, brows raised in question.

"Raven are a bit competitive when it comes to running. All refuse to be the first to call halt. It marks the weakest among the group." The boy did his best to hide his own labored breathing.

"You are a worthy runner, Ram," a Raven said. Others nodded agreement.

"But you believe I'm the weakest of our small company?" asked Gryphon.

Sani nodded, serious as ever. "Without question."

A few of the Raven chuckled as they each choose a tree and began climbing.

"Where are you going?" Gryphon asked Sani. The boy took hold of a low branch and hoisted himself up.

Sani paused and turned his head as though he didn't quite understand the question. "We're settling in to rest, before our next run. There is still an hour or two until first light. We'll resume our journey when the sun rises."

"Why climb when you will rest better on the ground?" asked Gryphon.

Sani reached for the next highest branch and pulled himself up. "Because only fools sleep on the ground in this part of the region."

Gryphon watched Sani and the others climb, each settling into a forked branch of his own tree. He considered Sani's warning, but the idea of climbing and sleeping on a branch held little appeal. He pulled out a woolen blanket from his pack and bundled it into a ball to act as a pillow. The moment his head touched the fabric of his people, Gryphon's eyelids drooped and sleep overtook him.

Rain fell on the metal roof of the weapons shed. When the door opened, Gryphon expected to see the Gate Master or another trainer come to deliver his yearly beating, but instead, Zo walked in, bringing with her mist that smelled of tree sap from the outside rain.

"You shouldn't be here." Gryphon looked beyond her to the door. He wanted to throw the lock but that was against the rules. Ram always obeyed the rules.

Zo stood wearing a simple tunic over leather pants. A woven belt accentuated her thin waist. She rubbed warmth into her arms as she walked among the shelves of the weapons shed. Her blue eyes struck him as they always had. Her dark hair fell in a perfect wave around her shoulders. She bit her bottom lip, wrinkling her forehead as if something were troubling her.

Gryphon stepped over his woolen blanket and approached her with open arms. He couldn't bear to see her concern even though he didn't understand its cause. But Zo just kept walking around the room, ignoring his offer to hold her. To love her.

The door creaked open and Zo scurried to the far corner of the shed. Gryphon planted himself in front of her as Zander walked in.

"It is that time of year, healer. Time to receive your gift."

No.

Gryphon charged Zander. He tried to grab him, to hurt him, but his hands—his whole body—couldn't connect with him. It was as if Gryphon were nothing more than a useless, powerless vapor.

Zander stood patiently by the door. "There is no way out, healer. Come to me and it will be easier for you."

Zo's perfect lips pulled back into a snarl. She snatched a short sword from a shelf and crouched low, refusing to leave her corner.

Zander sighed. "I suppose it will be more fun for us both this way."

"NO!" Gryphon yelled, but no sound came from his lips. He fought the space between him and Zander with wasted effort.

Zander ran at her and with one powerful swipe of his arm Zo's weapon clattered to the floor. She screamed and cried out in agony. Gryphon sank to the ground and covered his ears but her screams penetrated his very soul.

Panting, Gryphon startled awake. The sun hadn't fully risen. Sani peered down from his lofty perch but the others still slept. Gryphon rolled onto his side and refused to close his eyes, never wanting to see the inside of the weapons shed again.

Gryphon and the Raven ran most of the next day. By nightfall, Gryphon was again the one to beg the others to stop. Surrounded by the giant pines that dotted the region, Gryphon and the rest of the Raven leaned against trees as they ate a meal of dried meat and hard biscuits in silence. Gryphon greedily guzzled his water then choked, forgetting he needed air even more than hydration.

They'd managed to cover nearly four days of travel in two, bringing them dangerously close to the massive wall of Ram's Gate. Gryphon chewed on his humble meal and looked out at the dim forest surrounding him. These were his woods. He knew exactly where they were.

Chief Barnabas constantly had them scanning this forest for game and other clans. So many memories. Successes and failures. Moments of victory and loss. Zo, Tess, and Joshua had rested under the boughs of a giant fir only a few hundred yards from where he sat.

A part of him wanted to go to the tree and see it empty with his own eyes. Just seeing their tracks would bring some measure of comfort.

Gryphon, stiff with sore muscles, pushed himself off the ground and gained his feet. "I'll be right back."

Two of the Raven, including Sani, climbed to their feet as well. "Where are you going?" asked Sani.

"There's something I need to see," he said.

Sani exchanged silent looks with his fellow clansmen. Gryphon still found it strange that the small band of warriors looked to an adolescent boy as a leader. He was so young, but being the chief's son, his opinions weighed more than most. "I'll go with you," said Sani.

"I'd rather go alone," said Gryphon, stepping away from the rough circle of men.

"We are close to the Gate. You shouldn't travel alone," said Sani.

"Listen, boy. You might think I'm weak, but I can handle—"

"We don't trust you," Sani blurted. "You might betray us to your clan."

Gryphon stepped back. "You can't be serious."

"We want to trust you." Sani showed Gryphon his palms in surrender. "You have been honorable so far. But—"

"Fine," Gryphon snarled. "Follow me if you like."

Gryphon shouldn't have been offended. These men lost their homes and were separated from their families. He couldn't blame them for being uncomfortable with him. If anything, it reminded Gryphon just how alone he really was in the world. No one would ever fully trust a Ram. Certainly not the Allies. He had Joshua, but his conversation with Gabe before they left the Nest had severed even that little thread of peace.

What was he doing with these Raven anyway? Could he risk traveling to the Allies to see Joshua one last time? He wanted to believe the boy would see reason and settle within the protection of a clan, but Gabe had a point. Joshua wouldn't want to stay with the Allies if he knew Gryphon wasn't welcome.

Gryphon and Sani picked their way through the forest, weaving between bushes and briars until Gryphon spotted the familiar cluster of granite boulders next to a thick fir tree with low-hanging boughs.

"I'll only be a moment."

Gryphon left Sani by the boulders and dropped his pack on the ground before falling to hands and knees and crawling under the heavy boughs. The familiar smell of pine and lemongrass carried with it sweet memories. A miracle had taken place in this shadowed sanctuary. Two miracles, actually. Both at the hands of Zo.

Yes, she'd miraculously healed Joshua from a deadly stab wound, but she'd also healed Gryphon. His wounds were less obvious but equally profound. His whole life, he'd tried to compensate for his father's failings, but only when he and Zo held each other under this tree did he finally feel centered. She'd made him feel capable. Strong.

These Raven didn't trust him to take a simple walk through the woods without supervision, but she had trusted him with her and her sister's lives. Her belief in him had made him invincible.

And then he failed her. His own mess brother ended her precious life.

"She wasn't pretty in death."

Did she die beneath the boughs of this tree? Did little Tess see it happen? How much did Zo suffer?

Digging his fingers into the ground, Gryphon pushed his forehead into the loose soil and fought a sob. How could someone hurt her? He should have fought harder. He should have found a way to take her away from this place. Gryphon's hands and arms shook. He clutched two fistfuls of his hair, his forehead still pressed to the dirt. He couldn't delay his revenge any longer.

Bursting out from under the tree, he couldn't catch his breath. Couldn't get away from the tree fast enough.

"What happened?" Sani asked.

"We need to leave. We can't rest here tonight."

Sure-footed Sani stumbled to catch up with Gryphon. "I don't understand."

"I know."

When they reached the Raven warriors, every man stood.

"What happened?" one asked.

Gryphon adjusted the straps of his pack and said, "We're leaving."

Sani must have given a signal to the men, because they all gathered their meager possessions and, without speech or ceremony, took off into the gathering shadows of night.

Zo BLINKED, and looked between Boar and Stone. "You can't be serious."

Boar shrugged. "It's a fair trade. I give you three people in exchange for one." He took out his own knife and spun it on one finger with a practiced hand before catching it.

"Zo is a healer and our guide. She's too valuable." Stone crossed his arms.

Zo whipped around and glared at Stone. Was the man seriously negotiating with Boar, as if she were no more than a valuable commodity? Stone above anyone else knew what it meant to belong to another person.

"What you don't seem to appreciate, Nameless, is that my little band here," he stretched out his arms toward his men, "can be a nightmare to your people. We will slow you down. Pick off your people one by one. You will never rest without fear, always wondering if we are surrounding you, planning our next attack.

As crazy as Stone was, Zo knew he couldn't reasonably allow his people to suffer just for one person. Yes, she was a healer, and yes, she was the only person who'd traveled to the Allied Camp, but her life wasn't valuable enough to sacrifice so many. She balled her fists and closed her eyes, waiting for Stone to agree to Boar's terms.

"I am willing to trade with you, Boar. I'm willing to give you something valuable to gain back what you've stolen from me. But Zo is a big reason we've escaped the Gate. I can't reward her help by trading her to you."

Boar offered an exaggerated sigh. "I was afraid you'd say that." He gestured to one of his men who, without hesitation, produced a knife and dragged it across the Nameless woman's throat.

"No!" Stone yelled. Zo's knees wobbled beneath her. Stone's men drew swords. The bleeding woman crumpled to the ground and the entire ring of men seemed to inhale at once. Then everything happened fast. Stone's hand clamped down on Zo's arm as he shouted, "Attack!" The Nameless charged the Clanless. Swords clashed. A few of Boar's large, Kodiak-looking men pulled the other three Nameless hostages away. Stone held firmly to Zo's arm and dragged her back toward the Nameless camp. At his command, the men who hadn't fallen to the Clanless covered their retreat. Boar didn't offer chase.

The image of the woman being killed replayed over and over in Zo's mind. When the forest was quiet again, and there was no sign of Boar's men, she said, "We can't leave her." Boar considered Zo for a moment then nodded. "You're right."

He sent two of his men to retrieve the woman, saying it was too dangerous to let Zo go herself. The men were fast. They returned with faces of stone and laid her reverently on the ground where Zo could administer to her.

Blood covered her neck and chest. A familiar gurgling sound accompanied what Zo knew to be a severed trachea. Without air, the woman had died quickly. Even if she could perform a healing blessing, it wouldn't bring this woman back from the dead.

Zo, who had wept more in the past few days than she had since her parents were killed, didn't have another tear to shed for this stranger on the ground, who'd escaped slavery only to die a savage death. This woman's death was only the beginning of the terror Boar had promised to inflict on the Nameless refugees.

Stone placed a hand on Zo's shoulder, but she shrugged it off. For so long after her parents' murder she had reserved her anger only for the Ram. But from her time spent in Ram's Gate, she had come to realize her anger had less to do with the Ram and more to do with horrible people—people who strut around the world and take and take and *take*, just because they can. Zo expended so much time trying to preserve life, that the immorality of murder—of *taking* life—shocked her to the core. She'd never get used to it.

"We'll get the others back," said Stone. His face was white. Even his lips drained of color as he looked down at Zo and the woman who'd died because of his decision. "We will protect our people."

Zo didn't mean to laugh, but she did, a dark, sinister thing that snaked out of her mouth without permission. "You don't even know how many men they have, Stone. How can you possibly know that you can defend us against them?"

It was the wrong thing to say. She should have been thanking him for not trading her to Boar. But with her fingers soaked in the blood of an innocent woman who'd unwittingly died in her place, it was hard to be grateful for anything.

Shame came much easier.

A heavy raindrop landed on Zo's forehead and dribbled down into her eye. Another met her arm, and another the back of her neck.

"We can't stay here," said Stone. He scooped up the woman's body and they made a solemn walk back to deliver the news of their failure to the Nameless.

CHAPTER FOURTEEN

Little by little, Gryphon fell back from Sani and the rest of the Raven warriors as they ran. Sani glanced over his shoulder to check that Gryphon was still following, eyeing the growing distance between them with distaste. The more time he spent with the boy, the more he struggled to believe he was only thirteen years old. What thirteen-year-old ran around pledging his life to others? He spouted nonsense about honor when he wasn't even old enough to grow whiskers. The boy had some nerve.

The forest thickened with pines and spruces, forcing them to follow winding game trails. Gryphon lost sight of Sani on a turn and made a quick decision.

He darted east, leaving the trail for an untamed path through the dense forest.

It wouldn't be long before Sani realized Gryphon's absence and came looking for him to fulfill his duty as

'*Atiin*, but Gryphon knew this mountain and was confident he could easily avoid them.

He sprinted a half mile east then, ducking between a pair of lichen-covered boulders, crumpled to the ground knowing he would never see Joshua again.

I'm doing this for him, he reminded himself over and over again. Joshua deserved a life that Gryphon simply couldn't offer. Gryphon pressed his palms into his eyes. Without Joshua to care for, his focus fell to the one thing he had left to fight for: Zo's memory. And he'd start by hunting Zander and Ajax. They'd feel every ounce of pain Zo had before she died, even if it was his final act in this life.

It wasn't long before the sounds of snapping branches and murmuring voices reached him. They were close enough that Gryphon easily distinguished Sani's high-pitched tone from the other Raven, but distant enough that Gryphon didn't bother running. The Raven didn't seem to look for long before they moved on. Even the son of a chief couldn't convince the warriors to give their time to a lost cause. And if they mistrusted him enough to think he defected to warn the Ram, they'd run with even more haste than they had up to now.

Gryphon lay hidden between the boulders into the afternoon, long after the sun peeked over the horizon. Waiting. Hating the cruel blow life had dealt him. More hungry for revenge than for any morsel of food. He ran a hand over his face to feel the product of almost two weeks without shaving. His dark beard grew fast and thick and it wouldn't be long before even his mother wouldn't have recognized him.

Gryphon plucked a blade of grass and tore it into strips, thinking about his mother and how she ought to have made his list of things and people to live for. Beneath her rough exterior, she had loved Gryphon, even though a chunk of her heart wasn't available to him.

Yes, he assumed it was because his father had abandoned them when he was a baby. She'd let the disgrace govern her and Gryphon's lives, insisting that his father's shield be hung above the family hearth—an ever-present monument to their shame. But as a boy, Gryphon couldn't understand why the decisions of his father were his fault. Gryphon hadn't left. He'd been right under her nose all that time. Searching for new ways to please her and ease her pain. She'd been so young when his father left, probably close to Gryphon's age. Her whole life forfeit because she didn't move on. Gryphon would have forgiven her emotional neglect a thousand times over. But forgiveness was never sought and, consequently, never offered.

He bit off a piece of grass root and stared at the clouds shifting in the sky. His thoughts were broken by the faint sound of breathing behind him. People didn't sound like that when they breathed. It was more like the slow and heavy pant of a dog. A very, very large dog. He craned his neck to look back, afraid to make any sudden movements.

Two bear cubs with brownish-black fur backed behind their gigantic mother. They seemed to whimper at her feet. The mother wore a shaggy brown coat. Her long muzzle stretched into a wet, black nose raised to the sky as she sniffed the air.

Gryphon flipped onto his stomach and eyed the massive creature. Its head was easily as wide as Gryphon's shoulders, and standing on four legs, the beast's back would have met his chest. He'd heard of mess units spotting Kodiak bears, but they mostly kept east to the Kodiak Hills. Men whispered stories about the size of these beasts, but people exaggerate, and Gryphon hadn't believed them. Until now.

Again, the bear sniffed the air around Gryphon. She sneezed and shook her head, as if disgusted by what she smelled. Tossing her head from side to side, she clacked her teeth together, her mouth opening and shutting.

Gryphon slowly pushed up onto his hands and knees. "Easy, girl. I'm not going to hurt your cubs. I'll leave."

The bear grunted and charged forward, then stopped only five yards away. With claws like daggers, it swiped at the air as it backed up.

Gryphon shifted into a crouch and picked a dead tree branch off the ground. "I'm leaving. I'm leaving. It's all right. I'm leaving."

He took a half step backward and the bear charged again, this time stopping just outside the reach of its claw swipes. The fur on its neck stood on end and its ears lay flat to its head.

This was no longer just about defending her cubs. She seemed hungry, and he was prey. The giant Kodiak pushed onto its hind legs. The force of her growl sent Gryphon stumbling back.

Gryphon raised the stick above his head and shouted his own battle cry before launching the stick at the bear's face like a spear. The stick flew wobbly through the air and struck the bear's nose. The roar that followed forced Gryphon to cover his ears.

The Kodiak charged forward and pushed up onto its hind legs. This time, when it swiped out with a paw, all the bear's weight went into the blow. Gryphon ducked and scrambled back against a tree. He scoured the ground for some kind of weapon to defend himself.

Just as the bear reached him, an arrow shot from somewhere behind Gryphon, connecting with the beast's shoulder. The bear howled in fury, biting at the arrow, desperate to pull it free of its body.

Gryphon spun around and gaped at the sight.

A woman stood on the shoulders of a man, a bow in her hands with an arrow aimed at the bear. The man at the bottom of the human totem kept a wide stance to support her weight and held the girl by the ankles.

"Don't turn your back on her," the woman said, her accent clearly Raven. "She's threatened by my size and knows now that my bite stings, but an injured Kodiak is a very dangerous creature."

Gryphon shook his head in wonder and obeyed the woman, turning to face the beast that seconds ago had almost killed him.

"Good, now back away. Good. Almost there. Now stop."

Gryphon stood level to the pair of Raven, panting and unable to keep his hands and legs from shaking.

The Raven man said, "Now it's your turn, bear. Back up before this girl squashes me into nothing." The man didn't seem at all taxed by the weight of the Raven girl. The bear snorted and whined as it backed away, but no one relaxed until it disappeared over the crest of a nearby ridge.

The Raven girl jumped to the ground, and Gryphon turned to thank the strangers but was met by a drawn bow, its arrow pointed at his head. "Who are you?" she hissed. The Raven man also had bow drawn, any humor he shared with the woman gone.

"You have Sani's beaded bracelet hanging about your wrist," the girl said. "What have you done to my brother?"

If this was Sani's sister, that also made her Chief Naat's daughter. "Months ago, when I was on a scouting trip with my unit, we came upon a flock of Raven," said Gryphon. "We attacked. I had the chance to kill Sani but instead spared his life. I've since left my clan to warn your people of a coming invasion. Sani recognized me and claimed he is my *'Atiin*. I just came from the Nest with him after helping convince your people to flee."

The woman sucked in a quick breath. "They left the Nest?"

"Impossible," said the man. His head was shaved on both sides, leaving a cropped strip of hair running from forehead to nape.

"They escaped the Ram by boat and are headed to meet the Allies in the south."

The woman lowered her bow and tugged on the man's sleeve. "They're safe, Talon." She wiped a tear from her cheek. "They're safe."

Zo didn't bother telling Joshua and Tess about Boar's desire to have her. They only knew Stone and Boar couldn't come to terms.

Eva stared at Zo across the burial pyre and offered a sharp nod, her Ram way of saying, "*We will fight this.*" Zo appreciated the show of support even though it was accompanied by a husband's wails, as smoke carried a murdered wife's ashes to the heavens.

The fumes of death constricted Zo's throat. Stone had spared her life, but at what cost? Now that Stone knew the Clanless were targeting them, he'd have everyone on high alert for the rest of the journey. If they could just survive another week, Commander Laden's scouts would surely spot them and send help. Just another week, and Zo and Tess would be completely safe for the first time in months.

After the short burial service, the Nameless refugees strapped their belongings to their backs and, as one compact group, marched south. Stone ordered they travel like they slept, with their best fighters traveling along the perimeter of the group. However, walking the game trails of a forested mountain pass forced the group to thin out like marching ants.

Zo tugged both Tess and Joshua close to her sides. They walked behind Stone and Eva, who held hands. Eva carried a knife in her free hand, and Stone, a spear. Their eyes constantly scanned the forest for signs of movement.

Joshua leaned over and whispered in Zo's ear, "You're keeping things from me again."

Zo watched Tess hop forward and kick a rock along

the game trail. "Not now, Joshua." She tilted her head toward Tess.

"I can handle more than you think. If I'm going to protect you and Tess, I need to know *everything* that's going on, Zo."

Tess must have heard her name because she abandoned her rock and pretended to be fascinated by a hole in her shirt.

"You are not my protector, Joshua. You're brave and strong, but if anyone is responsible for the lives of our little group," she hugged them both closer to her sides, "it's me. Do you understand?"

Joshua grumbled about her being worse than Gryphon and kicked his own rock down the trail. It knocked into the back of Stone's heel. The Nameless leader turned and scowled at the boy then resumed his scouting.

Joshua's head drooped even lower, till his chin rested against his chest.

"Cheer up, Ginger," said Zo. "We're only a week outside of the Allied Camp. I'm sure when Commander Laden sees what a skilled fighter you are, he'll put you in charge of something important."

"Yeah, probably make me the Master of Cleaning Weapons. Or maybe the Captain of Washing Dishes." He sighed. "I just...I wish Gryphon were here, is all." The muscles in his neck flexed and he looked out into the woods, his head turned away from Zo, likely to hide his tears.

Me too, Ginger. Me too.

CHAPTER FIFTEEN

The Raven twins who saved Gryphon's life were called Talon and Raca. They wanted to know everything that happened with their people at the Nest. Several times during Gryphon's tale they shared knowing looks, but they never interrupted.

"What I don't understand," said Talon, when Gryphon finished explaining how he, Sani, and a group of Raven warriors escaped the Nest, "is what compelled you to leave Ram's Gate in the first place. I've never heard of a Ram abandoning his clan."

Gryphon thought of the shield hanging over his family hearth and swallowed. "That is a story for another day." He had no desire to talk about Zo and Joshua.

"So Sani is on his way to meet up with our father and the rest of the Raven at the Allied Camp?" asked Raca.

"Your father is the chief." The family resemblance was hard to miss. "You're Sani's siblings."

Raca smiled. "Sani is the baby in the family. A strange boy."

Gryphon nodded and took a long drink from his water skin. He wiped his whiskered face and cringed at just how unkempt he must have appeared. And smelly. No wonder the bear attacked.

"If he is your '*Atiin*, why aren't you still with him?" she asked. There was a note of sympathy in her voice that made Gryphon bristle. He refused to be the object of anyone's pity. A Ram trait that followed him from the Gate.

"I am going my own way."

Talon's eyebrows rose. "And which way is that?"

Gryphon lifted the water skin to his lips again and paused. "I have a score to settle. I'll say no more about it."

If there was one thing his encounter with the bear taught Gryphon, it was that he was very different from his mother. He wanted to live. But more than that, he didn't want to be a victim. If given a choice between predator and prey, he chose predator. No more running from problems. From now on, he'd run toward his destiny.

Revenge.

"I have a few questions of my own," said Gryphon, hoping to wipe the pitiful look off of Raca's attractive face. "Why stand on your brother's shoulders to face the bear? Without him holding you, you'd have two arrows pointed at the bear instead of one."

"We didn't want to kill the animal. Only to scare it

away. Did you not see her little family? The poor beast was only startled by you and attacked to save her cubs."

A part of Gryphon wanted to challenge Raca's logic. If the cubs died they wouldn't grow up to attack another man. But in his heart, Gryphon knew that line of thinking was flawed.

The clans weren't so different from that bear. They, too, were afraid of what was strange to them and wanted to protect their families. They attacked when they should find a way to make peace. To coexist.

"The Kodiak Clan fights like that bear," said Talon. "Have you ever crossed them in battle?" He tugged on a leathery piece of dried meat and chewed with his mouth open.

"Once or twice, but I've never engaged a Kodiak beyond the wall of my mess's phalanx of shields. My people raided their clan before I was old enough to earn my shield and pledge a mess."

Talon nodded. His eyes unfocused while he chewed —probably thinking about how much he despised the Ram. "To them, the larger the man, the greater the man." Talon smiled with a few chunks of food in his teeth. "They like big women too." He held his hands in a provocative way in front of his chest.

Raca smacked her brother upside the head. "Quiet, Talon." And then to Gryphon she said, "Forgive him. He needs to get back to his wife."

Gryphon smiled and tried not to think about the fact that only a few months ago he considered Raven, and others outside the Ram, less than human. The thought brought him so much shame it was hard to swallow the final sip of water from his water skin. He climbed to his feet and dusted off his backside. "I should be going," he said. If he didn't get back to Ram's Gate soon, he'd lose his chance at killing Zander and Ajax before they went back inside the Gate.

"What about the redheaded boy?" Raca blurted. "He claimed you were his mentor. Will you abandon him?"

Gryphon froze halfway through the motion of putting on his pack. "What did you just say?"

"The boy." Raca bit her lip, no longer looking at Gryphon, but instead reading Talon's silent cues to stop talking.

"How do you know about Joshua?" Gryphon said each word carefully. This young woman's answer was so fragile to him.

"We shared his fire two nights ago. He keeps interesting company." The Nameless covered an impressive amount of ground before setting up camp for the night in a large clearing. Children used to working fields aren't strangers to endurance, but by the time Stone and Eva settled on a stopping place, most of the small ones hung on the thin coats of their weary parents if they weren't already resting on their mother's hip or their father's shoulders.

Zo recognized this portion of the mountain because the trees were blackened and bare and the ground scorched from a fire that must have happened in the last year. Zo remembered traveling through this part of the mountain with Gabe when she was on her way to deliver herself up as a Nameless spy for the Allies. It was hard to imagine Tess traveling these woods behind them. They had taken two full weeks to get to Ram's Gate, traveling at a much slower pace, but still, the fact that she had managed to stay hidden, that her short legs had carried her so far, was a miracle.

Needing the comfort of her touch and the reassurance she was still alive, Zo tugged Tess closer to her side before the girl wiggled free and ran to say something to Joshua.

Stone hopped up onto a fallen tree trunk and the Nameless went quiet. "The Clanless will come back and try to take more of our people. We must be ready to defend ourselves tonight." Tight whispers scattered across the camp, but died when Stone continued. "Gather your firewood in pairs. Men, build your campfires, arm your women, then report to me in twenty minutes with a torch in hand."

Stone shouldn't have any doubts that the Clanless knew their location. A toddler could follow the tracks of a group this size. They were less like tracks and more like a trampling of the earth.

Joshua hopped over to Zo and dropped a dead badger that he'd caught earlier that day at her feet. "Stay here with Tess. I'll get the wood!" He sprinted away, not yielding to Zo's calls for him to come back.

"You stay here," Zo said to Tess. "I'm going to go kill that boy. I'll be right back."

Tess wrinkled her nose with a smile. She knelt and scanned the ground for more rocks—something of a nightly tradition.

Zo knew it wasn't smart to set out into the woods alone, but she couldn't let Joshua go without her. That boy! He was so excited about taking care of Zo and Tess that he forgot his own age. Sure, he was a decent fighter, especially for a thirteen-year-old, but he was still just a boy.

A boy Zo couldn't bear to lose.

The evening brought with it new shadows that shifted as she walked through the woods, away from camp. A large bird cawed from its perch in the trees. Curious, Zo approached it and the bird pushed off from the thin branch, using its powerful black wings to ascend into the darkening night.

Where are you, Ginger?

A dead branch snapped, but the sound echoed around Zo, making it impossible to tell from which direction it came. She wanted to call out for Joshua, but didn't dare alert her enemies to her whereabouts if they lurked in these blackened woods that offered so little cover.

"Zo!" Joshua called from the direction of the camp. He didn't know how foolish it was to announce that she was missing. He and the rest of the camp didn't realize she was the reason they had to fear the woods. She was the reason that the Nameless woman was killed this morning and that two other men were somewhere—hopefully alive—with Boar and his Clanless band of savages.

"Zo!" he called again.

Zo sprinted toward the clearing and practically tackled Joshua when she found him at the edge of the forest, carrying so much firewood she couldn't even see his face over the pile.

"You are in so much trouble right now." Zo kissed his

cheek, killing the power of her threat, but too relieved to care. "Pairs, Joshua. You're supposed to go in pairs. Didn't you hear Stone?"

Only then did Zo notice the lanky Nameless young man at Joshua's side, carrying his own large pile.

"Oh. I didn't realize…"

The little Zo saw of Joshua's face turned red as his flaming hair with the embarrassment of being reprimanded in front of another boy. "See you at the meeting, Ruff," said Joshua, striding away on his long, awkward legs.

Zo jogged to keep pace with him. "I'm sorry for embarrassing you. I'm responsible for you, Joshua. I don't want you hurt."

Joshua didn't answer until he reached the place near the center of camp where Tess and their traveling packs rested. Tess had gathered enough rocks to make a small fire ring. She went right to work with the twigs Joshua gathered to make a teepee structure perfect for lighting a fire to cook their meal.

Joshua retrieved a thicker stick of pine and used his knife to slice two intersecting lines into the top. He refused to speak to or even look at Zo as he skinned the stick then wedged the shavings into the splits to create a capable torch.

"You can't blame me for being protective, Joshua," said Zo. She nudged his boot to try and coax a smile that didn't come.

Joshua stopped his work with the torch. "I'm the best fighter of the three of us. *You* can't blame me for trying to protect us."

"Of course not, but—"

"Let me *do* something, Zo. I want to help you and Tess. I *need* to do this…for Gryphon. Why can't you understand that?" He snatched his torch from the ground and stalked away to meet Stone with the rest of the men in camp. To take on his foolishly assumed role as "protector" in their unconventional little family.

Zo massaged her fingers into her temples, fighting away a throbbing headache. She glanced at the Nameless around them. Several men hurriedly worked on their torches with half the skill Joshua had. Gryphon had truly shaped the boy into something great. But Zo wouldn't allow Joshua to put himself at risk…not even for the sake of Gryphon's memory. There were others who could step in and protect the camp. Joshua and Zo had already done their part.

CHAPTER SIXTEEN

Gryphon jumped to his feet and grabbed Raca's shoulders, ready to shake her to get her to speak. "You shared a fire with my apprentice?"

Talon stepped in front of Raca. "You will not touch my sister in such a way, Sheep."

Gryphon backed away. He hadn't meant to scare the girl.

"Stop playing guard dog, brother." Raca gently pushed her brother away, then said to Gryphon, "We met them a few days ago. They said they were tracking the Nameless refugees to the Allied Camp. But…" Talon glanced at his sister and frowned. "These are dangerous mountains, Gryphon. We've heard a wild man has rallied the Clanless in the area. A banished Ram named Boar."

"What does that have to do with my friends?" said Gryphon.

"Nothing, only we've heard from several wandering Clanless that Barnabas has offered a mighty reward for the person who brings him you and a Wolf healer called Zo. I didn't want Raca to mention the boy only because I didn't want to raise your hopes that your friends were still safe."

"What are you saying?" Gryphon remembered hearing the name Boar several years ago while he was still training for the opportunity to join a mess. A man by that name was banished for gruesome crimes committed against his own wife.

"The Clanless man we met says Boar is completely crazy. He's bullied many of the Clanless into following him, creating something of a small army in these mountains."

"An army of desperate men."

Talon nodded.

"I worry for your friends, especially the Wolf. I'd imagine Boar would do anything for enough leverage to reinstate his citizenship with the Ram."

"I doubt Boar would be interested in Tess. He'll know that bringing an innocent little girl back to the Gate won't buy him anything."

Both Raca and Talon wrinkled their noses in exactly the same way and at exactly the same time. "Tess?" Raca asked. Then her expression cleared. "No, we're talking about the other girl. The older Wolf. The healer."

Gryphon held his breath. The Raven woman had to be confused.

"Zo," said Talon. "The one Joshua claimed you were in love with. The one Boar is hunting."

Gryphon shook his head and momentarily closed his eyes against the aching hope. "You're wrong. She died outside Ram's Gate." He paced the ground in front of them. "This girl. What did she look like?"

"Tall. Brownish-black hair. Stunning blue eyes…"

"It's not possible." Gryphon sank to his knees. He gasped, remembering to breathe. "What did you say to her? How did she answer?" He found himself repeating, "It can't be" over and over.

A soft hand touched his shoulder. Raca's concerned eyes met his. "She was kind to us. Invited us to sit at her fire and warned us of the Ram invasion. Unless there is another Wolf healer named Zo crossing this mountain, your friend is still alive," said Raca.

Gryphon gasped and jumped up, scooping Raca and Talon into one gigantic hug. "I could kiss you both."

"Please don't," said Talon.

Zo was alive.

Torches staked around the perimeter of the camp flickered in the wind. They lit the rim of the charred and blackened forest more than the Nameless camped in the clearing. If fear had a taste, it was burnt and bitter. Zo watched as the torches cast only half of the naked trees in light. They were gnarled fingers of wood that seemed to reach out at them. Zo couldn't look away from their reaching fingers as she muscled down the badger stew concoction Joshua and Tess made for dinner.

"Do you like it?" Tess asked. She'd taken a hand to "spicing" their meals with different kinds of plants and flowers she picked along the trail. The previous night, she'd almost poisoned them by adding wild foxglove to the cooking pot, before Zo had stopped her.

Zo chewed and chewed on a stringy leaf that, even boiled, didn't want to be broken down. "Delicious."

Joshua sat down next to them after meeting with Stone and the other men in camp. Zo felt like the term "man" was used a little generously in Joshua's case, but didn't want to argue with him anymore.

"What did Stone say?" Tess asked before Zo had the chance.

Joshua picked up his wooden bowl and served himself a big helping of stew, wrinkling his nose a bit at the smell. "He's divided us into five groups with ten men to a group. Each group has a leader and the leader will report to Stone."

"Smart," said Tess as she chewed.

There was a lot of chewing going on around their little cook fire.

"I'm not a unit leader," said Joshua, "but the men in my unit are happy to have me at their side. Said at least they had someone who knew how to fight." Joshua's grin turned goofy, revealing his age, until it rested on Zo. He dropped his gaze to his humble meal and chewed.

He was happy. Validated. And he couldn't share his excitement with Zo because she had made him feel weak when he wanted to be strong. Tess reached her little hand out to touch Joshua's leg. He flinched at first but Tess wouldn't be avoided. She scooted next to him, this time touching his arm.

After whispering a blessing of comfort Zo had taught her, Tess said, "You can be brave and miss him too." She dropped her hand and went back to focusing on her food.

That night, Zo only asked Joshua once if he would give up his watch. "I could talk to Stone. He'd release you from your position. No one would think less of you for it." The idea of him sitting on the perimeter of the camp—with Boar's men waiting to strike—made her ill.

But Joshua shook his head and walked away from Zo and their dying fire to take up his watch.

Eva also took a watch shift, much to Stone's grumblings. She clutched her two favorite daggers and calmly waited for the Clanless like one might wait for a pie to bake.

Every moment of Joshua's watch was agony for Zo. She kept seeing Boar carelessly order one of his men to drag a knife across that Nameless woman's throat. And worse still, she kept imagining men wild and hungry enough to eat another human being. The Ram had some savage customs, but even *they* didn't resort to that level of inhumanity. And Joshua was out there on the fringe of the camp with only a makeshift spear for protection.

When he returned to sit on the blanket to remove his shoes for bed, Zo pretended to be asleep.

"I know you're up. You don't have a watch shift, Zo. You should be sleeping."

She kept her eyes closed and mumbled what she hoped was a convincing, "I am."

"Liar." He didn't sound mad. Just tired.

Before Zo could properly apologize for hurting the boy's feelings, a number of the torches surrounding the camp went out at exactly the same time. Dark figures retreated back into the woods.

Men shouted and a cry sliced through the night like a dagger. Then other cries joined the first and chaos broke out in the camp.

"Please, heaven. Not again!" cried Zo.

Joshua sprinted toward the perimeter of the small encampment barefooted. Zo moved to follow him when a pair of hands clamped on her shoulders. "You're no fighter, healer," said Eva. "You're too valuable to go and get yourself captured."

"But these people. I should help them." In a twisted sort of way, it was her fault the Nameless suffered tonight. How many families would be ruined before Boar left them alone? How valuable could one person be?

I'm not even a real healer anymore.

With the torches extinguished, it was impossible to tell by the shouts and clamoring of weapons exactly how deadly the attack was. With every clang and cry, Zo held Tess more fiercely to her. After the initial attack, others followed. They never engaged the Nameless for more than a few minutes before pulling back again. Fear and anticipation, their greatest weapon; darkness, their battle color.

Helpless whimpers of children and worried mothers filled the camp throughout the night. Zo wanted to grab Tess and Joshua and run, but he hadn't come back yet. And even if he had, the fight was on the perimeter, and leaving the protection of the circle meant capture, if not death.

"Why are they doing this?" Tess whimpered in between attacks. "What do they want?"

Zo kissed the top of her head, but couldn't find a voice to answer.

This madness had to end. The Nameless had endured too much already. But could Zo tear what remained of her little family apart again? Could she do that to Tess and Joshua?

Did peace always demand sacrifice?

Dawn came with the charcoal smoke of dead fires blended with the haze of fog. Joshua's wiry form cut through the morning veil and only Tess asleep in Zo's arms kept Zo from jumping up to embrace him.

He slumped wordlessly into an exhausted heap at her side and curled into a ball. The cries of the Nameless were a white noise to Zo's ears—no more noticeable than the wind brushing past her ears in subtle gusts.

Tess stirred in her arms. "Joshua?" she asked, as though her little spirit could sense his.

Letting her sister slide from her hands, Zo said, "Help me, Tess." They rolled him onto his back so they could look after his wounds. "I'll stoke the fire, if you'll start on these scratches." Zo pointed to a few shallow scrapes on his arms that were practically nothing.

A startling thought hit Zo like a knife to the gut: others would be hurt. Others would want her, a healer, to come and tend to them. Stone had said she was valuable. But what if he discovered her gift was waning? Would he be angry?

She couldn't give herself over to Boar, but she also couldn't stay here knowing she had the ability to end these people's suffering. Zo stood up and let her medical satchel fall next to Tess. "Look after him, bug. I'm going to talk to Stone."

Boar and his band stole three more people from the Nameless and wounded half a dozen others. Zo spent the better part of the day begging Stone to give in to Boar's demands, but he wouldn't listen. After another long day of hiking, Zo sat in the dirt with the rest of the Nameless refugees. Tess slept in a ball on the ground at Zo's side. Beside her, a young child wept into her mother's bosom. "I don't want to fall asleep, Mama. The bad men will come again."

Looking around at the frightened faces of the camp, Zo wondered what the Nameless would think if they discovered she was responsible for their fears? That their nightmares would end the moment they handed her over to Boar?

Zo brushed her fingers through Tess's hair. She should run dead into the woods and shout for Boar to take her in exchange for the stolen Nameless, but how could she leave her sister and Joshua? Two orphans who considered her their only family in this world.

One by one, the stars came out. Men and boys stood surrounding the perimeter of the camp, too tired to be truly effective. At some point, these men had to sleep. Joshua included. Men took their meals on foot, always carrying a weapon in their free hand. No one in the camp spoke.

The twilight hour passed. The forest was still, save for a light wind rustling the leaves and the occasional call from the crows that seemed to follow them. Zo and the rest of the Nameless waited for an attack. But it never came. Eventually, the women and children around the camp relaxed into sleep. A few men leaned on their spears, their eyes fluttering between worlds.

Joshua walked wearily toward Zo and Tess and their low-burning fire. "Stone-made-me-rest." His words slurred with exhaustion. He dropped to his knees beside Tess and fell forward. Only when his breathing dropped into a sleeping pattern did Zo close her eyes. Maybe Boar decided she wasn't worth the fight. Maybe he'd moved on.

CHAPTER SEVENTEEN

She's alive. She's alive. She's alive.

Gryphon repeated the words over and over again in his mind. He could barely slow his brain down enough to process anything else as he, Raca, and Talon raced across the mountainous terrain.

If Zo was alive, that meant Ajax had risked everything to spare her. It also meant Gabe had lied.

Gryphon thought back on his time with Gabe. Had the Wolf ever come out and said Zo was dead? It had definitely been inferred, but had he said the actual words?

Gryphon decided it didn't matter. Gabe lied by letting him believe she was gone. The snake must have seen the way he'd suffered over the past weeks. With a few simple words he could have ended Gryphon's torment.

But he hadn't. He'd even convinced Gryphon that

not returning to the Allies for Joshua was the noble thing to do.

Gryphon gasped as realization dawned.

He'd almost walked away from Joshua forever. All because Gabe wanted Zo for himself.

"He's a dead man," Gryphon growled. But his anger was still overshadowed by the plain truth that Zo was alive, or at least had been when she left the hiding tree outside Ram's Gate.

"Who's a dead man?" asked Talon.

Gryphon gathered his pack. "Never mind. Let's cover some ground."

They hadn't gone more than a mile when they heard the moans of what might have been a wounded animal. Talon darted off the game trail and after a few minutes called for Gryphon and Raca. "It's a woman," he said.

Soggy leaves and long grass made a bed for a creature so small she might have been a child were it not for her withered hands and white hair. Gryphon dropped his pack and knelt beside the old woman, taking her icy cold hands in his. She had no blanket and no supplies. She appeared to have lain down in this soft patch of earth to die.

"Who's there?" Her weak voice was rough and parched of water. She rolled over to face Gryphon.

He jumped at the sight of the Historian. She was little more than a skeleton and one of her eyes was missing, with blood dried and crusted around the swollen socket. "Troy's son? Is it really you?"

"Yes," he choked. "I'm here. I'll help you." Though she looked far beyond his help.

The Historian was Barnabas' grandmother and the former Seer of Ram's Gate. She had betrayed Barnabas by helping foster the Nameless insurrection. The last time Gryphon saw her she had helped him and his friends escape the Gate.

"The Raven. Did you warn them?" she asked.

Gryphon might have grinned at her knowledge of his dealings. She always seemed to know what he was about. But after seeing her like this…he couldn't muster a smile.

"They escaped before the Ram had a chance to reach them."

Her features lightened in obvious relief. "Joshua…" she smacked her wrinkled lips together, "the Wolf healer and her sister?"

"All fine and traveling with the Nameless refugees." He hoped.

"Barnabas wants you, Troy. He'll do anything to have you." He accepted her icy hand, her skin translucent and frail.

Gryphon didn't bother correcting her misuse of his name. Troy was his father. "I can't believe Barnabas banished you. Did he discover your work with the Nameless?"

The Historian nodded. "Told me I saw too much." She lifted a bent and bony finger to her gnarled eye socket.

How could he do such a thing to his own grandmother?

"He knows about the Allies. He knows Troy. The Ram will march…" The Historian coughed. "Preparations…for the Great Move are…"

Gryphon lifted the back of her head and poured water onto her dry tongue. "Try not to speak."

"Help me die, Troy. Please. I'm in…so much pain," she wheezed as Gryphon wiped water from her chin.

"I…I'm not brave enough." If only Zo were here. She'd know just what to do to keep this woman comfortable until she passed away peacefully.

Raca knelt down on the other side of the Historian. "I will help you pass, old one." She looked up at Gryphon, searching his face for permission.

"I…no. You can't—"

The Historian used what remained of her energy to reach up and press her palm to Gryphon's cheek. "You're like him. I've always thought so." She coughed again. "When you see him. Tell him…how proud…" her hand fell and her one eye shut.

Gryphon felt for a pulse at her neck. It came, then seconds passed before it beat again.

For the last time.

Gryphon rested his forehead against the Historian's shoulder and whispered, "Great men are mighty in life and in death." A common Ram prayer spoken over the dead as they pass from this life. Strange that it triggered a buried sense pride for a clan he had betrayed. For a people who no longer claimed him as their son. "Rest in peace, old friend. Thank you for everything."

Raca and Talon retreated a good distance from the Historian's lifeless body. He assumed they didn't want to have the old woman's spirit haunting them for the rest of their lives, or something ridiculous like that. Shaking his head, Gryphon searched the ground until he found a good-sized rock with a point strong enough to cut into the dirt. He knelt next to his unlikely mentor and dug into the ground, thinking about the Historian's final words.

The Great Move was something whispered about among the ranks of Ram mess units. It would be his people's most extreme effort to secure a bountiful future for the Ram and their posterity. Gryphon couldn't imagine his people leaving behind their mighty city and the towering Gate that defined them. But then he also couldn't imagine Barnabas exiling his aged grandmother—a woman upon whom he'd doted.

Muscles burning and mind reeling, Gryphon set his rock aside. Only then did he notice the cuts and calluses from using only a rock and his bare hands to dig the shallow grave. His minor injuries were nothing compared to the fate of so many people around him—people he hadn't been able to protect.

Afraid he'd break her, Gryphon tenderly lifted the Historian into his arms and then laid her in the earth to rest forever.

AT FIRST, Zo thought the fire catapulting across the sky was another nightmare. Only when one of the balls of woven brambles and flame crashed near them—shattering on the ground around the sleeping families—did she realize it was real. The Nameless cried out as they fought the flames. Bedrolls, packs, and the clothes upon their backs caught fire. The men stationed along the outer edge of the camp couldn't attack the demons in the woods and help their families douse the flames at the same time.

Beyond the perimeter, Zo saw Clanless clutch balls of woven wood, light it ablaze, and launch it into the camp before Stone's men could get to them.

Zo turned to find Joshua shielding Tess like a mother bird protecting her chick in the fold of her wings. Beside them, a little girl screamed as her mother rolled around on the ground, desperate to suffocate the flames eating her shirt.

Zo grabbed her blanket and jumped on the woman. When the fire was completely out, Zo pulled the woman and her child under a lone cedar tree in the center of camp. Joshua and Tess followed.

The light of the flames surrounding them was bright enough to see the exposed, melted skin on the woman's back. Her cry was barely audible over the commotion of the camp—a deep, throaty sound that bespoke a lifetime of hopeless suffering.

The fires around the camp diminished. The skies cleared, and the stars became visible to witness the suffering of those burned and the loved ones who had to stand by and watch their pain.

Zo hooked her arm around the lowest branch of the tree and pulled herself up to get a better vantage. "Bring us your injured," she called out. Jumping down, she unrolled her charred blanket on the ground. "Joshua, my kit. Tess, I'm going to need your help with—"

"The blessings," Tess interrupted. "I know." They locked eyes for a moment and a hundred small messages passed between them. Zo's apology for not telling her sister about her broken ability. Tess's forgiveness and confidence that Zo would recover.

The burned and wounded formed a line before Zo and Tess and, one by one, their wounds were tended and blessings given. By the time they finished, the first light of day crested the eastern horizon. All the color left Tess's face as she crumpled into Joshua's lap like a kitten. "Will you stay with her for a while?" Zo asked Joshua. The boy nodded—the freckles of his nose hidden under a layer of ash—and leaned his head back against the cedar tree, halfway lost to sleep already.

"I'm going to speak with Stone," said Zo. When she closed her eyes all she could see was the charred, melted skin of the innocent. People—children—paying the price for her freedom. What had happened last night would never happen again.

"No." Stone folded his arms over his muscled chest.

"But you lost another five men last night. And the injured…" Zo worked to control a tremor in her voice. "Do you not hear the cries of the Nameless? One person is not worth the lives of so many." Zo sighed. "Your only choice is to give me over to Boar. I can defend myself against him."

Stone barked a "Ha!" and resumed his pacing. "You're just a girl. Practically a child."

"Commander Laden entrusted me with the task of spying inside Ram's Gate," said Zo. "I'll handle Boar."

Somehow. The Clanless leader had proven himself to be much more clever than they'd originally thought.

Zo cleared her throat to purge another tremor of fear from her voice. "And besides, you don't need me anymore. You know how to get to the Allies without me."

Stone grumbled and paced some more while Eva studied Zo, her ever-present daggers in hand. She tilted her head to the side and said, "I think Zo is right. If she is willing to go, it isn't cruel to let her." She walked over to Zo and offered a military nod. "Let her take the honorable path."

Zo didn't know whether or not to be grateful to Eva.

Stone growled and continued making tracks in the dirt.

"This is your only option, Stone. Stop pretending like it isn't. These people you're leading aren't fighters. They're farmers. If you don't give in to Boar, you won't have anyone left to save."

Before the Nameless set out for another day of hiking, Stone called a meeting with his little army of men, leaving Zo and Tess to organize their packs and bedrolls. Zo did her best not to stare at her little sister. She wanted to memorize every angle of her face, every shade of blond in her hair. When they finished, Tess asked if she could play with some of the children in the camp until it was time to leave.

"Stick to the center of the circle," said Zo.

"I will. I will." Tess shot away like a stone from Joshua's sling.

Zo dipped her hand into a familiar pocket of her medical satchel and found a short piece of graphite and paper. The same paper and graphite she'd used to write messages to the Allies while serving as a spy inside Ram's Gate.

If she was going to give herself over to Boar and his band of Clanless, she needed to make certain Tess and Joshua would be cared for. She had a feeling Boar would come soon to see if Stone had changed his mind about making the trade and wanted to be ready. Her cold hand shook as she wrote.

Commander Laden,

I write to you not as your spy, but as your adopted ward and friend. I have been ransomed to the Clanless leader, Boar, in exchange for the lives of many Nameless. I chose to do this against Stone's will. Please accept these people—these freemen who once bore the title "Nameless." They have risked everything to join you and have more reason to fight for our cause than most, though they lack the skill. Feed them. Clothe them. But most of all, respect them.

I've told Tess and our good friend, Joshua, that I've gone ahead without them. They will be very upset to know that I've lied to them when they arrive at the Allied Camp and discover I'm not there. They are my family. If I don't find a way to return to the Allies, I need you to look after them for me. They have no one else.

For the cause of freedom,
Zo

Zo dropped the piece of graphite and massaged her hands into her face. How could she do this to them? How could she leave? Zo folded the letter and tucked it into a hidden pocket of her shirt.

"What is that?" Joshua said, startling her.

"A letter for the Commander Laden of the Allies," said Zo. "Stone's asked that I go ahead with a few of the men to ask for help against the Clanless."

"Why you?" Joshua scrunched his freckled nose.

"I'm the only one Laden will listen to, and I know where I'm going."

Joshua folded his arms. "I'm going with you."

Zo knew he wouldn't accept her lie without a fight. "Who will look after Tess if you come with me?"

"She can come too."

Zo whispered. "People are dying, Joshua. I am planning to run the entire way. Tess will slow me down. She can't come."

"It's too dangerous."

"I won't be alone, Ginger." She sighed. "Who knows? I might be safer away from this camp than in it."

Joshua seemed to consider that. "I don't like it. We shouldn't split up."

"We don't have a choice." Zo understood how he felt. When you've gone through something as traumatic as escaping the Gate, you tend to hold tighter to the people you care about in life.

"When will you go?" asked Joshua, his head sunk low.

Zo surprised him by pulling him into a tight embrace. He was just barely taller than her, making it easy to rest her head upon his shoulder. She tried to infuse love, strength, and peace into the touch but knew that nothing extended from her beyond the surface.

She couldn't even give that final gift to Joshua.

"Be careful. Please protect Tess." She released him from her hug.

Stone approached. His head was newly shaven and a dark beard filled his face from ear to ear. "Are you ready?" he asked, eyeing Joshua with a frown lost in facial hair.

Tess chased another little girl in a circle around Zo and Joshua. Zo caught her by the back of collar, earning a wild complaint from Tess. "You said I could play!" Her words died when she saw Stone.

Zo knelt in front of her sister and commanded control of her emotion. "I'm sorry, bug. There's something I need to tell you."

As Zo explained, Tess's whole body seemed to sag with the weight of Zo's lie. Images of Tess as an adolescent, as a young woman, and a grown woman flitted across her mind. She'd be so beautiful, far more lovely and warm than Zo could ever be. Zo could only imagine the lives she might save and the love she might offer those around her. No doubt she'd marry and have children one day. Maybe a little girl whom she could teach the healing art—just like their mother had taught Zo.

"I don't want you to leave me," Tess whimpered.

Zo's control broke and a tear streaked down her chin. "I know, bug. Leaving is always hard. But Joshua will stay with you. You're now officially the healer of the camp."

Tess smiled sheepishly and hugged Zo. "I'll miss you," she said.

Zo kissed them both, forcing herself not to think that this would likely be the last time she'd ever see them again. "Look out for one another."

Following Stone to the edge of camp, she remembered something important. She sprinted back to Joshua and said, "Whatever you do, don't let Tess follow me. She has a habit of doing that."

CHAPTER EIGHTEEN

Gryphon, Talon, and Raca slowed as they reached a clearing that bore all the signs of the Nameless camp. It was the second abandoned Nameless campsite they'd seen that day.

Gryphon collapsed next to a trickling stream, not bothering to take his pack from off his shoulders, too tired to even roll over and stick his face in the water to drink.

Talon and Raca didn't fare any better. "I can't keep this pace much longer," said Raca. "I just want to clean the layer of dirt from my skin and sink into my bed." She flinched, probably thinking of how she might never go back to her home, her bed, again.

"Father will secure you a very fine bed once he reaches the Allies," said Talon, reading his sister's mind.

"Yes, and he will offer it to Sani, because he is his favorite." Raca smiled as she pulled off her boots to let her small feet soak in the stream. "Ah, that's better."

Gryphon might have joined her if he had the energy to pull off his boots.

"If you stop fighting his wishes and marry, father would make sure you had a hundred fine beds," said Talon. He was back to chewing on his dried meat rations. "Then perhaps we could both stop these tiresome travels."

"I thought you were ambassadors," said Gryphon, only just realizing how strange it was for the son and daughter of a chief to be wandering around the region on their own. Chief Naat had hundreds of men at his disposal to act as emissaries. Why risk his children with such a dangerous task?

"We *are* ambassadors, but my father sends me out with Talon, partly because I'm his best archer and my brother needs looking after, but mostly because he hopes I'll find a worthy husband and Talon is the only chaperone he trusts."

Gryphon's confusion must have shown clearly on his face, because Talon jumped in to add, "Father has two heirs in me and Sani. He hopes his daughter will marry the chief of another clan to bring stability to the region and further his influence."

Raca rolled her eyes. "That's one of the reasons we went to the Allies. Father wanted me to attach myself to Commander Laden since he's become the most powerful man in the region, apart from Barnabas.

Gryphon pushed up into a seated position and dropped his water skin into the stream. "How did you do?"

Raca laughed. Not an unpleasant sound. "Commander Laden is old enough to be my father. Besides, I didn't get the impression that he was looking for a wife."

Gryphon had a difficult time believing Laden wouldn't notice Raca. She was young and very pretty. She didn't seem like the type that would lead men to disinterest.

Raca said, "His mind is only for his cause. He's obsessed with overthrowing Barnabas. He eats, drinks, and sleeps it. I admire his drive, but I want a husband closer to my own age."

She held Gryphon's gaze and then quickly looked away. "They say that Murtog's wife was killed in the last Ram raid."

"The Kodiak Chief would squish you!" said Talon.

Raca grabbed a handful of mud and flung it in her brother's face. "Eww."

Talon laughed, unrepentant, and scraped mud off his cheek. "The Kodiak are too wild. Besides, I've heard that a good portion of them left the caves. The clan is scattered. Some men, when their families were murdered or taken as slaves, joined the Clanless. Others traveled to the Allies. But Murtog refuses to leave his caves."

"Just like your father refused to leave the Nest," said Gryphon.

Raca shrugged. "People cling to tradition and fear change. That's what makes your flight from the Ram so remarkable, Gryphon." She tugged on her boots and climbed to her feet. "You didn't have to leave, but you loved Zo enough to change the world for her."

Gryphon's cheeks reddened. "I haven't changed the world."

Raca frowned. "Right now we are tracking people who are free because of you. You did that for Zo, am I right? You left your home, your people, your family…all for her."

"Enough." Gryphon didn't want to be reminded about what he left behind. His pride. His family home and friends. His own mother. They would all hate him now.

"You changed the world for her." She nodded, satisfied that her point was made.

Gryphon cleared his throat. "These tracks are only about a day old. We should intercept them tomorrow." He wandered around the woods picking up dead branches and snapping them over his knee to break them down for firewood.

"She's lucky to have you," said Raca.

* * *

BOAR WAITED FOR STONE, Zo, and a small contingent of weary Nameless men a mile outside the charred remains of camp. They guarded eight Nameless who knelt in their midst, their hands bound behind their backs. Most of the Nameless captives' clothes and all of their shoes were missing, stolen by the desperate Clanless.

Only a Clanless would bother stealing the shoes of a former slave.

At Stone's command, the handful of men that acted as his guard stopped twenty yards away. Zo stepped up to Stone's side with her hands clasped in front of her, arms locked straight and knuckles white with fear.

"You came," said Boar. His gaze rested on Zo, and he showed his yellow teeth in a frightening grin. "I'm glad." He gestured down to the Nameless at his feet. "I think they're glad, as well."

"We will make the trade, Boar, but you stole nine of my men. I only count eight."

"I didn't realize Nameless could count," sneered Boar. Then he shrugged like it didn't matter. "Our agreement changed when you refused me. I planned to kill one of your men every night you prolonged our arrangement." He nudged one of the men on the ground with his boot. "Like I said, this lot is glad to see you."

"You filthy—"

"Take your men and leave the girl, and my band of Clanless will not bother you anymore." He almost sang his offer. His smile was so wrong that Zo took an involuntary step backward. Was this man psychotic?

Stone's skin turned a reddish hue. The muscles in his neck and jaw flared like he'd enjoy nothing better than to detach Boar's head from his neck.

Zo touched Stone's shoulder, trying to calm him before he tried to kill Boar with his bare hands. "Do this for Eva, Stone. Do it for your men and those suffering in camp."

Stone nodded and exhaled out his nose, but couldn't manage to speak, so Zo spoke for him. "We have a deal," Zo said. "I will go with you, but first you need to let our men go."

Boar licked his lips. He flicked his wrist at one of his men—the same gesture he gave when he had the Nameless woman's throat slit.

"Don't!" cried Zo.

But instead of cutting another throat, Stone's men cut the ropes binding the Nameless. The men struggled to their bare feet.

"Good," said Boar. "Now walk to me, my dear." He rubbed the side of his nose with his thumb and licked his lips again.

Zo took one steadying breath then reached inside her shirt pocket and handed her letter to Stone. "Give this to Commander Laden. It explains everything and will ensure a future for the Nameless, as well as Tess and Joshua."

Stone's eyes asked forgiveness as he accepted the missive.

"Walk!" shouted Boar.

Zo flinched under the command but hiked up her pack and stepped away from Stone and his guard. The walk lasted a lifetime. Each step marked a hundred days with those she loved that she might never experience. A memory of time wasted that she'd never get back. She should have told Tess more stories about their parents. Why didn't she teach her the lullabies their mother used to sing to them when they were small? Tess would never sing them to her children. Those precious memories would die with Zo.

Zo stopped just outside of Boar's reach. "Now let them go."

Boar nodded and the Nameless men scrambled away from their wild captors. Zo felt their stares at her back. Their guilt. Their relief.

Boar held out his hand, like he was talking to a young

child or perhaps a very close friend. "Come along, Healer. We have ground to cover."

Zo would rather swallow a knife than take his hand. But there was a wild glint to his eyes. Unsteadiness in his outstretched hand. For some reason, the cruel side of Boar didn't frighten her as much as the calm and calculated side. She had a distinct impression that the longer she played the docile creature the longer she might live.

And she needed to live to teach Tess those lullabies.

Zo reached out and accepted Boar's hand.

CHAPTER NINETEEN

The next morning Gryphon ran with more energy than he had since leaving the Nest. Today he would see Zo and Joshua and Tess. *My family.*

It was strange how people had the ability to create holes in your life. With them, he knew the emptiness he'd felt for abandoning his clan would be filled. A little voice in the back of his head reminded him that he would still never be welcome with the Allies, but he shoved the thought aside. There was too much to be grateful for today to worry about the trials of tomorrow. With the people he cared for by his side, everything would find its way of working out. It simply would.

Gryphon reached the crest of a hill and, not three hundred yards away, saw the Nameless caravan trekking through the sparse, blackened forest. "Praise heaven." Finally, he'd see Zo and mark the task of emotionally bringing her back from the dead complete. He took off at a full sprint, leaving Raca and Talon to trail behind.

"Zo! Joshua!" He shouted with all the breath he could spare. "Tess!"

People from the Nameless caravan stopped and turned back. When they saw him closing the distance, some cowered while others ran around in a panic. Gryphon couldn't blame them. He likely appeared as wild as any Clanless they'd encountered on their journey south. A motley line of men formed a barrier between Gryphon and the rest of the people. They linked rudimentary shields and held Ram spears in their hands. All aimed at his chest.

Gryphon stopped twenty yards away with hands raised to show he held no weapon. He gaped at the men before him—former slaves of his people—poorly mimicking Ram formation. Talon and Raca appeared beside him, breathing hard.

Before anyone had the chance to exchange words, a redheaded boy burst through the line of men, knocking one Nameless to the ground as he sprinted for Gryphon. "I knew you were alive! I told her you were! I knew it!"

Another, higher-pitched shout sounded from behind the line of men and then Tess appeared on hands and knees, crawling between the legs of bewildered men who only now seemed to recognize Gryphon.

Tess scrambled to her feet and ran toward him just as Joshua tackled Gryphon to the ground. The boy wept openly, unable to wipe his tears fast enough. "Gabe told Zo they killed you. She hasn't been herself. Everything is going to be all right now."

Tess jumped and squealed as she landed on the pile of Ram. Gryphon wrapped her into a big hug then held her at arm's length to get a better look at the enormous smile that seemed to reach every corner of her tiny face. Her striking eyes, so characteristic of a Wolf, shone through the dirt on her cheeks. Eyes like her sister's, but with just a bit more green. "You precious girl." He kissed her forehead and pulled her in for another hug. "I'm so relieved you're safe."

Tess put her hands on his cheeks and whispered a little blessing. Feelings of peace and tranquility emanated from her small hands.

"You're improving, little one." Gryphon tapped her on the nose and the spell was broken.

"I've needed to," said Tess. She cupped her hand to Gryphon's ear. "Zo's not well. She's losing her gift, but she doesn't want anyone else to know. Not even me."

Zo was a remarkable healer. The idea of her losing her gift seemed about as likely as the sun setting tonight and not rising tomorrow. Healing was a part of her.

"Where is she, bug?" Gryphon scanned the crowd of Nameless that had gathered. It was strange that Zo hadn't come out to meet him like Joshua and Tess. Did she regret kissing him? Did he complicate things with Gabe so much that she wished he'd never returned? The thought didn't feel true, but then neither did the idea of Zo caring for him to the degree he cared for her.

Stone stood at the front of the group of Nameless refugees with Eva at his side. The grim look on the crazy leader's face made the bottom of Gryphon's stomach drop out. He climbed to his feet with Tess and Joshua still firmly planted at his sides, and together they walked to meet Stone.

"Gryphon," said Stone, his tone matching his name. "We need to talk."

BOAR'S HAND was a dead fish, cold and moist. He led Zo through the woods with the small contingent of men surrounding them. A handful of larger men with shaved heads and full beards clustered at the rear of the pack. They constantly glanced over their shoulders to see if they were being followed.

"No one will come for me. You can tell your men to relax."

Boar smiled. "I should go back and kill every one of them if they *don't* make an attempt to get you back." He shook his head. "You are a valuable asset, my dear. A young Wolf healer is a fine prize. But a young Wolf healer hunted by the most powerful man in the region is a prize even greater than all the gems in the Kodiak Caves. The Nameless are fools for letting you go."

"How do you know about Barnabas?" asked Zo, stunned.

"I helped get the information out of one of his scouts a few days ago."

Was that why they hadn't seen any other scouts? Had Boar's band of Clanless killed them?

"So you're taking me back to Ram's Gate?" She kept her face forward, unwilling to so much as look at the man who still insisted on holding her hand. "What do you hope to gain from Barnabas?" asked Zo.

The Gate! She couldn't go back to that place. She couldn't!

Boar licked his chapped and peeling lips. "My citizenship."

"And your men?" Zo looked around at the concave faces of the Clanless.

"Theirs too," grunted Boar, but something about his tone was off. Did the others not hear the lie or were they blinded by the hope of belonging to the most powerful clan in the region? Barnabas would never accept anyone other than a Ram into his clan unless they offered themselves up as Nameless. Several of the men encircling them looked like they might pass for Ram, but the giants in the back of the group were decidedly Kodiak in origin. They'd be killed the moment they passed through the gate.

The smell of fire warned that Boar's camp was nearby. They reached a steep rock wall, and Boar released her hand as he navigated the rock face. When he reached the top shelf, about twenty feet up, he called, "Your turn, my dear," his smile more menacing than a hundred threats. "That is, unless you'd like one of my men to help you?"

The idea of any of these men touching her propelled her to the wall. She managed the climb without any difficulty and dusted off her hands at the top.

"Such valuable hands," said Boar. "I hear the man who entices a healer is wealthy for life." He stared at her hands entranced, then blinked hard and shook his head. "I felt your sister's touch. Her little hands brought me a great deal of peace. I can't imagine what a more experienced healer might be able to do." He licked his chapped lips again and smiled. "Perhaps you'll show me before I return you to Barnabas."

The urge to spit in Boar's face nearly overtook her. Instead, she ignored him and scanned the horizon and the view their raised position offered. She felt his stare. It was a sticky film on her skin, leaving her violated and somehow worthless.

"This way, my dove." The shelf narrowed as it wrapped around a corner then opened up wide enough to accommodate Boar's band of Clanless. Cook fires smoldered as clusters of haggard men looked up at Zo. Most of the men were large, carrying the round faces and dark eyes of the Kodiak clan. They wore their long, coarse hair in a mass of disheveled braids down the center of their backs.

Most barely spared a glance for Zo.

Boar led her to a small tent in the far corner of the shelf, and with a flourish, opened the flap for her to enter. "A place to rest while we prepare to leave."

Zo eyed the dark little space and hugged her arms to her chest. "I'm not going in there."

Boar's smile slipped in slow motion. The skin around his neck reddened and a few of the men in the camp climbed to their feet.

A thousand chills ran the length of Zo's spine as Boar began to shake.

"Please go, miss," a quiet voice called from somewhere in the camp.

Boar's head snapped around. "Who said that?" Spittle flew from his mouth.

No one spoke. A few men backed away.

Boar leapt to the Clanless man closest to him and threw his knee into the man's stomach even though the man hadn't done a thing to deserve it. As the victim groaned and sunk to his knees, Boar said, "No one talks to her. Am I understood? No one!"

The men in his camp nodded and muttered, "Yes, sir," then went back to their business, doing their best to pretend Zo wasn't there.

"*Kindly* get in the tent, Healer."

Zo dropped to her knees and crawled into the dark space that reeked of man-sweat and fire. The shelter was only large enough for one. Facing the flap opening, she scooted backward, not daring to take her eyes off the door of the tent until her back met cold mountain rock.

This would be a horrible place to die.

CHAPTER TWENTY

"What do you mean, she's not here?" Gryphon crowded Stone, getting right in his face. He knew the Nameless revolutionary was a volatile man, but Gryphon welcomed the challenge as adrenaline coursed throughout his body. She was supposed to be here. He'd staked all of his hopes on it.

Stone crossed his arms. "Back up, Ram, and I'll tell you."

"I'll kill you, Stone." An open threat that didn't make any sense, but Gryphon was past logical reasoning. He took a step back and pulled the dagger from his belt the Raven had gifted him. "Talk."

Suddenly a knife pricked the skin of his back shoulder. "Relax, Gryph. And put your blade away. We are all on the same side now." Eva walked around Gryphon to stand next to Stone. She spun the knife around her fingers like she used to do during training sessions when they were little. Ever the showoff.

Gryphon sighed and sheathed his knife, embarrassed by his volatile temper. "I'm sorry."

Eva nodded and sheathed her own blade. She held out her hand to Stone and the large Nameless set a folded piece of paper in it. Eva handed the paper over to Gryphon.

"What is this?" Gryphon asked.

"A letter written by Zo for Commander Laden. It explains everything." Eva gestured to the paper. "Open it. Read it."

Gryphon handed the letter back to Eva and frowned. "I don't know how to read." Reading was taught in the home, but Gryphon's mother hadn't bothered teaching him the skill. She'd always said a man was judged more by his physical ability than his intellect. Looking back, Gryphon wondered if it had been just another way to punish him for looking too much like his father or if it was simply blatant neglect. He couldn't decide which answer hurt more.

Eva plucked the letter from his hands and opened it. Gryphon craned over her shoulder just to see Zo's script.

When Eva read, *"I have been ransomed to the Clanless leader, Boar, in exchange for the lives of many Nameless. I chose to do this against Stone's will,"* Gryphon grabbed the letter from her and squinted at the words as if he could somehow make them say something different.

His nostrils flared as he fought to maintain control. "How long ago?"

Stone said, "A day. My scout says they headed north." *Back toward Ram's Gate.*

"The Nameless were being taken every night. Many

people were burned in a fire attack. Boar threatened to hunt us all down, picking us off little by little until we delivered Zo," said Stone. "I refused him, but after nearly ten men were taken, Zo couldn't stand it any longer."

"So you let her go," said Gryphon.

"Zo is the reason we are all free." Stone got in Gryphon's face this time. "I would never trade a human being like livestock. I've lived that life, Ram. You, who have kept slaves, have no place to judge me."

"Stop." Eva wormed her way in between Stone and Gryphon. "Arguing will not bring her back."

She was right and Gryphon didn't want to waste another moment in this camp. "What can you tell me about Boar? How many does he command? What are his possible weaknesses? Strengths?"

Gryphon listened to Stone's retelling of his encounters with Boar. How he didn't hesitate to kill the Nameless woman when Stone wouldn't trade Zo for Ram weapons. His cunning lies. How they were desperate enough in their hunger to eat other people to survive starvation. His strange fascination with Zo.

Gryphon pinched the bridge of his nose, forcing away his fears. What horrors was she facing by the hands of this wild man? "You mentioned Ram weapons. Do you still have some?" asked Gryphon.

Stone nodded and led him to a small cart of tools and weapons that they'd managed to bring from the Gate. Gryphon lifted the familiar weight of a Ram shield and a small surge of hope filled him. He strapped a short sword to his hip and, with reverence, picked up a metal-tipped spear with his throwing hand. Looking down the shaft, he found the oiled wood straight. An accurate tool. Gryphon itched to launch it, to feel the familiar flip of his wrist as he released the perfectly balanced weapon.

"I can spare to send a few men with you," said Stone.

Gryphon shook his head, still studying the length of the spear. "I only need one." Then to Eva he said, "Where is Joshua?"

At Gryphon's request, Talon and Raca agreed to help escort the Nameless refugees to the Allied Camp. But as they prepared to leave, Raca returned without her older brother. "Need any help?" she asked.

"Only a promise that you'll look after Tess until we return," Gryphon said as he and Joshua filled their packs with some of Stone's limited supplies.

"We're only a day and a half 's journey from the Allies. She'll be fine. I can't say the same for you and the boy."

Joshua didn't raise his head from his task but scowled just the same. He didn't like being referred to as a boy, even though he was one.

"You should take me with you." Raca reached out and touched Gryphon's sleeve, the gentle contact that, for some reason, made him freeze. He looked up from his pack and met her dark eyes. Eyes very different from Zo's, but beautiful all the same.

"My bow could save your life." She swallowed and dropped her gaze.

Gryphon felt Joshua studying them and stepped away from Raca's touch. "Thank you, but Joshua and I can handle ourselves. We'll get Zo back."

Raca nodded. "Be careful." She walked away without a second glance.

Stone did his best to direct them to the meeting place where he last saw Zo before Boar led her away. It wasn't hard to find, and once they did, the jumble of tracks made it difficult to distinguish Zo's footprints from the rest.

Gryphon walked around the perimeter of the tracks, not wanting to disturb any evidence that might help them get Zo back. A smaller set of footprints stood in the midst of what he guessed to be ten men.

Ten men. Zo without protection. They didn't have much time. But she was alive a day ago, and if what Talon and Raca said about Boar was true, he would keep her alive, so long as he managed his men.

"We have our tracks, Joshua," said Gryphon.

Joshua nodded. "I'm right behind you."

They ran until the sun was high above their heads. "Zo always does this!" said Joshua. "She puts herself in danger to protect me." He mumbled something about her not thinking him capable.

"You're not much better," said Gryphon. "At least she didn't stab herself in the stomach." Gryphon cringed as the image of Joshua and Zo in the prizefighting ring flooded his memories. The Ram punished Gryphon for his crimes against the clan by putting the two people he cared for most in the ring. Only one was allowed to leave alive.

"That was different!"

"Ha!" Gryphon barked as they secured their packs. Joshua slid his weapons in place and tucked his trusted sling into the leather holster Gryphon made for him when he turned eleven. It secured to his thigh with a leather strap so not to get in the way of other weapons. Gryphon knew for a fact that Joshua carried a pocketful of small rocks wherever he went, even though most boys his age preferred a knife. Not only could the boy knock a squirrel from a tree or stun a rabbit before it found its den, he could actually aim to preserve the meat—a difficult feat for such a small, fast target.

"Being placed in that ring with Zo was a very difficult situation," said Gryphon, slipping into his mentoring voice. "Did you have any other options beyond killing yourself?" He planted a hand on a partially felled tree trunk and jumped over the log.

"I wasn't thinking about that!" said Joshua. "All I could think about was saving Zo. One of us had to die. I didn't want it to be her."

Gryphon nodded, catching the resentment in Joshua's tone. The boy was growing in his skill, but he still jumped to the defensive whenever Gryphon tried to correct him. "There was nothing you could do? No resources you could have exploited?"

"Too much was happening. Everyone watched us, cheering and calling for blood. I had no other option."

"But looking back, can you find a solution that wasn't obvious to you before?"

Joshua groaned. "Why does that matter now? Nothing I think of now will change the past."

"But it could prepare you for hard decisions in the future." Gryphon tapped Joshua's arm and they slowed to a stop. He tossed Joshua his water skin then leaned against a thick tree trunk with arms folded across his chest. "Think."

Gryphon had trained Joshua better than to argue with the exercise. This line of questioning was common practice for the pair.

"I could have fought her."

Gryphon nodded encouragement, knowing the boy took a minute or two to warm up.

"I could have tried to reason with the guards that threw us into the ring…maybe offer them money…or something else of more value to them than my life." He started pacing in front of Gryphon, using his hands to help him communicate. "I had information that was valuable. Maybe if I demanded to see the Seer it would have bought us more time."

Gryphon nodded. "If you took that gamble and were given the chance to speak to the Seer, what would you have told her?" asked Gryphon.

"Nothing. I would have kept my secrets. The whole thing would be a ploy to get us out of the ring."

"What if I hadn't come for you in time? What if you were tortured for information?"

"You would have come. You always find a way."

"What if I didn't?"

"I could handle a little torture." Joshua shrugged. "Dying is dying. People do it every day."

Gryphon frowned. "What you did for Zo in that prizefight was beyond brave. It was the most selfless thing I can imagine a person doing. But don't toss around ideas of torture like it wouldn't affect you. That's flippant and irresponsible."

"*Sorry*," said Joshua, though he clearly wasn't.

"Let's try again. What would you do if they tried to torture you for information?"

"I'D FIGHT THEM, okay? I'd use everything you've ever taught me to fight them. I'd find a weakness and exploit it. I'd survive!" he yelled. "Happy?"

Gryphon lost his battle to suppress a smile. "Good answer."

He stowed his water skin and hiked up his pack. "No more throwing yourself into danger. You've already proven your courage. Now let's concentrate on your skill and intellect." He ruffled Joshua's red hair and together they ran north.

DURING THE FIRST hour of sitting in Boar's dark tent, Zo flinched every time she heard the Clanless leader's voice. After the second hour, Zo inched to the front of the tent and peeked out of the narrow opening to study the men in the camp. She figured Boar couldn't be that angry with her as long as she stayed inside.

Men milled around the camp, some sharpening weapons, others breaking down ragged tents. Very few of the men wore wool or woven material. Instead, their bodies were cover in worn leather and fur. Their skin was the kind of brown that might have washed away with a hot bath or some time out of the sun.

How would she ever escape so many men?

Zo didn't see Boar among the Clanless. The way he talked about her value, Zo didn't think he'd leave her alone for long. Not a single man so much as looked in her direction, which either proved their dedication to their tasks or their fear of Boar.

How could men so large, with such an advantage in numbers, fear Boar? It didn't make any sense, unless they truly believed Boar's lie that he could buy their membership into the Ram Clan.

One of the men left his place by a fire, looked over his shoulder, then walked toward Boar's tent. Some men hissed at him to stop, exchanging worried glances, but no one followed him.

Zo backed into the tent as the Clanless man drew near. They were cannibals, desperate men who couldn't be trusted.

"Please, miss. I won't hurt you." He raised his palms to placate her and looked over his shoulder again, checking for Boar. Gray hair blended with the black around his ears, but thick muscles corded his meaty arms. "I am Ikatou. My wife and daughters were taken as slaves in a Ram raid." He looked over his shoulder again.

Zo noticed that a few men had wandered to the corner of the shelf, perhaps to act as lookout for their friend.

"I hear you were a Nameless. You might know my family." He rattled off a list of names that didn't mean anything to Zo.

She shook her head. "I'm sorry. I don't know them."

The large man's shoulders slumped, as his whole body caved inward with disappointment. "Of course." He walked back toward the fire, but Zo called after him. "Wait."

He whipped around and held a finger to his lips. More men stopped what they were doing to stare at the exchange. "Boar is lying to you," she said. "I've lived inside the Gate and I know Barnabas. He will never respect Kodiak, Raven, or Wolf. He would likely enslave you, or if you show any resistance, kill you before you had a chance to defend yourselves."

Men near on the opposite end of the shelf waved Ikatou over. Someone was coming.

"You're walking to your deaths," Zo hissed as Ikatou and the rest of the men went back to their work. A few of the men Boar kept close to him turned the corner, followed by Boar himself. Zo inched to the back of the foul-smelling tent and hugged her knees to her chest.

Boar barked orders too muffled by the tent for Zo to discern. Then a head popped in front of the tent opening, causing Zo to gasp. A stone jabbed against her spine as she pressed her back more firmly to the mountainside.

"My scouts have returned. Time to move." Boar extended his hand to her like he had earlier that day, a sickly smile plastered on his red-blotched face.

Zo couldn't bring herself to move toward him. "Back with the Nameless refugees, you said your people ate human flesh to survive. It was a lie to get us to fear you, wasn't it?" She didn't know why it mattered at this point —she was too valuable to kill—but she needed to know. She couldn't imagine a man like Ikatou doing such a thing.

Boar's smile widened. "The more the Nameless feared my band, the more likely Stone would make a trade."

"Clever," said Zo. She placed her hand in Boar's and let him help her from the tent. As always, his hand was cold and moist. Would she be forced to hold it like a small child all the way to Ram's Gate?

Out of the corner of her eye, Zo caught Ikatou whispering to a few of the other Clanless. Other Kodiak, if she wasn't mistaken.

Boar had fooled the Nameless, but she could be clever too.

If she could turn enough of them against Boar, she might have a chance of escaping before they reached the Gate. She might even convince the Clanless to join Laden's cause in the process.

What would Laden think if she returned with a small contingent of Clanless and a few hundred Nameless? Hopefully it would be enough to appease him when she told him that she didn't want to fight the Ram anymore.

If she survived this mess, she would take Tess and Joshua to the Valley of Wolves and do her best to forget any of this ever happened.

CHAPTER TWENTY-ONE

W hen the sky turned a murky gray and the sun dipped below the mountainous horizon, smoke from a fire rose above the trees only a few hundred yards away.

"Campfire," said Joshua, pointing at the smoke before Gryphon had the chance to point it out himself.

"Observant." Not being aware of his surroundings had always been one of Joshua's weaknesses. As they traveled toward the fire, Gryphon slowed their pace.

"What do we know about them?" asked Gryphon.

"Nothing. We haven't seen them yet." Joshua's voice was too loud.

Gryphon turned back to him and held a finger to his lips, then whispered, "We know they have a fire."

Joshua nodded, picking up the thread Gryphon left for him. "Which means they're either cooking food or burning for warmth. They don't need it for light yet."

Gryphon nodded. "Go on."

"They are not threatened by others knowing their location or they aren't used to traveling outside of a clan and don't know any better."

"Which is more likely?"

Joshua answered, "They're not afraid."

"Which means?"

"They're strong. Probably stronger than us."

Gryphon smiled though Joshua couldn't see it from his position in front of him.

Joshua whispered, "But overconfidence is also a form of weakness. It will be harder for them to spot us, and their fire will help us see them clearly."

"Excellent, kid."

Gryphon knew he wasn't perfect, but the idea of someone else training Joshua in the ways of manhood made him ill. They belonged together, and somehow, once they rescued Zo and got back to the Allies, Gryphon would find a way to convince Commander Laden to let him stay. With Zo, Tess, Joshua …

And Gabe.

Gryphon swallowed the acrid anger rolling up his throat. Gabe. Zo cared for the lying Wolf. Gryphon had seen her love for him when he and Gabe fought each other in the ring. He'd even spared Gabe's life for Zo's sake. Now he wanted nothing more than to take it away.

As they approached the camp, the deep tones of male voices made him pause. Gryphon held up a fist. "With me," he whispered.

Joshua had the wild look he sometimes got when he wanted to argue. Standard practice would be to split up, Gryphon circling the perimeter in one direction and

Joshua the other. But Gryphon wasn't ready to split up. The boy's life was worth a great deal more than any information they could gather from separating.

Gryphon inched forward, careful with his steps. Joshua shadowed him so closely he trod on the heel of Gryphon's boot. One glance at the boy was all the scolding he needed. A few more steps and the foliage divided enough to offer a decent view of the camp.

What Gryphon saw made him flex his hands around a nearby branch.

Joshua gasped and then covered his mouth with both hands as Gryphon pushed his head down to duck beneath thicker foliage.

One of the men in the camp turned his head in their direction, but after a few moments seemed to give up on the notion that he'd heard anything.

Gryphon raised his head enough to survey the camp, practically shaking with the need to launch his spear into Zander's gut. All of his mess brothers gathered around a fire. Their once clean-shaven faces now bore weeks of growth. Zander sharpened the metal tip of his spear while others mumbled conversation too quiet for Gryphon to hear. Just seeing their round shields and their familiar faces made Gryphon want to waltz into the camp and put an arm around his brothers and at the same time break every one of their necks. When you belonged to a mess, you put your life in your brothers' hands almost every single day. Those bonds ran deep. Maybe even deeper than blood. And even if they hadn't liked it, they had all betrayed him on Barnabas' order.

Ajax sat apart from the rest of his mess brothers. He

held his head in his hands with elbows resting heavily on knees. Was he thinking about his young family? Sara, his wife, must be frantic with the task of keeping their new baby safe from the Seer. Ajax's baby was born with a deformity of the lip. Zo said she could help him with surgery, but a baby born outside of perfection in the Gate was not given such opportunities at life.

Gryphon wished he could talk to Ajax. Comfort him. Thank him for not killing Zo like he'd been ordered. He'd proven himself a true friend. More loyal to Gryphon than even his own clan.

Zander was a different case.

"Are they still after you?" Joshua's whisper barely reached even Gryphon's ears.

Gryphon nodded but put a fist to the ground. Now wasn't the time for talking.

"The Nameless tracks lead south," said Lincoln—one of Gryphon's mess brothers—as he entered the clearing from the other direction. Lincoln was known for his knowledge of the region as the mess unit's navigator. "But there is another set of tracks that leads north. Smaller in number. Probably a Clanless group."

Gryphon held his breath, shaken by how close they had come to being discovered.

Zander nodded. "For now we follow the Nameless. Gryphon and his little flock of Raven will head in that direction. They'll have decided on a place to meet up with the rest of the Birds."

What would happen if Zander and the rest of his mess followed the Nameless tracks all the way to the Allied Camp? His brothers were strong, but one mess unit couldn't withstand the might of the entire Allied resistance. They were walking to their deaths. His fear for their wellbeing mingled with his hatred. Strange that love and hate could be felt at the same time for the same people. He'd felt that for Zo when he first learned of her betrayal in sending bottles downriver to his enemies. He felt it for his father every day of his life.

Regardless of his confused emotions, Gryphon couldn't let them reach the Allies. If they weren't spotted, they'd learn Commander Laden's location and would surely deliver that information to Barnabas.

He couldn't let that happen.

Gryphon grimaced and gave the signal for them to leave. There was no sense in fighting them with Joshua present. Zo was their first priority now. He would have to decide what to do about his brothers later. For now, he needed to get as far away from them as possible.

***

THE ONLY TIME Boar released Zo's hand was to drink from his water skin or point orders to his band of men. And as soon as he finished, he greedily took it again, like she was his oxygen, the only thing keeping him alive. Whether out of perverse affection or fear that she'd escape, she didn't know. Even though his touch made her ill, Zo always accepted his hand. She'd save her rebellion. Bottle it up and strike when opportunity provided a real chance for escape.

The same eight men surrounded her and Boar as they trekked north, leaving a contingent of men to walk at the tail of the group, Ikatou and his Kodiak friends among them.

Boar practically hissed if any of the men so much as looked at Zo. A viper protecting its prey. She might have felt safe with the man if he weren't carefully leading her to her torture and certain.

They approached a small river crossing; a high plank of timber ran from bank to bank above the water. "The wood is only strong enough for one," Boar explained to Zo in a voice one might use with a small child.

Zo fought the urge to roll her eyes. A few of Boar's men walked ahead over the makeshift bridge. When it was Zo's turn, Boar released his grip on her hand. "I'll carry your satchel." He held out his hand for Zo's medical kit.

"I can manage," said Zo.

Boar's lips pressed into a firm line and his nostrils flared, reminding Zo exactly how dangerous the man could be. She didn't want his grubby hands touching something that belonged to her mother, but instinct insisted she hand it over before his fiery temper flared.

"Fine." She lifted the leather strap off her shoulder and reluctantly gave him her most prized physical possession. Wiping the sweat of his touch off on her pants, she stepped onto the plank.

"Hold the other end steady," shouted Boar. His men fell over themselves to obey, one even going so far as to climb down the steep bank and brace the board in ankle-deep water.

Zo stretched her arms out wide for balance and

walked toward the center of the plank, the river rushing beneath her.

A dangerous idea came to her as she reached the deepest part of the river. She looked down at the water then back at Boar and the rest of the men crowded behind him, waiting for their turn to cross.

Boar waved her onward as he paced the riverbank. "Just keep going. You're nearly there." The breeze coming off the water made his dark hair fly around his grizzled face.

Zo wasn't the strongest swimmer, and the chance of her plan actually working was slim at best. But a slim chance was better than any other option available to her. If she didn't escape these men before they reached Ram territory she was as good as dead anyway.

She took a teetering step forward and flailed her arms, pretending to try and save her balance.

Boar shouted something in panic and lunged after her onto plank, but didn't make it two steps before Zo hit the water. The water came over her head, so cold that she bit through her tongue. Her body cartwheeled in the strong current. Rocks jabbed her on all sides. When her feet finally found purchase on the muddy floor, she pushed off and was rewarded with a breath of air before the river pulled her back down. Her back connected with a large rock and the spinning cycle of chaos ensued once more before she managed another breath, but it wasn't enough to satisfy her burning lungs.

I don't want to die, she thought as she spun through the rapid moving water. *I don't want to die!*

As if in response to her mental plea, someone

grabbed her arm and then her waist. Together Zo and the man holding her pushed off the ground for air. "Swim to the side!" came the strangled voice of Boar, her rescuer.

Zo closed her eyes, kicked her legs, and allowed herself to be grateful to leave the river, even at the hands of her enemy.

The current was less violent near the bank. Zo's feet found purchase on the rocky floor. She reached to accept the hand of one of Boar's men, who yanked her from what could have been a watery grave.

Panting and soaked to the bone, Zo collapsed onto the ground with her cheek pressed into the dirt. The Clanless pulled Boar out of the water next. His hair and clothes hung from his trim frame like matted fur on a wet dog. A long cut stretched across his forehead like a misplaced frown. Blood gushed down his face and into his eyes like red tears. Every muscle in his shoulders and arms flexed as he stomped toward Zo.

He fell before he reached her.

A few of his men rushed to his side. Another thrust Zo's medical satchel at her and ordered, "Help him."

Zo's icy hands hugged her mother's satchel to her chest. "No," she said, scrambling backward. She bumped into the chest of another of Boar's men. She looked over at Boar sprawled out on the ground then down at the satchel in her arms. A clear memory of her mother sprang to the forefront of her mind.

Zo was young, maybe eight or nine years old. Her family had a few sheep that they used for wool and milk. Zo remembered them well because it was her job to care for them. They followed her around whenever she entered their pen. If she turned left, they turned left. If she ran, they ran. It was one of her favorite forms of entertainment.

Until they were slaughtered in a raid.

One of the men who committed the crime was injured and

Zo's mother called for him to be brought to her healing tent. Zo cried and cried over the loss of her sheep and when she learned what her mother had done, she stormed into her mother's healing tent and yelled, "Don't heal him, Mama! He killed my sheep."

Zo would never forget the disappointment she saw on her mother's face that day.

"I am not this man's executioner, Zo," she said. "I am a healer. If I do nothing I am as guilty as he is."

Even as a child, Zo didn't have her mother's humanity. Her incomprehensible ability to love and forgive. Besides, this wasn't about revenge over sheep, it was about self-preservation. Boar's injury might be the key to her escape.

Zo fought a niggling voice in her head that wouldn't be dismissed. *"Heal him."* It was absurd and utterly foolish, but as those two words gently penetrated her consciousness, a blanket of warmth spread over her body. *"Heal him."* It was her mother's voice. She'd forgotten just how soothing it could be. Deep and smooth and achingly beautiful. Zo clasped her hands and pressed them to her chest. Remembering brought so much pain, but strangely, comfort too.

Zo raised her head to the heavens, wiped at a tear, and sighed. *This is for you, Mother.*

"Step away from him," she ordered. The men parted to give her space. "Someone build a fire. I need boiling water. And you might as well set up camp. We're done traveling for the day."

Zo tuned out the clamor of men at work around her and gave Boar her full attention. Placing clean linen from her satchel on his forehead, she leaned over him to apply pressure and said, "I'm going to try to help you. But something inside me is broken, and I have no love for you." Blood soaked the cloth. She pressed harder. "It will be difficult."

She knew her words likely didn't make much sense to Boar. He closed his eyes at her touch and said, "I'm still taking you to the Ram."

Zo used her free hand to rummage through her kit. "I know."

CHAPTER TWENTY-TWO

Gryphon divided his time between watching their backs and answering Joshua's endless questions about his time spent in the Nest. Several times he had to remind the boy to keep his voice down. This was especially true when Gryphon told Joshua about Sani.

"What?" He practically shouted, earning him a stern look from Gryphon.

He pressed both hands over his own mouth, his cheeks reddening in chagrin. "Sorry," he whispered. "But you're telling me a kid my age thinks he's responsible for protecting you?"

Gryphon nodded, and then scanned the woods once more. They were too quiet for his liking, but then that might have been Joshua's fault. "He calls himself my *'Atiin* and claims that until he saves my life, he is honor bound to guard me."

"Guard you?" Joshua shook his head like the idea was

ridiculous, and then paused to add, "Is he bigger than me?" His chest inflated and he stood up tall, as if to remind Gryphon how much he'd grown over the past year.

"He's actually pretty small. But he's fast and really good with a bow. He also sounds and acts much older than he looks. Quiet. Dignified. A chief 's son." Gryphon shrugged.

Joshua nodded and the skin around his neck flamed red. He was bothered by something, but Gryphon couldn't imagine what. Together they walked in silence. Was Joshua jealous of Sani? Did he feel replaced because of the handful of days Gryphon had spent with the Raven boy? The idea was beyond ridiculous.

When he wasn't talking, Joshua tracked almost as well as he did, noticing irregular bends and breaks of the plants and the unsettling of leaves and grass. Boar's men left humongous footprints. Every time Gryphon singled out Zo's small tracks, painful hope exploded in his chest. She was still alive, or had been when they passed through this part of the mountain.

It wouldn't be long now.

BOAR LEANED against a tree while Zo spooned broth into his mouth. "No more," he said, pushing her hand away. "All that salt is likely masking poison."

Zo rested the bowl on the ground by his feet and shrugged. "The broth is salted to help your body replenish the blood you've lost. You need the fluids."

Boar squinted, his animal eyes calculating in the flashes of light from the fire crackling at Zo's back. "You fell on purpose. You tried to escape."

Zo held her chin high and rummaged through her medical kit. She was low on several herbs. Constantly running for her life left little time to replenish her stock.

"You would have died in that river if I hadn't saved you," said Boar.

"Then I would have died on my terms. Not Barnabas'."

Boar frowned. His brow rolled into deep folds and he winced from the pressure on his fresh stitches. "Curse these!" He held his hands up to his forehead as though he'd like nothing better than to rip them out. Then he directed his anger at Zo. "Why heal me then? Why bother?"

Instead of answering, she turned back to her kit, ignoring the question.

"Ask something of me."

Zo lifted her head. "What?"

Boar growled, "Ask something of me."

"W-why?"

Boar narrowed his eyes, and spat, "I don't like feeling like I owe you anything, Healer. Ask something of me."

"Let me go back to my sister." Zo held her breath, afraid to even hope that it could be that simple.

Boar shook his head. "I can't give you that. Something else. Something reasonable."

"Wanting my life isn't reasonable?" Zo crossed her arms in front of her chest and turned away from Boar to stare at the hypnotic flames of the fire. Most of the men turned to look in her direction, but then quickly looked away—likely stunned that she had contradicted Boar and afraid of Boar's wrath if he caught them watching.

"Never mind," Boar's gravelly voice rolled.

"What about their lives?" Zo glared at Boar. "Have you been

honest with them? Do they know what will happen to them when they've passed through the Gate?"

The back of Boar's hand flew through the air and *cracked* against her cheek, knocking her flat on the ground. Hot pain pulsed where his hand connected with her face. She blinked away tears as her vision tilted to the right, then the left. A sob welled in her throat, but she refused to release it.

"Why do you make me do this to you?" Boar took her by the arm and helped her off the ground so she sat in front of him again. She tried to pull out of his grasp but he only squeezed her arm harder. He reached out and rested his hand on her pulsing cheek. A lover's touch conflicting with his brutality.

Zo's stomach flipped with nausea. Her only rebellion was to stare at the ground.

When he finally released her, she scurried backwards, putting as much space between them as she dared. Her cheek swelled to the point of pinching her eye closed and obstructing her vision. She rubbed her arm and wiped another tear.

To think she'd healed the man!

With a shaking hand, Zo took a sip of her own broth, wincing at the heavy salt. She almost wished it were poisoned. The anticipation of facing Barnabas' soldiers in some interrogation room had to be worse than one swallow of poison.

Zo's head snapped up as an idea struck her. It was crazy. But if there was one thing she'd learned inside Ram's Gate it was that giving up guaranteed defeat.

"Herbs," said Zo, turning back to Boar. "If you want to thank me for healing you, I'd like permission to collect more herbs for my kit."

Boar frowned again, this time remembering not to scrunch up his forehead. "Why herbs? They won't serve you inside the Gate."

Zo nodded and fiddled with a band of leather tied around her wrist. Gabe had given it to her months ago. *A present, just because,* he'd said.

"It's what I love the most, Boar. If you want to thank me, that is how you can do it." She turned back to the fire and her salty broth, mentally begging him to say yes.

The fire snapped and whizzed. Zo hugged her knees. Ikatou walked over and added wood to the hungry flames.

"Bear," Boar said to Ikatou. "Take the healer to collect her herbs. Bring her back before the sun sets or our band will hunt you down and kill you."

"I understand, sir."

Zo suppressed a smile and mumbled thanks as she gained her feet. Her head still throbbed from Boar's attack.

"Don't wander far, Ikatou, if you want to see your family again."

Ikatou's nod was solemn. He lifted a hand, gesturing for Zo to lead the way.

Boar couldn't have assigned her a better escort. When they put a safe enough distance between them and the camp, Zo said, "I'm so glad he sent you."

Ikatou held a finger to his lips as he scanned the forest then whispered, "I am not in Boar's inner circle. It isn't normal for him to give me such responsibility. This is a test. Others will follow us, so watch you words."

Zo nodded and turned her focus back to the ground. Occasionally, she let her gaze wander back to Ikatou. Sweat beaded on his upper lip. His hand never once left the hilt of the broad sword sheathed at his belt.

"How long since you've seen your family?" asked Zo, as she bent down to clip a stem of slippery elm using a small pair of shears she carried in her kit.

"Just over a year," said Ikatou. He tucked his thumbs into his belt.

Zo moved on from the patch of slippery elm in search of her real quarry. She only had an hour to find the flower. "I'm sorry for your loss. The raids affected many." She forced a lump down her throat and kept moving. She wanted to ask him why he'd ever want to become a Ram. Zo assumed it was less about belonging to a clan and a great deal more about reuniting with his family. People didn't behave rationally when it came to protecting those they loved—the last year of Zo's life proved as much.

"I knew several Kodiak who, when the Ram took everything from them, pledged servitude to the Ram to save their fatherless children," said Zo.

But Ikatou's children had a father. Had he been banished? Is that why he ran with Boar and the others?

These were all questions she didn't dare ask. She tried to change the subject. "Did you know Stone, the leader of the Nameless rebellion, is a Kodiak man born inside Ram's Gate? He's been a slave his whole life."

When Ikatou didn't respond, she worried she'd offended the man. He probably didn't appreciate Zo dredging up difficult memories of his past. "I'm sorry." She crouched to examine the leaves of another plant.

"I wasn't banished, if that's what you're thinking," said Ikatou, his voice barely over a whisper as he searched the tree surrounding them. "My wife, my daughters, they were all taken from me in the raid. Stolen like sacks of grain."

Zo didn't move, didn't breathe, for fear Ikatou would stop talking.

"We were out hunting, me and a small group of men. We didn't know they were gone until we came back." Emotion made Ikatou's speech thick and trembling. "I didn't have a chance to die for them. Didn't have a chance to fight." He coughed and looked away. "The cowards attacked us at our weakest possible moment."

He cleared his throat. "I wasn't there for my little girls. For my wife. Helping Boar is the only way I can get inside the Gate to save them."

The hillside took on a steeper upward grade and Zo slipped, jamming her knee on a rock. She crawled to a sturdier game trail. While Ikatou followed, Zo made a show of clipping a useless weed from the ground and adding the unhelpful stems to her slow-growing pile.

The sun was close to setting and Ikatou grew restless. "We need to start heading back," he said.

But Zo hadn't found what she needed. "Only a little longer."

Ikatou shook his head. "Your plants are not worth risking my chances of seeing my family again."

"Please. Five more minutes." Zo had been lucky to get away from Boar for even a little while. If she didn't find that flower, any chance of escape—as small as it was—would be lost forever.

She whispered, "There is a better way to help your family, Ikatou. I know people who can help you and all of the Nameless still living inside Ram's Gate."

Ikatou shifted from one foot to the other.

"Please. I just need five minutes." She poured every ounce of her desperation into the plea. If only her healing instincts weren't broken. She might have persuaded him to let go of his fear of Boar with her touch.

Ikatou glanced up at the setting sun then back at her panicked face. His sigh rolled like a growl. "Five minutes. But we head back in the direction of camp."

Zo could have kissed him.

She practically threw herself to the ground in search of the flower that might be her last chance of escaping Boar and his men. From the corner of her eye, she caught the distant rustling of leaves. Clanless. Following them. Making sure Boar's ticket back into the Ram didn't wander too far.

Some of Boar's men were like their leader. Wild. Stripped of humanity. But Ikatou and several of the other Kodiak were different, ruled by desperation rather than selfishness. Zo had to wonder if Ikatou and the others would turn on Boar if given a better offer—a chance to fight the men who took their homes and families.

"Ikatou," she whispered, still scanning the ground. "I can help you." Zo hoped her voice was low enough for only the Kodiak to hear.

Ikatou didn't answer, and she interpreted his silence as if it were an invitation. He would hear her out.

"I belong to a group of people, an allied force training and growing in number." She paused for effect. "Their whole purpose is to overthrow the Ram. They will free the Nameless." Zo didn't know if it was wise to assume Commander Laden planned to do any such thing, but it seemed like an obvious consequence of winning the war against the Ram. And if it meant gaining Ikatou and a few of his friends as allies, it was worth the risk.

"I know where they are camped. I am like a daughter to their commander. I can help you find a place with them. Get your families back by fighting the people who tore you all apart, not by helping them."

Then Zo spotted it. Thin stems held up clusters of the unique blue flowers of the monkshood. Though they appeared harmless, they were highly poisonous if ingested.

She nearly wept as she knelt next to the little plant that held within its veins great power. *Just like Tess*. She silently laughed as she clipped the precious stems. She'd almost forgotten Ikatou was there until he pulled her up by the elbow and dragged her toward the camp.

"We have to hurry," he said.

Zo juggled her kit and freshly cut herbs, fighting not to drop so much as a leaf in their flight back to Boar.

"Can they defeat the Ram? It seems impossible," said Ikatou under his breath.

Zo thought of the Allied Camp filled with people like herself. People who had lost homes, loved ones, and pride, or who simply didn't want to stand by and wait for it to happen. "If anyone can lead a group against Barnabas, it's Commander Laden."

"I heard you tell Boar about your little sister," he grunted as they moved. The camp was in sight, but the men shepherding them from behind were still far enough away to allow whispered conversation. "Do you swear upon her head that your Commander will help free the rest of the Nameless? Would you swear it in your own blood?"

Zo had never lived among the Kodiak Clan, but most people had heard rumors about the clan's archaic customs, especially when it came to keeping promises. If a Kodiak promised something and didn't deliver, he was expected to make a drastic sacrifice—like chopping off a body part or roasting a hand over a hot fire. The bigger the grievance, the more drastic the consequence.

Zo had a feeling Ikatou would hold her to her word.

Will you swear it in your own blood? What did that mean to him exactly?

Time was up. The sun was setting. In a bold move Zo blurted, "I swear, and if you help me escape, I'll take you to him. You will see your families again."

Ikatou nodded and their pact was sealed. Zo hugged

the flowers to her chest and walked into camp, directly to her former place by Boar's fire.

"Did you find what you were looking for?" the Clanless leader grunted, the thread of his stitches lost in the bulge of his swollen skin.

Zo nodded. "Yes, I believe so."

CHAPTER TWENTY-THREE

Gryphon drank from the stream but couldn't slow his breathing enough to suck in the water. The ice-cold liquid numbed his chin. Blood rushed to his head as he leaned forward, causing his heart to beat in his temples.

"Be honest," Joshua said. "How much am I slowing you down?"

Gryphon choked out a laugh and grabbed his cramped side. "I don't know if I've ever covered so much ground in so little time. Even when I ran with the Raven."

Joshua gave him a pointed look.

"Really, kid. At this rate we might actually catch them before sundown." Gryphon hoped he wasn't being too optimistic. He hated the idea of Zo spending one more night alone with those animals.

After drinking all their stomachs could handle, they

set off at a slow jog to give the water time to settle. They covered another mile before Joshua broke the silence.

"What are you going to say to Zo when we find her?"

Until now, Gryphon hadn't thought about anything beyond just getting her back. "I'll think of something," he mumbled, suddenly consumed with thought.

What would he say to her? How would she react to seeing him after all they'd survived over the past few weeks? He knew she cared for him to some degree. Joshua and Tess said she'd missed him and mourned him, but he didn't even want to consider the possibility that she still might have feelings for Gabe.

"What about a song?" Joshua snickered.

Gryphon stopped running. "Not funny. Ram don't sing, kid."

Joshua continued at his usual pace down the trail. Gryphon had to stretch his legs to catch up to the boy. "I've heard you humming when you think no one is listening. Zo has too."

"She has?" Gryphon's heart beat faster. "When did she hear me?"

Gryphon could almost sense the cocky smile plastered to Joshua's smug face. "She told me you used to sing in the Medica when I was asleep, and you thought you were alone." They ran another hundred yards before he added, "She said you have a soothing tone."

Gryphon chewed on the inside of his lip. A song. The unsung melodies that had so often flitted through his mind—taking shape on the tip of his tongue—had disappeared of late. It was as though Zo's presumed death had killed that part of him. Even now, with her life in so much in peril, the music existed just beyond his mental grasp.

It didn't matter. Sharing his music with Zo seemed grossly embarrassing and entirely too honest. He'd look the fool while exposing his most naked thoughts. Never.

"It was just a suggestion," said Joshua. "Relax."

Zo spent the night using the sharp end of a rock to slice the monkshood into a pulpy mound. When finished, she coaxed the liquid into a bottle and firmly secured the wooden stopper.

Her fingers tingled with numbness from the residue of the plant as she rose to her feet.

Boar fell fast asleep after dinner, but his men watched her every movement—some watched in a way that made her uncomfortable. When Zo stood to rinse her hands in the nearby river, a man in Boar's inner circle asked, "What are you doing?" He carried himself like a Ram and Zo had to wonder if he had been banished from the city-dwelling warriors like Boar.

"Just wanted to wash my hands," said Zo.

The man gave her a quick nod, but kept his eyes fastened to her every movement, like a starving predator ready to devour his next meal.

Zo plunged her hands in the river and scrubbed. Boar's guard approached her from the side, either to be certain she wouldn't run or for some darker purpose. Both options seemed probable.

Zo pulled her hands from the icy water and practically ran back to her place by the fire and Boar. As dangerous as the Clanless leader was, Zo had no doubt he served as a sort of protection to her among this camp of wild men.

The following morning, while most of the men were packing up camp, Zo slipped the vial of monkshood in her pocket before rolling up her bed. One of the men at each of the three campfires tended a cook pot. Aside from Boar's, one fire was shared by Boar's inner circle, and the other by Ikatou and the rest of the Kodiak. Mostly they ate a stew-like concoction of broth and meat, with the occasional diced and boiled tuber. From the bland smell coming from the cook pots, this morning appeared no different.

When she thought no one was looking, Zo uncorked the vial and poured some of the monkshood into her and Boar's pot. When she looked up, she met Ikatou's questioning face. Zo didn't dare keep eye contact, but purposefully stared at the other cook pot. The one shared by Boar's inner circle.

How would they get the rest of the monkshood into that pot? How could she communicate her need for Ikatou's help?

Ikatou turned away from her and went about his business. Clearly, he hadn't understood her need. Zo would have to find a way to poison the other pot without his help and without drawing the attention of the rest of the camp.

Boar nudged her with a steaming bowl of stew, a ladle still dripping in his other hand. "Eat. We have to leave soon."

Zo tried to hide a tremor of fear as she accepted the bowl of deadly stew. Killing Boar wouldn't be enough. She needed to kill his inner circle as well if she wanted any hope of escaping this motley clan with her life.

Boar ladled his own food and together they sat on their folded bedrolls to eat. Steam curled off Boar's stew as he blew across its surface. "The swelling on my forehead is down, but I still have a bad headache," he said, conversationally. Then he took his first bite.

"That's natural. You lost a lot of blood. Fluids will help." She held her own bowl to her lips and pretended to drink.

The instant the broth touched her lips, the skin around her mouth tingled with a hint of numbness. She didn't let a drop in her mouth.

If Boar felt the effects of his stew too quickly—before the other men had a chance to eat—she was dead.

Behind them, someone shouted a curse and the camp turned to pandemonium.

Zo spun around to see Ikatou and a member of Boar's inner circle shoving each other. Ikatou ducked to avoid the other man's fist and answered with an uppercut of his own.

Boar set down his bowl, and as if he were excusing rowdy children said, "They get like this from time to time." He stumbled a little as he stood, and cleared his throat a few times as he moved toward what had become a full-fledged battle between Ikatou and his opponent. The other men formed a ring around the combatants, and Zo didn't squander the opportunity.

She inched toward the other fire and fumbled with

the vial of monkshood. She twisted the cork while it was still in her pocket, careful to keep it upright when the cork came free of the bottle.

Boar shouted, "That's enough," and a few of the men helped to pull the two apart.

But Zo still hadn't reached the other cook fire. She sprinted the rest of the way to the fire and instead of pouring the uncorked vial into the cook pot, she threw it into the stew, vial and all.

"We leave in five minutes if we want to reach the Gate and your new clan by nightfall," Boar ordered. He cleared his throat a few times, shook his head, and staggered toward Zo. "You look like you've never seen two men fight before," he said. He put his hand to his head and moaned, but didn't complain further as they sat back down on their bedrolls and picked up their bowls again. He lifted a shaking spoon to his lips.

Around them, other bowls were filled and the camp divided back to their own fires. The men of Boar's inner circle ate their stew as they talked while at Ikatou's fire, the men ate with shifting glances.

Zo looked back to find Boar lying on his side, the bowl of stew spilled and forgotten. He tried to clear his throat a few times. "What's…wrong with…me?"

Across the camp, one of Boar's men shouted, "What's this?" as he held up the empty vial. He examined it for a moment then looked directly at Zo. A few men cleared their throats; some scratched at their necks, as if that would bring some feeling to the numbness spreading throughout their bodies.

Boar tried to crawl toward Zo, but didn't seem to

have the strength to push his body off the ground. "You…" A gargling gasp escaped his swollen lips. Drool rolled down the side of his face.

Boar's eyes rolled back and with a sickening thud, his head connected with the earth. A sound she knew would haunt her dreams for the rest of her life.

She snatched up her medical kit and bedroll as the man holding her vial threw it into the fire. "Poison," the Clanless man wailed.

Bowls clattered to the rocky ground and every wild and haggard man from Boar's inner circle turned to Zo. She could tell they were feeling the initial effects of the monkshood, but it would take another minute or two to circulate through their bloodstream. Too much time.

Zo dove at Boar, pulling a long knife from the dead man's belt. Rolling onto her back, she fumbled with the blade as one of Boar's men ran toward her, his face twisted in rage.

Zo backed into Boar's corpse, her hand unwittingly planted against his lifeless face, and she screamed. It was as though time decelerated and hours passed in the moments that led up to her impending death by the hands of Boar's men. How could she let this happen? To come so achingly close to freedom just to have it ripped from her fingertips. Tess. Joshua. Her arms throbbed with the need to hold them, almost as much as they ached to hold Gryphon one last time.

Just as Zo's attacker lunged—his weapon arm raised above his head to kill—large Kodiak arms wrapped around his chest.

Ikatou growled, pulling the Clanless man away from

Zo. The wild man stabbed at the air in front of her face. Zo rolled and ducked behind Boar's corpse. She hid for two breaths before doubling her grip on Boar's knife and peeking up over the body.

The Clanless attacker lay motionless on the ground with Ikatou standing over him, panting. Behind Ikatou, men cried out in agony as the Kodiak engaged Boar's inner circle.

"Get out of here," Ikatou pointed toward the trees then ran back to join in the fight.

Zo, still clutching the knife, climbed to her feet. She retrieved her medical kit and stumbled backward, unwilling to turn her back to the slaughter.

Even though it was the last thing she wanted to see, even though these images would haunt her for the rest of her life, she couldn't look away. This minor massacre was her doing, and she needed to witness it, to claim it and carry the burden of her actions.

The last two fighters dropped to their knees, each clutching their throats. One fell forward, onto his face. The last man, Zo's final victim, looked beyond the Kodiak surrounding him and met Zo's gaze. He might have begged if he had any command of his lungs and throat. Instead, he stared until his eyes rolled up into his head and he too collapsed into the mud and gore surrounding them.

Zo tried to swallow but gagged. She couldn't stay there, not a moment longer. She stepped over Boar's dead body and sprinted into the cover of the forest. She tripped and fell on a dead branch, cutting a line of skin along her forearm. She stayed on the ground and watched the blood seep to the surface of her skin, shocked by what she'd done. She'd never killed a man before, let alone ten.

Ikatou, bruised and bloodied, stomped toward Zo, his chest heaving. "My portion of our agreement is complete," he said. "It's time to fulfill your promise of the blood oath."

CHAPTER TWENTY-FOUR

Three fires smoked, masking some of the stench of dead bodies scattered around them. Ten men. Clanless. "Check the forest. She might be nearby. Look for tracks. Whoever killed these men has Zo." Gryphon bent down next to a man matching Stone's description of Boar.

Was it possible?

Gryphon held his sleeve to his nose and circled the camp to look for clues that might help him find Zo. It seemed impossible that he could come so close to finding her only to have her slip through his fingers again.

Something crunched under his foot. Glass. He reached down and picked up a shard of what had been a glass vial. He'd seen something similar in Zo's medical kit. Unthinking, he brought the broken glass to his lips and closed his eyes, imagining Zo here now.

He dropped the shard and realized his lips tingled with numbness, a residue from the glass.

Gryphon went back to Boar's body and, fighting the rising nausea in his stomach, bent down to smell near Boar's mouth.

He gagged and stumbled over to the river to clear the rancid smell from his head. Poison.

Joshua knelt beside him at the river's edge. "I think I found a new set of tracks."

Gryphon dipped his hands into the river and splashed water on his face. It was cold and shocking enough to command his thoughts to plot their next move.

"She fought back, kid." He gestured to the men lying dead in the rocky soil. "She poisoned Boar. I found one of her vials."

"But all that blood. Those other men didn't die from poison."

Gryphon had to agree with the boy's logic, even though it forced him to admit that someone must have killed those men, and, judging by the gore, it most definitely wasn't Zo. She wasn't fond of killing or watching others fight. Gryphon remembered the first day he'd met her. She had been forced by Gate Master Leon to watch a prize fight and afterward vomited in an abandoned alleyway.

It wasn't hard to confirm Joshua's suspicion that the victors of this small massacre left as a group. It seemed the men gathered out in the forest, away from where the fight took place. Gryphon dropped to his hands and knees and pressed his fingers into a set of tracks. The ground was damp here and the impressions easy to read, the walls of the track intact. A fresh trail.

"What if they did something to her when they found

out she poisoned Boar? What if she's in trouble? What if—"

"Slow down, Joshua." Gryphon rested a hand on his shoulder. "Zo has been in trouble since the moment I met her. She'll get out of this. She'll find a way to survive." She had to, for Joshua's sake as much as his own.

How could one person have such a powerful impact on them in such a short amount of time? As a warrior, it was tactical to explore every outcome of a mission. To have a back-up plan in case things went south.

But Gryphon couldn't fathom going back to believing Zo was gone. He couldn't lose her, not again. He still couldn't believe a series of rational decisions had led him to this place in the mud, that he'd allowed himself to grow attached to a Wolf even after discovering she was an enemy spy. It was absolutely insane, but it felt as right as holding a spear in his hands. Natural. Like maybe he was born to care for her.

He hitched up his pack and ruffled Joshua's flaming hair. "Let's move."

BLOOD DRIED in long stripes down the length of Zo's arm as she hiked alongside Ikatou, the group's new leader. She didn't have the will to even attempt to heal herself. She didn't deserve it after causing the deaths of all of those men. Yes, they meant to hand her over to Barn-abas. Yes, they were the foulest form of human life, but that didn't matter.

She'd killed them.

Her mother would never have used knowledge that was meant for the good of others to cause harm. To take life instead of preserving it. But she wasn't her mother, and maybe in the face of saving so many others, that was all right.

Stretched beyond physical and emotional limits, her feet barely lifted off the ground as she pushed forward. Were it not for her desire to see Joshua and Tess, she would have sat down right in the middle of the trail and slept.

The group came across three giant boulders, each standing nearly twenty feet high, as though a portion of the mountainside broke free and shattered to form a tight circle of stone with one narrow entrance. Without ceremony or words exchanged, the quiet men stocked the circular shelter with enough wood to last them through the night.

To Zo's amazement, they also collected rocks.

Zo leaned against a rock wall and melted down into a sitting position. She was tired of walking and hungry from missing her morning meal. Too exhausted even to allow herself to worry about Ikatou's plans for a blood oath. She assumed it was just like it sounded. Maybe she'd cut her hand, and he'd do the same, and then they'd shake and call it done.

The Kodiak men didn't pay her any attention as they hefted rocks—some as large as Zo's head—to the center of the rudimentary open-air cave. When the pile rose several feet off the ground, they built a fire to block the only entrance. The confinement for a Wolf like Zo, who thrived in open spaces and vast farmland, made her anxious. She hugged her elbows and pressed more firmly against the wall.

The Clanless Kodiak murmured to each other in a strange dialect as they positioned themselves in a circle around the pile of stones. When everyone was in place, with legs crossed and hands resting open on knees, they all inhaled in unison through their noses. Their eyes closed. Their faces and chests lifted to a sky that threatened yet another spring rain.

The Kodiak held that position, and their breaths, for several moments. When they finally, on some unspoken cue, freed the captive air from their lungs, Zo realized she too had held her breath. She exhaled.

Then the shouting began.

Every man in the circle yelled at once. Their voices bounced off the stone columns surrounding them, fighting for dominance. It was impossible to make out more than a few words scattered in the cacophony of voices. Rather than bother with interpreting the words, Zo focused on the strain of their voices. They spoke of anger, loss, determination, and grief.

Over time she made easier work of interpreting the individual shouts. Some were angry she had killed Boar when he was their ticket into Ram's Gate and their only hope for seeing their families again. Some wanted to turn back and scale the walls and fight Barnabas even though it would ensure their death. Others argued that Ikatou was right in trusting the healer. They wanted to travel to the Allied Camp to see if there was really a force strong enough to free their families.

Zo pressed her hands over her ears as the voices grew louder and louder. Maybe they believed the loudest voice was the most correct. Or maybe they had lost their minds. What if they turned their anger onto her? How would she even begin to defend herself against so many men and so much rage?

Then as quickly as the shouting started, it stopped. The men in the circle, with chests pumping up and down and nostrils flared, took turns looking every man in the eye. The process was slow but Zo sensed its importance.

"We see each other," said Ikatou when they finished. "Our course is decided."

The men grunted as they climbed to their feet and each took several steps back. "Healer," said Ikatou. "It's time to seal our agreement." He beckoned Zo to stand with him next to the pile of stones.

The Blood Oath. Spears of cold fear stretched through her fingers and numbed her toes as she used the rock wall she'd been resting against to help gain her feet. Couldn't she and Ikatou do this privately? Couldn't he be convinced that she would keep her promise to help the Nameless inside Ram's Gate escape their slavery without some barbaric ritual?

Zo slipped past one of the Kodiak and approached the pile of rocks. Her legs seemed detached from her body, like she might have floated the whole way to Ikatou's side.

He spoke loud enough for his voice to bounce off the walls, but gave his full attention and energy to Zo. "We agreed to help you escape. In exchange, you agreed to a take us to your commander and help us free our families.

You have sworn it in words, but now you will swear it in blood."

Could Zo even make this promise? What if Commander Laden didn't defeat the Ram? Was she willing to bet her life that the Allies could defeat the undefeatable enemy? She hoped they could, but was it even possible? She'd been inside the Gate and witnessed with her own eyes the grueling training and the seemingly countless warriors—the grit of a society determined to defend its dominance in the region.

But Ikatou had made her a deal when she went searching for the monkshood. She'd sworn she would help him and agreed to the seal it in blood—whatever that meant. He'd kept his promise and now she would have to keep hers.

Ikatou removed a leather bundle from his pack and set it reverently into the open hands of another Kodiak. He unwrapped the leather, one fold at a time to reveal a beautiful curved knife. Zo had never seen a blade like it before. The metal didn't look like metal at all. It wasn't until Ikatou lifted it and tucked the narrow handle between two fingers that she realized what it was.

A bear claw. A massive bear claw secured to an intricately engraved stone handle. Ikatou raised the claw to the back of his hand, drawing a straight line from knuckle to wrist without breaking skin. "I will mark the back of your hands so with every action your promise is remembered."

Zo's tongue felt tacky against the roof of her mouth as she lifted her shaking hands over the fire.

"Repeat after me," said Ikatou, taking hold of one of

her hands. "I swear to do all that was promised in my own blood."

Zo repeated the oath and Ikatou dragged the claw across her skin. Zo gasped in pain as the claw cut and tore a jagged line. When Ikatou finished, he turned her hand over so blood dripped down on the pile of stones.

"I do willingly tie my life and blood to the task of freeing the Nameless," said Ikatou.

The words were even more terrifying than the claw. Still, she said them, and the second cut was made.

Zo staggered to one knee but held both hands out, allowing the stones to catch her blood.

"This seals our pact, Healer. We are allies until the day you break it."

CHAPTER TWENTY-FIVE

he tracks led south, away from the Gate. At first Gryphon thought the Clanless altered their course, hoping to approach Ram's Gate from a different angle, but now the truth was as clear as it was confusing. They hiked through the very forest from which they just came. Which also meant walking toward Zander and his mess brothers.

As a trained predator, Gryphon had little experience as prey. It might have been the excessive quiet or the thick clouds gathering overhead, but there was something strange about the woods as he led Joshua up the steep, graded mountainside. Even the trees seemed watchful today.

Or maybe it was just the hope of finally seeing Zo.

The shadows of the forest stretched long as night descended. Tracking was impossible without light. If they didn't find her soon, they'd have to make camp and begin again tomorrow. Gryphon couldn't stop thinking about the men that now had Zo. Without

Boar and his motivation to sell her to the Ram, what would keep them from harming her? Yes, they were heading south, away from the Ram, but that didn't mean she was safe. He'd heard too many stories about the wild Clanless that roamed these mountains.

"We have to find her tonight, kid." Something terrible was coming. He felt it.

Joshua, who had been silent ever since finding the massacre by the river, nodded. "There isn't much daylight." His hair was more copper than fire in the low light. He sagged under the weight of his pack, but never complained.

In the distance, a new noise buzzed higher on the mountain. The inhuman sound reminded Gryphon of the steady roll and crash of the ocean against the cliffs on the western edge of Ram's Gate, a sustained roar that barely breathed.

"What is it?" asked Joshua.

Gryphon answered him with a raised hand, signaling him to silence.

They stopped walking and just listened until, after several minutes, the sound died to nothing.

Joshua said, "Do you think…?"

Gryphon redoubled his grip on his spear and hiked his pack higher on his shoulders. "Run with me, Joshua."

If Gryphon and Joshua had heard the sound, that meant Zander had likely heard it too and would be drawn toward it. They raced through the trees up the mountainside, using the sparse light until there was no light at all. Gryphon's eyes adjusted enough to make out the shapes of rocks and trees, but he and Joshua stumbled often.

"How do you know we're going the right way?" grunted Joshua as he struggled to pull himself up over a rocky shelf. The ground grew so steep they spent as much time climbing as they did hiking.

The boy gave voice to Gryphon's own concerns. "I don't. It just feels right." Only a fool traveled blindly in the night; he'd lectured the point to Joshua countless times. But Joshua didn't balk or complain. He simply nodded as if what Gryphon said made perfect sense. "You'll find her, Gryph. I know you will."

Gryphon welcomed Joshua's faith, but it did little to ease his rising panic. If he was wrong, they'd have a very difficult time retracing their steps to pick up on Zo's trail. Valuable time would be lost—time Zo might not have.

"I think I smell…" Joshua lifted his nose to the sky and sniffed the air like a hunting dog, "fire."

Gryphon smelled it too. The air was thick with moisture from another impending spring storm, the night peaceful with little wind, which meant the fire had to be close. "It could be Zander and the mess unit," Gryphon warned as he and Joshua followed the smell of campfire. "We can't be too careful right now, kid."

They crested yet another climb and froze.

Not fifty feet away, pushed up against the rocky mountainside, orange and red flames licked the wood of a campfire. Surrounding the fire were tall pillars of rock; each stretched twice the height of a man. It was too dark to make out the black forms lying on the ground but Gryphon imagined one of those forms as Zo.

"With me," he whispered to Joshua. Adrenaline exploded within him. This was it. She was here. She was alive. He just knew it.

Together they crept toward the sleeping camp, sticking to the shadows outside the light of the fire. Gryphon's whole body yearned to sprint, but they kept every movement painfully slow. Nothing, not even a breeze, covered their careful steps. Only the subtle crack of the fire and the pounding rhythm of Gryphon's heart beating in his ears, and Joshua's heavy breathing.

Someone from the camp would be standing watch. If he could somehow take out the watchman without alerting the rest, they might have a chance of escaping. He could throw his spear, but a man could still scream with a spear in his gut.

Gryphon scanned the black trees for any sign of Zander and his mess. Every moment wasted could mean the difference between leaving with Zo and getting all three of them killed.

He touched his fist to the ground, calling halt. "Do you still have your sling?" he half mouthed, half whispered.

Joshua nodded, a thin smile spread across his face. He cupped his hand to Gryphon's ear to block the sound. "You want me to take out the watchman without waking the others."

This is why Joshua was so valuable to Gryphon. They'd worked and trained together long enough that the kid seemed to read his very thoughts. "You sure you can knock him out with that little thing?" Gryphon said.

Any other time Joshua would have scoffed at Gryphon's request and pranced up to his target like a peacock. But this was Zo's life hanging in the balance. He sat down on the muddy ground, his chest still pumping from the climb. "What if I miss?" He pressed his palms into his forehead.

"You won't," said Gryphon.

"But what if I *do*?"

Gryphon covered Joshua's mouth and looked over his shoulder to make sure the watchman didn't hear. They were still far enough away that he couldn't make out a man's form. The tall shadow standing near the rock—the watchman, if Gryphon wasn't mistaken—didn't move from his position.

Gryphon turned back to Joshua and tugged at a leather strap, freeing the boy's sling. Gryphon weighed the child's weapon in his hand and whispered, "I'll do it."

Joshua snatched the sling from Gryphon's hands and climbed to his feet. "You're a terrible shot." Too loud again.

"Kid, if you're doubting yourself—"

"I know, I know. If I doubt myself, I've already failed."

"Then I'll ask again." Gryphon placed the sling reverently in Joshua's smaller hands. "Can you do this?"

Joshua's fingers closed around his weapon of choice. "Yes. I can do this." He took a deep breath. "For Zo."

Zo RESTED with her hands by the fire but couldn't turn off her thoughts long enough to allow sleep to set in. She'd promised these barbarians she'd help free their Nameless families and packaged her life in the deal! It was pure madness. But she'd likely do it again if it ensured that she wouldn't have to walk into Ram's Gate as a bargaining chip for Boar.

What would she tell Tess and Joshua when they reached the Allies? *"Yes, I'm back, but don't count on me staying for long. I've got to help wild men free their families from Barnabas."*

Utter insanity.

Commander Laden would be furious that she committed herself—and vicariously, his men—to this new endeavor. Maybe she'd have a chance of freeing the Nameless while the Allies went to battle with the Ram, but that could be five years from now or even ten, depending on the growth and preparedness of Commander Laden's forces. Ikatou and his men wouldn't wait that long.

What have I done?

Zo turned to rest her head in the crook of her elbow, still making sure to keep the backs of her mangled hands facing the fire. Ikatou said she couldn't stitch the cuts; the wounds needed to heal naturally to create a proper scar. A lifelong reminder of her promise. Fearing infection, Zo relied on the heat of the fire to seal the wounds. That was, of course, assuming the bear claw used to make the cuts wasn't contaminated. She doubted Ikatou took the time to regularly clean the evil tool.

Restless, Zo rolled onto her back to study the wounds

with hands raised to the light of the fire. The flesh looked torn instead of cut. As it was, blood dried thick on clumps of ragged skin. Whenever she flexed her hand into a fist, the wound reopened and fresh blood leaked through the marred mess to add yet another layer.

Zo rolled over again, this time facing the fire. When she was only a little girl and her parents were still alive, Zo associated campfires with stories and songs, not a place to dry out gory wounds. She closed her eyes and imagined a melody from her childhood, a song Wolves sang when they pondered the state of the region. A lament with a melody so careful and clear, it brought tears to her eyes. If only she could hear it aloud. She hadn't sung since she was a child—did she even know how to sing anymore?

Zo wiped her eyes, smearing a streak of blood across her cheek, but paused when she spotted movement above one of the rock pillars.

CHAPTER TWENTY-SIX

While Joshua hiked over the giant boulders to peer down at the sleeping camp, Gryphon approached the fire head on. He crawled on hands and knees, only daring to advance when the man at the entrance of the cave wasn't looking.

To call the watchman large was a gross understatement. With the fire at his back, his features were cast in heavy shadow. The outline of a full beard turned half his face black. He certainly didn't fit the image Gryphon envisioned of the starving Clanless who roamed the land. This man had muscle to spare and, by the looks of him, ate like a chieftain.

He had to be a Kodiak, which meant Gryphon had more than met his match physically. He'd never fought a Kodiak outside of his mess unit's phalanx formation. If Joshua missed his target that would all change tonight. But instead of fighting just one Kodiak with his fists, he'd be devoured by a whole group of them. He should have told Joshua to run away if his stone didn't fell the Bear. Why hadn't he thought to do that? It wasn't like him not to think through a plan before putting it into motion. The thought of Zo sleeping so close by rattled every rationale he possessed.

Gryphon threw a rock twenty yards away, awakening the watchman from the trance men develop after hours spent staring at shadows. The Kodiak stepped away from his group to get a better vantage of the mountain. Above his head, he didn't see Joshua perched atop one of the giant stone pillars.

Just a few more steps, Gryphon urged. They couldn't afford for Joshua to fell the watchman so close to his men and risk the chance of waking the others. The untrained watchman might have heeded Gryphon's mental urgings, but this Kodiak-sized Clanless showed

his training by only glancing in all directions. He wouldn't be lured from his post.

What were they thinking? He and Joshua couldn't just walk up to a camp of wild Clanless and expect to fool them with only a decoy rock and a boy's woolen sling. As big as this man was, the chances of Joshua hurling a small rock with enough force to knock him out was as likely as Commander Laden and the Allies accepting Gryphon with open arms.

Gryphon waved to get Joshua's attention while not showing the Kodiak his position. They would just have to try again tomorrow, when Gryphon had time to craft a better plan that didn't rely solely on rocks and slings, and trust that Zander and the mess were miles away.

When Joshua finally looked in his direction, Gryphon

gave the signal for retreat. But instead of backing down off the pillar, Joshua shook his head and set a stone in the leather pouch of his sling.

That boy! Gryphon would kill him if they survived this.

Joshua let out a deep, silent breath, then whipped the sling over his head in one full rotation and released the stone. The entire motion happened in a blink. At the same time, Gryphon exploded toward the watchman, ready to kill the man if Joshua's stone didn't do its job. The rock whistled through the air and connected with the side of the Kodiak's head. The large man toppled into Gryphon's outstretched arms. He'd meant to break the man's fall, but the Clanless was so large he took Gryphon to the ground along with him.

Definitely a Kodiak.

Joshua stood on the stone pillar above his prey in humble triumph. A man.

With some effort, Gryphon rolled out from under the Kodiak. He pressed his fingers to the man's neck and found a pulse.

They didn't have much time.

More nervous than ever, Gryphon stood with his back against the nearest stone pillar and inched toward the opening. He listened for any movement in the camp but only heard the simmering crackle of the fire. He reached the edge of the pillar and held his breath as he turned the corner.

Flickering light from the campfire reflected off the giant rocks, highlighting portions of the sleeping figures on the ground. Gryphon's knees buckled when he spotted a smaller figure sleeping next to the fire, in the center of the group of Clanless. A blanket of shadow shrouded the figure's face, but female hands rested in firelight.

The air flew out of Gryphon's lungs, his hopes that she rested unharmed plummeted. Her hands—the hands that worked a miracle in healing Joshua and helped so many others—were crusted in blood.

Zo LOOKED UP, startled to see an enormous shadowed figure looming just outside the firelight. At first glance she assumed him to be Ikatou's lookout, but this man carried himself differently than the other Kodiak. And none of them stared like this stranger. He stood as still as the pillars surrounding their little camp, but his gaze cut through the heat of the flames and his shroud of darkness.

Zo sat up, still a little fire blind from staring at the flames for so long. The knot of hair she'd tied on top of her head loosened and dark, tangled strands tumbled about her shoulders and down her back. She considered reaching over to wake Ikatou from his heavy sleep and warn him of the stranger. It would be easy. He slept close enough she could smell the ripeness of his feet.

The shadowed man didn't seem to hold any weapons, typical of the Kodiak who preferred to kill with their bare hands. He was certainly large enough to be a Bear.

But he wasn't. Somehow she knew it.

Zo didn't understand the strange pull of her body as she pushed aside her tattered blanket and rose to her feet.

Who are you? She wanted to ask, but couldn't manage the words.

He lifted a hand to the light and beckoned her to him. She shook her head but inched closer to the fire just the same. Again, he waved her toward him, this time with more urgency then before. Ikatou stirred, the fire cracked, and Zo stood frozen, not daring to move any closer.

The shadowed man dropped his hands by his sides, and Zo had the distinct impression she'd let him down somehow. He shifted forward enough that a small amount of light touched his form. She blinked against the heat of the flames, searching the stranger's darkened face, but the fire lit only his whiskered chin. The gleam of a short sword peeked through the folds of a dark, hooded cape. A Ram blade.

Zo stepped back and inhaled to scream and wake the sleeping Kodiak, but it was too late. The man jumped over the flames of the fire.

In one graceful motion, he covered her mouth with his large hand and wrapped his arm around her waist.

There was something about the man's touch. Something she recognized. *But it couldn't be.* Zo's legs melted but the phantom before her didn't let her fall.

Gryphon?

It wasn't possible.

Yet, even his smell was familiar. *It couldn't be.*

Someone in the camp groaned. Gryphon's ghost didn't waste a second. He threw Zo over his shoulder as if she were a sack of grain and jumped back over the fire that blocked their exit from the rudimentary cave.

As they ran, Zo beat upon the ghost's back to get him to stop, but he didn't listen. Behind them shouts echoed off stone. Ikatou's voice rose above the rest. What if they thought she'd abandoned them?

Blood rushed to her head. She couldn't catch her breath to scream. Pain from the jostling of her hands and the pressure on her stomach mixed with a dizziness of being upside-down. This man ignoring her battle couldn't be Gryphon. Was her mourning so great that she'd attached his face and smell to another man?

He could have been a Ram scout. That made a lot more sense than any other explanation she could dream up. She kicked harder, grasping for branches of passing trees, unable to fill her lungs enough to scream.

Eventually her fight dwindled to a few sporadic fists against his back. Her eyes drooped closed, the running motion carrying her in and out of consciousness to a place of dreams, of loss and pain and longing so real her heart broke all over again.

CHAPTER TWENTY-SEVEN

Gryphon hugged Zo's legs as he ran wild with fear through the night. Joshua sprinted ahead of him, darting around trees, scouring the area for some place to hide, constantly looking over his shoulder to make sure Gryphon and Zo were close behind.

Thankfully, Zo stopped fighting Gryphon's hold a few minutes into the run. He'd refused to put her down so close to the camp in case she was too injured to run, and —even more vehemently— refused to consider why she fought him to begin with.

Zo was smaller than he remembered, lighter, but that didn't lessen the ache sprouting in his shoulder from supporting her weight. He winced and adjusted his hold, but it didn't help.

Slowing to a walk, he leaned forward and let her body shift so he cradled her in his arms. He couldn't decide if she was unconscious or simply sleeping. Had she lost too much blood from the cuts on her hands?

Why didn't she come when he beckoned? What did those savages do to her?

Her eyes fluttered open, but swiftly drifted shut again. Blood was smeared across her cheek and her head lolled back to face the dim light of the crescent moon. How could beauty be so frightening? It reminded him just how unworthy he was to even hold her, let alone try to claim her heart. Rejection from her would wound him in a way that a sword or spear never could.

Gryphon didn't realize he'd stopped walking until Joshua approached.

"I've found a place, Gryph," said Joshua. He reached out and touched his fingertips to Zo's where they hung limp in the air. The poor boy looked ready to fall over. "It's not the best, but—"

"Lead the way, kid. I'm sure it'll be fine." They needed rest and couldn't afford exposure to the Kodiak and possibly Zander.

Joshua led them to a tight cluster of trees, heavily furred, with boughs hanging close to the ground. Gryphon dropped to his knees still cradling Zo to his chest. Joshua cleared the ground of rocks and pulled a bedroll from his pack.

"This reminds me of the tree I woke up under after Zo healed me," said Joshua. His words slurred with need of rest.

Gryphon's throat tightened at the memory of being with Zo under that tree. The kiss they shared. Zo had called him her family. She'd clung to him with such intensity at the time, he'd had no doubt of her affection. Or was it merely gratitude?

He shook his head and bent over to lay her unconscious form on the bedroll. He cleared the ground next to her and unrolled his own blanket. "Here you go, Joshua."

Joshua shook his head. "I'm not taking your spot."

Gryphon dropped to the open ground near the perimeter of the tree to keep watch. "It's not my spot."

He'd trained himself long ago to soak in as much rest as possible without actually falling asleep. Tonight it wouldn't be hard to stay awake. As exhausted as he was, he doubted he could sleep even if he tried.

RAYS OF LIGHT kissed Zo's eyelids, but she wasn't ready to wake. A soft sensation caressed the skin around the wounds on the backs of her hands. Though her hands were still tender from the blood oath, she welcomed the touch, considering it just another form of light kissing her skin.

She'd dreamt of Gryphon working beside her on hands and knees, thinning a patch of beets. He didn't carry any weapons. His dark hair was tied back with a strip of soft leather. He looked over his shoulder and gave her a contented smile then went back to his task, the muscles in his forearms moving beneath his skin as he worked.

Zo became aware of the hard ground beneath her, the sun filtering through the branches of the tree overhead. She wasn't ready to wake up. Adjusting into a new position, she inhaled the scent of pine, and then slipped back into another dream to be with Gryphon. The farm was gone. Now she sat under the tree with Gryphon outside the walls of Ram's Gate. "I never left you," he said.

"Zo?" A voice, soft and deep. "Are you in any pain?"

Zo gave in to the morning and blinked against the light filtering through the needles of the fir tree above her and groaned. Painful pressure behind her eyes from exhaustion and the ever-present ache of her hands made waking unwelcome. She needed rest. She needed more time with Gryphon.

A gentle touch caressed her hand—a welcome contradiction to the pain from the cuts of the blood oath. Her eyes sank back into sleep, until her memory of the night before forced its way to the front of her consciousness.

The blood oath. The man who kidnapped her from the Kodiak! The Ram sword he carried!

Zo's eyes flew open. But what she saw made her think she was still dreaming. Lying on his side next to her, his head resting in his hand with a tentative smile playing about the corners of his mouth, was Gryphon. The sun hit his face in splotches, highlighting his eyes while shadowing his mouth.

"This isn't real." Zo frowned. She reached out and threaded her fingers through his chin-length brown hair. He leaned into the touch, and her hand found his cheek. His jaw clenched beneath her fingers. He hesitated then turned his face to kiss the tender skin of her palm.

"Zo, stop," she commanded herself out loud,

squeezing her eyes shut and pulling away. A tear rolled down her face. "Deep breaths and it will pass." She covered her face with her hands and curled her knees up to her chest, as if doing so would protect her heart. *Wake up wake up wake up.*

"Zo?"

Her head whipped up at the sound of his voice. That voice! The way he said her name. It couldn't be. It simply wasn't possible. Wasn't this figure just the product of her fatigued body and mind?

"G-Gryphon?"

He nodded.

"But…but you died," she gasped, tears blurring her vision. She thrust her hands out to feel along the boiled leather vest he wore to protect his chest. "A spear. Gabe told me. He said Ram spears never miss."

Zo sat up and ignored Gryphon's shock as she pushed him onto his stomach, face to the soil, and examined his back for a spear wound.

"I'm fine, Zo. I got away." She nudged him to roll back onto his back and fanned her fingers along his shoulders, his arms, his legs. Tears rolled down her cheeks, her breath coming in strangled spurts. "Ram. Spears. Never. Miss." She struggled and gasped through each word.

Gryphon took her by the shoulders and gently shook her from her delirium. "I escaped them, Zo. Now will you please breathe?" He wiped her tears and took up her hands and kissed them, one knuckle at a time, all the while fighting a little boy grin.

"How is this even possible?" she sobbed and

launched herself at Gryphon, throwing her arms around his neck and knocking him onto his back. His deep laughter made his chest rise and fall—Zo along with it.

Gryphon was alive!

He trapped her in his arms, his chin resting protectively above her head. "You're safe now. Everything is going to be fine." He played with the long strands of her hair, occasionally kissing the crown of her head. With her ear pressed to him, each strong *thump* of his beating heart brought new hope. A joy that thrummed energy throughout her own body. Gryphon rolled onto his side, taking her with him so she rested in the crook of his arm, staring up at him in wonder.

How could she, in only a few days, have forgotten how attractive he was? Dark brown hair framed his chiseled jaw. Heavy shadows rested beneath his golden-brown eyes. *Such kind eyes.* His Ram nose had a knot at the bridge from being repeatedly broken, but even that added to his rugged charm. "You're alive." It needed to be said. Shouted. Over and over again. That knowledge alone made everything bearable, as if a boulder had been lifted from off her chest and she could finally breathe again.

"What happened to your hands?" he asked, taking one up and kissing her palm. Zo closed her eyes at his touch and sighed. Joshua and Tess would be so happy.

"Joshua!" said Zo. "We need to get to the Allies. Joshua and Tess think you're dead."

"No, I don't," a familiar voice approached the tree, and Joshua dropped down to his knees, a ridiculous grin plastered to his face.

"I don't understand." Zo looked back and forth between the two. "Tess?"

"Safe with Stone and Eva and the rest of the Nameless. By now they will have made it to the Allied Camp. Joshua came with me to get you back. We've been tracking you."

"Oh, no." Zo remember the Kodiak and the blood oath she'd made. Ikatou would stop at nothing to find her. She was his only hope of freeing his family. If they discovered she wasn't really kidnapped, that she didn't leave with Gryphon and Joshua against her will …

She looked down at her hands and grimaced. How could she tell him about her promise? Especially now.

"Your hands, Zo," he said, mirroring her thoughts. "What happened?"

The truth would ruin everything. She wanted nothing but to reach out to him. To take his weathered face in her hands and brush away the deep shadows beneath his eyes. To trace the strong lines of his jaw and smooth the wrinkled concern from his brow.

"Can you still run?" asked Joshua. "Once those Kodiak discover our tracks, it won't take them long to find us."

This was an opportunity to escape her promise to Ikatou and the others. They'd have a difficult time finding the Allied Camp on their own. She could be free of her blood oath! No more Barnabas. No more leaving loved ones. Gryphon was alive! This was a second chance to have him in her life, and she refused to squander it.

She looked down at her mutilated hands. She shouldn't be held responsible for a promise made to those men. Barnabas would have tortured her for information and then killed her if she hadn't escaped Boar. She'd been desperate. It wasn't her fault that Ikatou's clan was raided. She hadn't forced the Kodiak from their homes, starved their children to the point of desperation …

"Zo." Gryphon took her by the upper arms, bringing her back to the present. "What's wrong?" He tucked her wild hair behind her ears and let his fingers slide down her neck. Her body responded with fire. A craving she never experienced with Gabe. How could she live without this man?

Zo sat up and scooted away from Gryphon. She cradled her wounded hands to her stomach, afraid she might be sick. "We need to go back." She couldn't push her voice past a whisper.

"To those Kodiak animals?" Gryphon thundered. "Not a chance."

Zo blinked, startled by Gryphon's resolve. "They saved me from Boar. I've promised to take them to Commander Laden and the Allies in return. I can't go back on my word." Not a complete lie, but not a complete truth either. She wasn't ready to tell him about her blood oath. Not yet.

"What happened to your hands, Zo? Did they do that to you?" Gryphon's expression darkened into something dangerous.

"Gryphon? Did you hear me? I have to help these people."

One of Ikatou's brothers shouted in the distance. "Fresh tracks. To me! To me!"

"Sorry, Zo." Gryphon gathered the blankets and

tightened the straps of his pack. "I'm not taking any chances with you. Run with me, or be dragged. But I promise you I will fight every Clanless wild man that comes near you."

"We've got to go *now*," hissed Joshua.

"Zander and my mess are in these woods, somewhere between here and the Allied Camp. They'll have an easy time tracking those Kodiak. You're safer with me and Joshua." Gryphon's hand cupped her cheek with such reverence. "Please run with me."

How could she refuse him?

CHAPTER TWENTY-EIGHT

Somewhere, repressed deep in the folds of his mind, Gryphon knew running was crazy. Seeing Zo—no, feeling Zo—altered all reasoning. He should have taken her back to the camp. It's what she wanted. Leave it to Zo to find someone to save while she herself was in mortal danger.

But the idea of entering a situation outnumbered, without control, with Zo under his protection, simply wasn't acceptable.

They ran for hours. Zo checked him if he varied from the southerly course. Both Joshua and Zo asked to stop, but Gryphon refused. Too many hunters in the forest. Everyone was against them. The whole world, it seemed.

Only when Zo tripped on a fallen log and collapsed to the ground in an exhausted ball did he come to his senses. He knelt beside her and lifted her from the ground onto his lap. Even after the run her body was cold, her skin pallid and sickly.

"I'm sorry. I just—"

Zo covered his mouth with bloodied fingers. "I feel it too. The urgency."

They'd cheated death. All three of them. "I can't lose you again," he said.

Joshua dropped wearily beside him. "You're going to lose us both if we don't stop to rest." The boy's teasing bordered too close on truth to be funny.

Zo nudged for Gryphon to set her down, and he grudgingly obeyed. They wouldn't rest here long. Not enough cover.

"Tell me how you escaped," she whispered, easing down to lie on her side. Days of trekking the mountain with little food showed in her prominent cheekbones.

"Barnabas decided to let Zander and his men sit out in the rain for a night. Ajax and Gabe helped me escape."

Zo sat up. "Gabe? That's not possible. He told me—"

"He lied, Zo. He wanted us both to believe the other was dead."

Zo shook her head. "He wouldn't do that."

"But he did. He came back with me to warn the Raven. He let me believe that Ajax, my best friend, killed you." Gryphon grabbed a soggy pinecone and ground it in his fists. "If I hadn't run into Talon and Raca, I would never have found you."

Zo stared into the distance, still shaking her head. "Gabe wouldn't do such a thing. It doesn't make sense."

Gryphon threw the crumpled remains of the

pinecone and barked, "Of course it does!" Didn't she understand? They both loved her. They both wanted her. This was Gabe's way of keeping Zo to himself.

Joshua voiced what Gryphon was too angry and too afraid to say. "Gabe doesn't want you to choose Gryphon instead of him."

Gryphon looked away, not daring to see Zo's expression. He knew she cared for him. But could that affection trump years of friendship, and maybe even love, between her and Gabe? It didn't seem possible.

"Where is he now?" whispered Zo.

Gryphon's throat wouldn't relax. "On a boat sailing south with the Raven. They'll approach the Allied Camp from the south to avoid the Ram."

Gabe had saved his life more than once. The Raven would have killed him in that field if Gabe hadn't shown up. How could he hate and admire someone so thoroughly?

"I hope he's alive," said Zo. "He's going to pay for this."

Gryphon whipped around, needing to see her face.

He didn't have the chance before she tucked her body into his side for warmth. The cold tip of her nose pressed gently against his rib cage. He draped his arm around her, drawing her even closer to him and lifted his other arm for Joshua to do the same.

"I'm good," the boy said, even though Gryphon saw him shiver.

"I didn't ask if you were 'good.' Now get over here." He pulled Joshua over by his collar and tucked him close to his side. The two people he cared for most.

"Thank you for saving the Raven," Zo mumbled into his shirt.

He squeezed her to let her know he'd heard.

GRYPHON WOKE to the feel of cold steel pressed against his throat. He stared down the blade to find Zander with the rest of the mess surrounding them.

"Get up." Ever the soldier, Zander kept his voice neutral, adding pressure to the sword until Gryphon had no choice but to rise. Zo and Joshua had fallen asleep resting on his shoulders. When his arms fell away, they stirred awake.

"Gryphon?" Zo gasped beside him. Joshua attempted to stand, reaching for the dagger he kept on his belt.

Ajax stepped in and kicked the knife out of the boy's hands before he could so much as point it in someone's direction. He pushed Joshua to the ground and planted a foot on his chest with enough force to make the kid groan.

How could Gryphon let this happen? He never fell asleep on watch, especially not in the middle of the day. He only meant to give Zo and Joshua a chance to rest, to have both of them huddled against him in total contentment. Gryphon didn't even remember closing his eyes.

The cycle was starting all over again, always coming back to the undeniable theme that he couldn't protect the ones he loved most. Zo would have been safer with the Clanless. Joshua should have stayed with the Nameless refugees. Everyone would have been better off if Gabe's lie were true—if he had died.

Why hadn't he killed Zander when he'd had the chance?

"Dispose of the boy and keep the healer." Zander turned a cool look at Ajax. "Since she's *still alive*, I'd like to handle her personally."

Ajax's scowl didn't fit him, his mouth better suited to laughter. "You know the orders, Zander," he said without moving to obey. "Barnabas wants Gryphon and the girl alive. The Seer believes she has information about the gathering of the clans."

Gryphon and the other brothers of their mess gawked at Ajax. All their lives they'd been programmed to accept a higher-ranking officer's word without question. Ajax publicly reminding Zander of Barnabas' orders bordered on sedition.

Zander's neck and cheeks flared red. His hand trembled on the sword still pointed at Gryphon's throat. His eyes were sunken and his skin a pallid gray. "I know our orders, Second." Zander's nostrils flared, his chest pumping. He turned back to Gryphon.

"Second?" Gryphon raised an eyebrow at Ajax, earning a stern glare from his best friend.

"Someone had to take your place, Gryph," said Ajax. He dug his boot harder into Joshua's chest, as if to prove a point. Gryphon couldn't decide if it was an act or not. He'd like to think his friend was on his side, but Ajax had a family to consider inside the Gate. He couldn't overtly help Gryphon without risking his wife and newborn son.

Gryphon watched Joshua from the corner of his eye

and made sure to keep Zo behind him when he turned back to Zander. "I'll come quietly if you let the healer and the boy go free."

"I'm not leaving you," said Zo quietly. Her hand gripped the back of his calf where she knelt.

Zander laughed. "For once, I agree with your little pet." He sidestepped Gryphon and bent down to speak to Zo. "He should have kept you at his farm with the other animals. Now he has to share you with the rest of us."

Gryphon's fist flew without his permission and landed squarely on Zander's cheek. Bone shattered beneath his knuckles and Zander hit the ground hard. Gryphon's mess brothers converged. Zo rushed into his arms. He held her for one fraction of a moment before strong hands pulled them apart amid Zo's shrill protests.

Joshua fought free of Ajax and charged in to help, but one of Gryphon's brothers threw an elbow into his face. Ajax caught him and dragged him away from the chaos. The boy hung limp in his arms.

"Don't touch him!" Zo cried at Ajax. "How can you do this?" she yelled. "How can you betray your best friend?"

"Shut her up," yelled Zander as he climbed to his feet.

Noah, a tall, lean man with light hair and a thin mouth, grabbed Zo's wrist. She whipped around and clawed at his face before he caught her other wrist and kneed her in the stomach. Doubled over in pain, her moan reverberated in Gryphon's ears.

Zander pressed his fingers to his cheek and winced.

"You're cowardly enough to hit a man when he's not looking? I taught you better."

Red tinged the corners of Gryphon's vision. He had to draw Zander's attention away from Zo and Joshua. He leaned forward, away from the arms that bound him, and spat, "You're afraid of me, Zander. You always have been."

Zander wiped his bloody lip on his sleeve and stepped toe to toe with Gryphon. He schooled his features and kept his sword hand loose at his side.

Fear wasn't Zander's problem, but pride was another matter.

"Not once, in all of our training sessions, did you spar with me. Why is that? Even now, you need the whole unit to subdue me so you can obey orders like an obedient, shoe-kissing grunt."

"Gryphon, please don't," Zo whimpered.

Everyone watched Zander as color rose up his neck. When he finally spoke, his voice was ice, every word crisp and cutting. "You're no better than the Clanless who roam these mountains. You fight only for yourself. You belong to nothing and so you are nothing." He signaled to his men by patting the air at his hip. A signal to stand down no matter what followed.

The hands holding Gryphon dropped away, and the Ram fanned out in a ring around him and Zander.

"These men are my brothers." Gryphon looked around the circle at the men he'd long admired. Only Ajax met his gaze. He'd expected as much, but hoped for more.

Zander gritted his teeth and tightened his grip on his

sword. "You. Are. Not. Our. Brother." The metal of Zander's blade caught and reflected sunlight as he reared back to strike. Gryphon knew the attack was coming and dodged, just catching the tip of the sword on his boiled leather vest.

Scrambling backward, Gryphon fingered the tear in his armor with one hand while drawing his own sword with the other. "What about your orders?" he said, adjusting his stance to keep a safe angle and distance from Zander. "It's not like you to think for yourself."

Zander attacked again. Gryphon deflected three rapid strikes but missed the fourth, earning him a long cut on his left bicep. He wasn't used to fighting without a shield to protect his weak side. If it was a test of throwing spears or fighting hand to hand, Zander wouldn't stand a chance against him, but swords were another matter, and Zander—being his captain—knew it.

Zander pushed Gryphon back. Metal clanged. Each strike Gryphon blocked vibrated all the way up his arm. Zander lunged, driving him back further still. Gryphon's heel connected with a large rock, and he fell onto his back. Before he could get up, Zander had the point of his sword pressed against Gryphon's exposed chest.

"I taught you everything you know, traitor. You never had a chance."

It was true. Not with swords. Not surrounded and outnumbered with Zo and Joshua's lives to consider.

"Drop the sword."

Gryphon didn't have a choice. The unhelpful weapon clinked on rock as it hit the ground. One of Zander's men collected it and stepped back to his place in the ring.

"You deserve this," said Zander as he pushed the tip of the sword into the skin over Gryphon's heart. He shifted the grip so both hands shared the hilt for leverage.

"Barnabas wants him alive!" Ajax yelled.

"There was a struggle," Zander said panting, his lips curving upward in wicked pleasure. Sweat ran down the side of his nose. "Accidents happen."

This wasn't happening. Not after all they'd endured to get here. Adrenaline like fire coursed through Gryphon. It filled his shoulders and arms, down to his fingertips.

He had to save them. He had to find a way. Zander said he was Clanless, but even if the Allies never accepted him, that wasn't. true. He might not fight for a chief, but he certainly fought for something.

Zander reared back. His sword cut through the air, parallel to the ground, toward Gryphon's neck. A piercing cry rent the air.

Gryphon closed his eyes and in a translucent moment of time imagined little Tess cupping his cheeks, whispering, *I don't want you to die.* Then Sani. *My life is linked to yours.* And lastly, Zo. Her eyes communicated everything words never could. A hope for something more. A chance to see if a Ram and a Wolf could have a life together. If they could prove it possible, Gryphon couldn't help but hope that others would follow their example. Set aside differences and find peace.

Just before the blade could split his skin, he lay back and swept Zander's legs out from under him. Gryphon sprang from his back to his feet in one motion and charged Zander, weaponless.

He wasn't that good at swords anyway.

Gryphon jumped on Zander. He landed a punch to Zander's kidneys and another to his face before Zander retaliated, hitting him so hard in the nose that lights exploded behind Gryphon's eyes.

They both staggered to their feet. Zander charged. His sword hacked down toward Gryphon's weak side. Unthinking, Gryphon raised his shield arm. The blade bit into his flesh, connecting with bone. Lodged there. He pulled away, crying out in agony, and Zander's sword stayed fixed to the bone below Gryphon's elbow. The pain was so blinding he couldn't even hear Zo's screams and sobs.

They stood facing each other, panting and stunned. Then panic exploded across Zander's face as he realized his attack wasn't enough.

They collided, two immovable forces connecting in the air. Gryphon's powerful hands surged with adrenaline as they clamped down on his mess leader's head. Years of worshipping this man conflicted with the need to end him. All his training, all his beatings, had prepared him for this bittersweet moment. His hands did what Zander had trained them to do. Zander's neck bone cracked as Gryphon severed it from his spinal cord. The bone popped under Gryphon's hands, the cracking sound both heard and felt.

Gryphon and Zander hit the ground at the same time.

Zander, however, did not get back up.

Zo GASPED as Gryphon crawled to his feet with Zander's sword still lodged in his arm. A lesser man would have passed out from the pain, but Gryphon held his arms out to his sides, blood dripping off him like sweat, and glared into the eyes of the men he used to call his brothers.

"Barnabas claims we Ram only take what is rightfully ours, but it's a lie. We've become thieves. Plunderers. I love my clan, but I cannot fight for a chief who would send me to kill the helpless only for dominance. I will defend my family," he gestured to Joshua and Zo, "but I will not live with innocent blood on my hands."

Gryphon staggered and dropped to one knee. "My conscience won't allow it." His eyes rolled up into his head, and he fell face first onto the earth.

Zo closed her eyes and concentrated on sending a feeling into the tall Ram holding her captive. *Sleep. Numb. Weakness.* The usual doubts came along with the fear that she'd never be able to heal again, but they were amplified by the foreign task set before her. Her training as a healer had been centered on loving her patients, offering energy to heal, and comfort for distress. She'd never tried to instill a negative emotion—she didn't even know if it was possible.

Weakness. Weakness. She mumbled the blessing that usually accompanied her healing but used her love for Gryphon to fuel the pull. Nothing happened. She concentrated harder and focused all her love for Tess, Gryphon, and Joshua into the pull.

A thin thread of something drew into her body, so subtle at first. she wasn't sure exactly what it was. The Ram's arms pinning her own to her sides slackened.

Weakness. Exhaustion. Sleep.

Zo mentally tugged harder on the thread of energy coming from the Ram until that thread turned into a steady stream. The Ram's arms loosened even more and his body swayed, his skin cool to the touch.

Zo pulled even harder. Her hands burned from the energy. Her cuts wept fresh blood as a new kind of pain registered beneath the coursing river of power washing through them.

The Ram holding her collapsed to the ground.

Zo was at Gryphon's side in an instant. She wrapped both hands around Gryphon and pushed energy with every ounce of strength she possessed. His eyes shot open and he sat up, even though the sword was still wedged in the bone of his forearm.

"Joshua." Zo wiped at the tears invading her vision. "I need your help." She looked around for her kit until remembering she'd left it with the Clanless when Gryphon abducted her. It didn't matter. The healing energy that had been dormant since Gryphon left flowed through her with more power than she'd ever experienced before.

Ajax released Joshua without a fight. The rest of the Ram stood by watching, probably just as shocked by what they'd witnessed as Zo. "What should I do?" said Joshua, kneeling beside her and Gryphon.

"Hold down his arm, Ginger." She leaned over Gryphon and held his face, brushing the hair from his forehead. His eyes barely. opened at her touch, but his uninjured arm wrapped around her waist, pulling her closer to him.

"I have to remove the sword. It's going to hurt." She swallowed hard.

Gryphon nodded and closed his eyes fully. "Not as much as losing you," he mumbled.

Zo leaned forward and pressed a chaste kiss to his unsuspecting lips. The hand at her back pulled her possessively closer, sending sparks of pleasure throughout her body. She pulled away, breathless but determined to help him, delirious with hope, even without her kit.

She took the hilt of the sword and looked up at the men surrounding them. For a thin moment, she'd forgotten they were there. Ram were loyal to their leaders. She imagined many of them wanted nothing more than to jump forward and drive a knife into Gryphon's heart for killing Zander. For now, they waited, some looking to Ajax for a command.

A flicker of movement from the shadows outside the group caught Zo's attention. A large man with shaved head and full beard hid in the shadows, partially covered by a tree.

Ikatou?

He held a finger up to his lips calling for her silence, while he and his men surrounded the Ram.

Zo dropped her focus back to Gryphon and the sword wedged into the bone of his forearm. "We're going to do this on my count," Zo spoke louder than necessary. "One." Then she whispered under her breath, "Kid, something's about to happen." Louder, she said, "Two." Then she whispered again. "Whatever you do, stay on the ground with Gryphon. Don't get up and fight."

"Three!" Zo pulled up on the hilt of the sword.

Gryphon howled. At the same time, the Kodiak charged the Ram with a deafening battle cry.

"Link!" Ajax shouted, but he was too late. Three of his mess brothers took swords through their stomachs at the Ram call to formation.

Zo pulled Joshua down next to Gryphon. "Don't move. They won't hurt me." She knelt with one hand on Gryphon and one hand on Joshua in the midst of the fierce confrontation, pushing as much love and peace into them as possible.

Ajax dodged the attack of a nearby Kodiak and ran straight for Zo, Gryphon, and Joshua. Zo threw her body across Gryphon and Joshua. Her men. She closed her eyes, every muscle in her body bracing for Ajax's attack.

But instead of a sword, a hand took her by the shoulder. Zo's head whipped up and she looked Ajax directly in the eye.

"Take care of him, Healer."

Behind him, Ikatou charged, his mighty long sword held high above his head to offer Ajax a killing blow.

"Look out!" said Zo, half a moment before the sword fell.

Ajax rolled to his side and sprinted out of the circle of fighting. "Retreat," he called. Those of his brothers not hewn down by the Kodiak broke free of their fighting and fled the clearing.

Ikatou and the rest of the Kodiak dropped their weapons and tugged at the front of their shirts, roaring at the retreating Ram. Zo assumed it was Kodiak tradition. Their large lungs must have carried the victory call for miles. Joshua clamped his hands over his ears while Zo stripped the sleeve off Gryphon's wounded arm and used it as a tourniquet to slow the bleeding.

"Zo?" Gryphon tried to sit up, but Zo pushed him back down.

"Be still. I can help you." And she could! The swirl of movable energy coalescing inside her confirmed as much.

"I…can't move my fingers."

Zo winced at the implications and put more pressure on his arm. "Zander's sword sliced through a muscle that runs along the top of the forearm. It's the same muscle that controls your ability to make a fist. It'll heal with time, but it's a slow process. I'm more worried about your bone. If you're not careful, the fracture could turn into a full break."

"Ajax." He moved his injured arm and sucked in a sharp breath of air, his teeth clenched together so tight she feared he'd accidently bite through his tongue if he didn't stop trying to speak. She rested. her fingers over his mouth. "He got away, and so did most of your brothers in retreat." She couldn't imagine how conflicted Gryphon must feel, fighting for an ideal he believed in against people he had devoted most of his life to protecting.

Gryphon shook his head and pulled her fingers from his lips with his good hand, but still clung to her. "Ram don't retreat. Ajax saved us. He'll be punished for it."

The Kodiak shouting stopped. Celebrating a victory that wasn't truly theirs. They embraced each other with burly hugs and sharp pats on the back.

When Ikatou turned to face Zo, a flurry of emotions crossed. his face. Relief. Betrayal. Concern. Distrust.

"I need to make this right," Zo whispered to Gryphon. "Will you be all right?"

He nodded. "Go. The kid and I will wait here."

She walked over to the waiting giant, the man who gave her the hideous cuts on her hands.

"I didn't run away," she said.

"It was the Ram unit. I know." He looked beyond Zo to Gryphon. "Is that one a friend?"

Zo paused. Did Ikatou really believe that Zander had kidnapped her from his camp? "Yes," she said, swallowing. "He and the boy freed me from the Gate. I owe them my life."

Ikatou, all muscle and business, rested a hand on Zo's shoulder, startling her. "I'm glad you are safe." She didn't know if he was glad only for the sake of his family and their agreement or for hers as well. She wanted to believe it was both.

Ikatou whistled to one of his men. A man ducked behind a tree carrying her mother's medical satchel.

Tears pricked the corners of her eyes. "You brought it." She had the strange desire to hug the Bear—this man who had cut open her hands for the sake of his family.

"You haven't forgotten your promise?" asked Ikatou. "You will fulfill your blood oath?"

Zo chewed on her bottom lip and showed him the backs of her hands. "I haven't forgotten."

Ikatou's whole body seemed to relax. He roughed up her hair. "For such a small person, you are capable of great things, Tumanoko."

"Tu-man-o-ko?" Zo pronounced each syllable with care.

"My people's word for 'hope.'"

Zo hugged the medical kit to her chest and stepped away from Ikatou, but turned back to add, "Thank you."

Zo walked back to Gryphon.

"Everything all right?" he asked as she settled to the ground next to him, still clutching the medical satchel to her chest.

"He thinks Zander kidnapped me. We're going to make it to the Allies, Gryphon. This nightmare is almost over." She still hadn't told him about the full obligation of her blood oath to Ikatou and the others, but now wasn't the time.

Joshua hovered over her as she cleaned Gryphon's wound, applied the proper medicine, and dressed it. When she laid her hands over the bandage, she thought of her mother as she whispered the healing blessing.

At last, she was a healer again.

CHAPTER TWENTY-NINE

Gryphon walked with his arm in a sling beside Ikatou as Joshua consumed all of Zo's attention behind him. Joshua asked endless questions about the Allies and the new life ahead of him. Since Gryphon had spent the last two days holding Zo's hand, sharing memories of their very different childhoods, and just being near her, he didn't mind sharing her with the kid.

Looking over his shoulder to make sure Zo and Joshua were still close behind, he and Zo locked eyes. The side of her lip curled and they shared a moment as Joshua continued his litany of questions.

"What claim do you have over the girl?" Ikatou said, startling. him out of his line of thought. Gryphon had nearly forgotten the large man beside him. "You're too young to be considered her guardian."

"She is my family," said Gryphon.

"A sister? That's impossible. You're a Ram. She's a Wolf."

Gryphon smiled at the thought of being compared to Zo as a brother. If Ikatou looked between them for some sign of similarity, he wouldn't find it. Zo was a Wolf and stunning, all long lines and grace. He was built like a boulder, with too much nose and temper.

Gryphon shook his head. "I'd do anything to keep her safe. We are not the same blood. But she *is* my family."

"Would her father agree?" Ikatou raised an eyebrow.

Gryphon bristled. What right did this Bear have to question him? He had far less claim on Zo than even Gryphon had. "Her parents are gone from this world."

Ikatou nodded. "How do I know you aren't a spy sent by Barnabas to learn the location of the Allied Camp?"

Gryphon's face burned hot. "Is that what this is about?"

"A lone Ram? A deserter? Your kind doesn't leave the Gate without a purpose."

"I had a purpose," Gryphon snarled. The constant throb in. his arm only added to his anger—a reminder of his losses. He was lucky he still had an arm after Zander's strike.

"If you're not a spy, why did you leave?"

He decided the simple truth was better than throwing his last good fist into the man's face. He lowered his voice. "Because I'm in love with her." He glanced back to see if Zo heard, but her attention was all for Joshua.

"She and the boy are all I have left." His Adam's apple leapt up and down.

Ikatou eyed Gryphon from the side. "If she were my daughter, I would kill you and not take the chance."

"You could certainly try." Gryphon's good hand hovered over the hilt of his sword.

Ikatou shook his head and looked out across the horizon. They'd been walking downhill all day with a clear view of the lower portions of the mountain range. "It's not my place to interfere." They walked a few more steps. "But I've lived among Clanless men. I know what that honorless breed is like. She deserves more than a man without a banner."

Gryphon had battled that same reasoning since he left the Gate. But having her here with him. Seeing her smile, as though some of the momentous weight that once sat upon her shoulders was lifted, feeling like he had something to do with that…it mattered. He mattered, to her and to Joshua.

"She is my clan now," he said.

Ikatou narrowed his eyes. "If you hurt her, I swear on all the jewels of my homeland, I'll kill you."

"If I hurt her, I'll deserve it."

AFTER EVENING MEAL, most of the men fell asleep around the fire. Zo, Gryphon, and Joshua sat awake watching the flames. The fire cast every angle of Gryphon's face in a different light and shadow. His thoughts were completely lost to Zo, as unpredictable and blurred as the shadowed planes of his face. Light or shadow, Zo loved it all with such frightening adoration that it brought about as much agony as it did pleasure. Nothing in life lasted forever. The death of her parents taught her as much. The more a person gained, the more they had to lose.

Joshua threw a piece of bark into the fire; his eyes glued to the hypnotic movement of the flames. "Will the Allies like us?"

"People of the Allies are highly secretive. They won't appreciate your presence." Zo squeezed Gryphon's good hand. "Not until they understand what you've done for them." She looked up into his piercing gaze and melted. "What you've done for me."

"And Gabe will be there too," said Joshua, matter-of-factly. Gryphon looked away and the moment soured into something different. Something forced. She waited a minute before pulling her hand free of Gryphon's to throw another log on the already healthy fire. She folded her arms around her legs when she sat back down, considering Gabe and his betrayal.

"Will you take a walk with me?" she said to Gryphon.

"I'll come." Joshua hopped up and dusted leaves and grass from his pants. "Where are we going?"

Gryphon kept his expression guarded. He hadn't moved from his position on the ground.

She looked away from the fire to hide her blush. "I actually need to speak with Gryphon." She cleared her throat. "Alone."

Despite his injury, Gryphon was standing almost before she had time to turn back and face them. She smiled, her cheeks even hotter than they were before, and reached for his good hand. "We won't be long, Ginger."

"I'll just wait here, alone, by myself then," Joshua grumbled as they headed into the darkness.

The moon above reminded Zo of the symbol of the Allies. Something growing, waxing, and beautiful. The small light it afforded made their walk perilous but also gave the stars a chance to really shine.

Zo didn't immediately speak, didn't trust herself to say what needed to be said without sounding like a complete fool. Gryphon cared for her, she knew that much, but did he crave her the way she did him?

"If you need time to sort things out with Gabe, I'll understand."

Zo's head shot up and she tripped on a low hanging branch. Gryphon saved her from falling by wrapping his uninjured arm around her waist. She clung to him as he righted her, desperate to absorb his strength for just a little longer. She turned and looked up into his handsome face, past the gentle curve of his lips, until their eyes met. He cleared his throat and Zo turned back to the trail.

His hand supported her back as they made the semi-blind trek. through the trees until the foliage opened up to a small sloped clearing just large enough for the two of them. Lemongrass carpeted the ground. The sweet aroma made Zo sigh with pleasure as they sank to the earth. The ground slanted enough to make lying on their backs the perfect position to watch the stars.

"I don't deserve this," said Gryphon. He propped up his head with his good arm while his splinted arm rested on his stomach.

"Yes. You do," said Zo. She held her breath, questioning her own bravery for a moment before scooting next to him and resting her head against his good shoulder. His arm came down around her before she had a moment to feel awkward.

Did Gryphon feel it too? The unwinding of all the hurt she'd ever endured. She was still so young—seventeen was hardly the time to think about choosing one man to be with forever—but she couldn't help imagining what it might be like to belong to Gryphon. To have him belong to her in return. After a while she rolled onto her side. Her body pressed against his in delicious ways. "Gryphon?"

He watched her with a hunter's attention. "Yes." His voice caught as he spoke.

Zo brushed her cheek against his. Whiskers tickled her face.

Gryphon let go a long, shuttering breath. He glanced down at her lips then leaned in. His mouth hovered inches from hers, waiting for her to close the distance.

Zo pulled away. She'd brought him here for a reason. If she didn't tell him now, it would only be harder later.

"Forgive me," she whispered. The gold in his eyes reflected the stars. "For dragging you into all this. I've ruined your life." She cupped his face in her hands and let her lips lightly brush against his. "I'm so sorry."

She barely had time to say the words before his kiss silenced her. He pulled her closer, removing what little space existed between them. Zo's hands slipped from his face and settled comfortably against his chest. Their lips moved against each other's in a natural rhythm. She'd never kissed a man like that before. She didn't know where her lips stopped and his began. One thing she did know is that when the heavens and earth were formed and man was created, at some point Gryphon's lips were molded to fit hers.

Zo pulled away and dropped her head to rest in his neck. Her heart pounded in her ears.

"Zo?" Uncertainty laced Gryphon's deep voice. "Is everything all right?"

But Zo wasn't ready to look up into those eyes again.

"Is it Gabe? Is it too soon?"

At that Zo did raise her head. "Gabe is like a brother to me, Gryphon. I know you must hate him, and I'm ready to kill him myself, but he is still the closest thing I have to a family."

"Did you just say *brother*?"

Her cheeks burned. She felt herself melting under the intensity of his gaze. He lifted her chin with his forefinger, studying her from under the hood of his dark brows. Whatever he saw in her expression gave him courage.

"If I promise not to kill Gabe, will you let me call you mine?"

"You don't have to, you know."

Gryphon's brows shot up. "Excuse me?"

This is what she'd been hoping to communicate all night. "Gryphon, you've done so much for me. You're selfless and brave and kind and…I don't want you to feel like I'm your only option. We don't have to be together for you to find a home with the Allies."

A wide grin spread across Gryphon's face. "Answer the question, Zo." He reached up and gently knotted his hand in the hair at the nape of her neck. Possessive. Strong.

Zo couldn't remember a time when she'd ever felt so blissfully content. Didn't he know? Wasn't it obvious? "Why ask for what you already have?"

Just in case words weren't enough, she took his face in her hands and thoroughly, deliciously kissed him.

CHAPTER THIRTY

Gryphon woke to the feel of raindrops hitting his face. It wasn't quite morning, and Zo lay tucked into his side, her head resting peacefully on his shoulder. They needed to get back to camp before Ikatou came looking for them.

I've lost myself to a Wolf. He let his head fall back against the grass and smiled. He couldn't ever remember being so happy.

A brown flurry of movement a hundred yards away caught Gryphon's eye. He stared out through the thick maze of pine trees, unblinking, but didn't see the movement again. Was it an animal? It had seemed tall enough to be a bear. His gut clinched. *Not again.*

Careful to rest Zo's head gently against the ground, Gryphon sat up, unhooked his wool cloak, and covered Zo to protect her from the rain. He paused to tuck a strand of her dark hair behind her ears and fought the desire to linger to watch her sleep.

He pulled a knife from the sheath above his ankle and turned back to face whatever beast threatened them, cursing his useless arm and hand, still bound in a sling. Raindrops rolled into his eyes and he blinked them away. The rain-soaked earth absorbed all sound as Gryphon moved so he could keep an eye on Zo, scanning the area where he last saw movement. He used the trees for cover, stepping quickly from one to the next. His teeth chattered, and his breath smoked the air.

Thunder rumbled in the distance. Gryphon looked back to make sure Zo still slept. When he turned around again to search the trees, Ajax stood not five feet in front of him. His brother and best friend held up his hands in surrender.

"What are you doing here, Jax?" Then realization dawned. If Ajax was here then the rest of the mess wasn't far behind. "Where are the others?"

"We're camped at the summit. I came alone so we could talk."

Gryphon stepped closer to Ajax and rested his good arm on his brother's shoulder. "You're going to be in trouble when Barnabas learns you retreated."

Ajax offered a tired smile. "It's actually worse than that."

"What do you mean?"

His large friend took a deep breath; his shoulders raised and dropped under Gryphon's hand. "After you escaped, we reported everything to Barnabas." He shook his head. "Barnabas banished the mess as punishment. We've been running rogue ever since."

Gryphon shook his head. "No." He refused to believe

it. No wonder they were so desperate to capture him. No wonder his brothers wouldn't so much as look him in the eye.

Gryphon swayed on his feet, then rolled back from his heels to sit on the soggy ground. Water seeped through his pants and rain pelted his body, but he didn't care. "What have I done?" he muttered, covering his face in his hands. "What about your families? Sara, and the baby. Are they all right?"

Ajax didn't answer, but he didn't need to. Gryphon understood life inside the Gate for the family of a banished soldier all too well.

"I…I'm so sorry. What can I do, Jax? How can I fix this?"

Ajax went still, his voice barely heard over the rain. "There is something you can do."

"Name it, brother."

Ajax stared at the ground, unwilling to meet Gryphon's eyes. "The only way Barnabas will let us regain our citizenship and the honor of our families is if…we bring him your head." He seemed to have a difficult time swallowing. His voice took on a desperate tone. "The mess. They see me as their leader now. I'm responsible for them, Gryph." His head fell forward into his hands. "I don't know what to do!"

Gryphon swore and stepped away from Ajax.

Zo. How could he possibly walk away from Zo now that they finally had each other? "I want to help you, Ajax. But I…I just can't."

Gryphon jumped as Ajax dropped to his knees at Gryphon's feet. "It kills me to beg you, brother, but think of their families." He wiped rain from his agonized face. "Think of my family. Of Sara. How will I protect her and our baby if I'm not allowed near them? You know what will happen if the Seer finds out about the baby."

Ajax threaded his fingers through the grass at Gryphon's feet and made a fist with shaking hands. By now the Seer would likely know about the baby and the birth defect. The malformation of the child's lip was something Zo claimed could be fixed in a minor surgery, but the Ram didn't accept any born outside perfection.

Gryphon dropped to the ground next to his friend and rested a hand on his shoulder. "We will find a way around this, Ajax. I'll find a way to help you."

Ajax slowly lifted his head, his face coming level with Gryphon's, his chin trembling. "If you ever considered me a brother, you will help me save my wife and son."

Ajax's words ripped through Gryphon's chest. "I'd do it for you, Gryph."

Gryphon swore and turned away. A knot in his throat made speaking impossible. He couldn't believe this was happening, couldn't fathom the words that tumbled out of his mouth next. "I will give myself over to Barnabas." A pause. "But there's something I must do first."

"What's that?" Ajax didn't pull his eyes from the ground.

"I need to get Joshua and Zo to the Allies. It's the only place they'll be safe."

Ajax frowned. "You would send Joshua to fight against us?"

"I would send Joshua away to live, brother. He has no future with the Ram. Even you can see that!"

Ajax shook his head. "You and that blasted boy. You set your mind to protecting something and you'll change the stars to do it. You would make…"

"What?" Gryphon asked when Ajax faltered.

Ajax looked him square in the eye. "I was going to say that you'd make a good clan chief someday, but…"

"But there isn't going to be a someday. Not for me," said Gryphon.

Ajax swore. "I'd follow you to hell and back, Gryph. But the others, I can't abandon them. I have to think of Sara." He smiled weakly. "I guess we're not that different after all."

"Go back to the Gate," said Gryphon. "Tell them I'll come and turn myself in in a month. Maybe two." How would he explain this to Zo? Why did taking the honorable road require him to hurt those he loved? He'd need that time to get Joshua settled. To say goodbye. He closed his eyes and counted to ten before opening them again.

"That won't work," said Ajax.

"Why?"

"Because the chief has ordered the Ram to relocate to the south. They're leaving the Gate. The Great Move is officially underway."

"The Great Move?"

"We're marching on the Valley of Wolves. Barnabas sees it as our new home, and final battleground in his quest to control the region."

"The Wolves—"

"Don't stand a chance," said Ajax.

Gryphon looked back in Zo's direction. "I will not come with you today, brother."

Ajax's face looked tired, stretched and folded in misery. "Meet us outside the entrance to the Valley of the Wolves where the two rivers meet in one month's time."

"I'll do it." A rush of fluttering nerves swirled inside Gryphon's gut as he agreed to his fate. "I...I swear upon my honor, I will do this thing." It reminded him of walking to the shed to receive his yearly beatings. He'd been terrified, especially without a father at his side to reassure him that everything would work out. Only he wouldn't limp away from this appointment like he had as a child.

They clasped hands in a firm shake. Ajax placed his other hand on top of the pile to seal the pact. "I'm sorry, my friend. I'm so sorry."

Gryphon looked back in Zo's direction. "Me too."

***

Zo AWOKE to a gentle nudging at her shoulder.

"We need to get back to camp before the others worry," said. Gryphon.

Zo reached her hands above her head and stretched before. allowing Gryphon to help her up. She leaned her head into his side with his arm draped along her back as they walked back to camp in the early light of morning.

Zo touched her lips, swollen from kissing Gryphon, and silently prayed Ikatou and the others wouldn't notice.

They entered the camp to find the Kodiak and Joshua still asleep. Zo dropped to her bedroll and Gryphon lay down beside her, pulling her into the protective curve of his body. It seemed that within moments of shutting her eyes, Ikatou was calling the camp to action. As they packed up their belongings, Zo found Gryphon staring at her. She smiled, a blush warming her cheeks. It took her three tries to properly tie off her bedroll with those liquid brown eyes watching. Careful of her injured hands, she threaded her arm. into her pack and stood next to Gryphon and Joshua.

"We're going to see Tess today," she practically sang.

Around them, men spoke to each other in excited whispers, as they prepared for the final leg of their journey to a new future.

"I can't believe I'm saying this, but I've actually missed Tess's cooking," said Joshua.

Gryphon's smile didn't reach his eyes. He stared out to the horizon where the sun's rays peeked over a distant mountain range. He hadn't spoken since he woke her early that morning. Probably overwhelmed by the possibilities of living with the Allies.

"Lead the way, Wolf," Ikatou called to Zo when the Kodiak were ready to move out.

Zo set an aggressive pace that the others—with their longer legs—matched with ease. They trudged downhill and found a familiar path marked by the passage of the Nameless refugees. All trails on this side of the mountain filtered into a narrow slot canyon.

Walls of granite towered several hundred feet above them on both sides, like God had driven a giant ax through the mountain. Several places were barely large enough for Gryphon to squeeze through sideways. The trail curved back and forth like a snake. Zo looked to the narrow patch of sky high above. They were so close now.

"Does it ever end?" Gryphon asked a few paces behind her. He panted, bracing the walls as if they needed his strength to keep them upright. Beads of sweat rolled down from his hairline. The Kodiak seemed perfectly at ease sandwiched between the giant slabs of stone.

"Only a little further," said Zo.

After four more turns the way opened up to reveal a green meadow with a multi-colored carpet of flowers and ferns. Beyond that, a valley dotted with cook fires.

The Allies.

Gryphon put his hands his on knees. "Tell me there is a different way out of this valley."

"You didn't enjoy that?" Zo walked up to him and placed a comforting hand on his back, a smile tickling her lips. Gryphon was good at everything. The idea that he was claustrophobic didn't fit with his character. "It gets easier with practice," she said.

"So there really isn't?"

Zo couldn't help the bubble of laughter that rolled up her throat. She reached up on her toes and threw her arms around his neck, kissing his cheek. "Welcome home, Gryphon."

ACKNOWLEDGMENTS

This middle child of the NAMELESS series is a story about belonging. I've been accepted, included, and supported by so many wonderful "clans" throughout the process of writing this book.

Each is beautiful and different in its own, blessed way.

The most obvious clan worth mentioning is my crazy-supportive family and friends. They've gone to great lengths to spread book love in the form of costumes, food, words of encouragement, beta reading, babysitting, tribal face paint, acting, tweeting, and the list goes on and on. They are the metaphoric hands that hold me up— hands I know will be there to catch me if I fall or allow myself to be overwhelmed with self-doubt. Their faces are many and extend well beyond my husband and three little rascals, including: parents, brothers and sisters (in-laws included!), grandparents, aunts and uncles, cousins, nieces and nephews, and good, good friends. I'm a firm believer that we can all do great things when great people surround us.

Huge thanks to my more immediate Writing Clan. To Amy Jameson who wears many hats, namely, agent, editor, dream weaver, counselor, travel companion, and friend. To the brilliant writers in my life: Lois D. Brown, Margie Jordan, James Lewis, Jo Schaffer, and Tahsha Wilson. And to priceless beta readers such as Brad Walker, Amy Beatty, Jonathan Ryan, Kristen Whitely, Jen Bradford, the hunky Mr. Clint Jenkins, and Brad Walker (Did I. mention him already?).

I must also thank the many book bloggers who've taken the time to review and tweet my books. I'm extremely tempted to list out the members of the Blogging Clan one by one, but the. fear of forgetting someone makes me scared to try. I will say that your reviews for this series have been beautiful, powerful, and ridiculously validating for me as a writer. Thank you so much.

As always, I will end by sending thanks and love to my little, eternal clan. Clint, Casey, Liberty, and Boston, thank you again for your loving support. You are the root of all happiness in my life.

ALSO BY JENNIFER JENKINS

Nameless Trilogy

Nameless

Clanless

Fearless

Lingering Seas Novels

To Kill a Curse

Of Blood and Fire

The Order of Chaos

Standalone Titles

A Necessary Madness

Teen Writer's Guide: Your Road Map to Writing (non-fiction)

ABOUT THE AUTHOR

Jennifer Jenkins is the author of seven published novels and one non-fiction guide to creative writing. She serves as the Executive Director of Operation Literacy, a national 501c3 nonprofit dedicated to promoting children's literacy. She has taught at universities across the country on the subjects of writing, story, leadership, and entrepreneurship. She divides her free time between reading, taking spontaneous trips, researching random events from the past, and fostering her adrenaline junkie addictions.

Learn more at http://authorjenniferjenkins.com.